L'Amérique

A Novel

Thierry Sagnier

L'Amérique

A Novel

Thierry Sagnier

Apprentice
House Press
Loyola University Maryland

First Edition

Paperback ISBN: 978-1-62720-174-2
Ebook ISBN: 978-1-62720-175-9

Design: Julia Cardali
Marketing: Meg Kennedy
Development: Rachel Kingsley

Printed in the United States of America

Published by Apprentice House

Apprentice
House Press
Loyola University Maryland

4501 N. Charles Street
Baltimore, MD 21210
410.617.5265 • 410.617.2198 (fax)
www.ApprenticeHouse.com
info@ApprenticeHouse.com

Chapter 1

In Jeanot's room off the main corridor were two bunk beds. Jeanot slept in the top one and when either of his sisters visited, she could have the bottom bunk. There was one chair, a floor lamp with a faulty bulb, and a false fireplace which Jeanot knew was the lair of unspeakable beings who no longer scared him. The focus of the room, though, was a large square table on which he kept his display of lead cowboys and Choctaw, Navajo, Kiowa and Apache warriors. He'd been told the Indians were from these specific tribes by the man in the toy store who'd sold him the small figures. In truth, Jeanot wasn't sure the man knew his American Indians at all.

Jeanot's Papa built the table from boards he found in the building's cellar. The boy watched as his father sawed the ancient greying wood to the proper size, then used a hand-drill to make screw holes. Papa told Jeanot to put soap on the screw threads. "Like this," Papa said, and he moistened the screw threads with his mouth, then rubbed them against a bar of brown soap. He sank the tip of the fastener into the drilled hole and handed Jeanot a screwdriver, placed the blade in the screw's groove, and said, "Now turn it to the right." Jeanot did and got the screw about a third of the way in. "It won't turn anymore," he said, and Papa took over.

It took two hours to build the table. When it was done, it didn't wobble at all but stood as rock steady as any piece of furniture in the house, steadier, even, that the family dining room table that *did* wobble, and that Papa simply couldn't cure, though he'd tried.

That same afternoon, Jeanot's Maman knotted and dyed an old tablecloth a sand color in the kitchen sink. She balled several wads of paper, wetted them and sprinkled them with white flour from the kitchen. She put them in the small oven and lit it, and twenty minutes later, when the balls dried hard, she glued them to the table, draped the tablecloth over everything, and then tacked it into place. The tabletop became a North American desert of varied sand-colored hues with mounds made by the lumps of *papier maché*.

Maman painted the adjoining wall blue, with white clouds and a fierce yellow sun that baked the tablecloth desert. She put birds in the sky, vultures and eagles and a giant Andean condor she and Jeanot had read about in *Paris Match*. Below the sky she painted a verdant plain with buffaloes, gazelles and cows, because, she explained, she had always liked painting cows. Cows, said Maman, were so many fun colors; black, and brown, and white, all at the same time. She painted more cows than gazelles, but Jeanot didn't mind.

Together, Jeanot and his mother made teepees from fabric remnants and dowels.

"Like this," she showed him, gathering and tying the sticks together at one end. She made a cone, cut a small swatch of fabric and used clear brown glue to stick the fabric to the dowels. Then using a very small brush and oil paints, she decorated the teepees with images of stars, moons, horses, bears and antelopes. And cows.

For a long time the diorama was the focus of Jeanot's world. Every holiday brought new braves and cowhands, some wielding lariats and pistols. The building's Russian concierge, Sergei Kharkov, gave Jeanot a Cossack on a steed. The tiny figure wore a fur hat and brandished a shiny saber and it never entered Jeanot's mind that a Cossack might be ill at ease in an Indian village.

The Cossack was followed by a set of plastic dinosaurs that for a while terrorized the village until the braves laid the last one low. Then appeared a fur-swabbed seal-hunter in a kayak, wielding a harpoon. This was problematic until Maman created a pond on the far side of the table using an old cracked mirror and blue and white paint.

Pour Papa et Maman, Isa et Flo, Louise et Tatie. Merci à tous !

"You see? He fits right in," she said.

Jeanot was doubtful at first. "There aren't any seals in the desert," he told her.

She thought about it for a moment then shrugged. "It's America. Anything can happen."

In 1955 in Paris, France, everything about *Les États Unis* was miraculous to a boy like Jeanot. He read voraciously and devoured three magazines a week; *Tintin, Spirou,* and *Mickey. Tintin* was excellent, by far his favorite, full of the serialized adventures of the magazine's namesake, Tintin, a young reporter who traveled to the moon, defeated bad guys, and discovered treasures with his best friend, the drunken sailor, Capitaine Haddock. *Spirou* wasn't bad and featured Lucky Luke, a sharpshooting cowboy in perpetual chase of the Dalton Brothers. *Mickey*, Jeanot thought, was really for little kids. He was fast outgrowing the magazine whose only saving grace was a weekly center page on *Les États Unis.*

He gleaned other information on the miraculous land across the Atlantic from his parents' subscriptions to *Paris Match* and *L'Écran.* There was, as well, a large soft-covered book on the wonders of the world. There he learned about the Grand Canyon, geysers, Kodiak bears, the Rocky Mountains, the Great Lakes and the American Civil War, *la Guerre de Sécession.*

The magazines, however, didn't answer every question. Jeanot found some things confusing, still. Puritans and settlers seemed interchangeable. Was George Washington still president, or was it Monsieur Roosevelt, in his wheelchair? Jeanot even heard some people say France had lost the war and it was American soldiers who had saved *La Patrie,* but that was patently ridiculous. The Germans, *les Boches,* had been defeated by men and women like his own parents, soldiers who had answered the call of the mythic Général de Gaulle, a giant of a man, three meters tall and strong as an oak tree.

Maman who loved American motion pictures, would come home from shows raving about the latest film. She'd seen *Oklahoma* three times with Jeanot and from that show, he had deduced that everyone in America sang, and rather well at that. This was further borne out by the guitar-playing Gene Autrey and Roy Rogers. Maman never missed anything featuring Tyrone Powers, whom she maintained looked a lot like her Roland, though Jeanot could never see any resemblance between his Papa and the American movie star.

Personally, Jeanot enjoyed *The Living Desert* and saw much of America as a place of shifting sands, moving rocks, dangerous snakes and lizards, and flash floods. Obviously, l'Amérique was a place far more dangerous than peacetime Paris. Most days, Jeanot walked to school by himself, crossed streets, bought his own magazines at the corner kiosk, and once or twice a week was sent to the *boulangerie* to buy bread. He might not be able to survive a living desert, but he knew his own neighborhood as well as the courtyard of the building where he lived.

Occasionally his father spoke of l'Amérique. Papa had been there as the traveling secretary to an important British person, and had gone to such places as Chicago, New York and Saskatchewan, which was almost as fun to pronounce as Massachusetts. Maman always said, *"Maches ta chaussette,"* which meant, "Chew your sock," but the joke was old and now Jeanot only smiled.

"Well," said Papa, "You wouldn't believe the buildings. They're ten times taller than here, where we live."

Jeanot knew his father was subject to exaggerations. Even his mother accused him of talking too big, saying things like, "Pft, Roland. What nonsense. Jeanot's too smart to believe all this, aren't you?"

Jeanot would nod yes, because he remembered the story his Papa had told once with a completely straight face about jumping out of an airplane.

Still, buildings that big? There'd been a story in *Tintin* about a building in New York City that was 381 meters tall, sixty meters taller than the Eiffel tower which, as every schoolkid in France knew, was 325 meters high. Maybe his Maman was right. In America, anything could happen.

Chapter 2

Events took a distressing turn when Jeanot and his family moved to the third floor apartment on rue de la Terrasse. Jeanot heard Mathilde, the maid, whispering about it outside the bathroom as he brushed his teeth one night. Oncle Yves, Maman's brother, had apparently "become smitten" with Papa.

Jeanot wasn't certain what that meant. Did men become "smitten" with other men? Surely not, or at least, not in the same way that Papa was "smitten" with Maman. Perhaps this was some sort of strange adult terminology with which he wasn't yet familiar. Jeanot didn't care about the state of Oncle Yves affections, but he was sure Papa would be mortified, if it was true. Not everything that Mathilde gossiped about, Jeanot knew, turned out to be true.

Oncle Yves was a charming man whom Jeanot didn't much like. He was the friend of famous people, and he claimed all sorts of connections to celebrities of whom Jeanot had never heard, but whose names apparently impressed everyone else in the room. Oncle Yves said that Ravel's "Left Hand Concerto" had been written for him "to strengthen that side of my body. As a child, I was a naturally weak leftist." He was 'a horizontal friend' of Cocteau's, lunched with Poulenc, advised Coco Chanel, knew Frank Lloyd Wright and claimed to inspire Edith Piaf. Jeanot had heard, at least, of Piaf; who hadn't? Papa was not impressed, Maman was and planned a party with Yves and his famous friends as honored guests.

Oncle Yves practiced the piano six hours a day, which to Jeanot sounded like the worst kind of torture. He read newspapers infrequently and listened to the radio only when classical programs were broadcast; programs which bored Jeanot to distraction. Yves was one of the rare humans Jeanot actively disliked. He'd once called Jeanot an idiot for using the salad fork to eat desert, and Jeanot had not forgiven him.

On April Fool's day 1952, Maman hosted the *soirée*. Mathilde hissed to Louise, another seasoned maid, that the party was "for Madame's new friends, only to impress the old ones."

Mathilde and Louise were driven to a frenzy of housecleaning. Two of the younger *soubrettes*, Solange and Corinne, were hired to serve; Monsieur Boyer, a former butler, mixed drinks, and Rémi-Pierre, the concierge's adopted son whom Jeanot quite liked, found employment announcing the guests.

Babette and her parents were the first to arrive. She grabbed Jeanot by the arm and dragged him to a corner of the room. They sat on the floor and she told him about each of the guests as they entered.

Babette was Jeanot's best friend. Two years older than him, she was full of information, self-assured, and inventive when necessary. He had known her since before he could walk, and remembered taking his first few steps with her help.

She knew all the guests. Her parents, she said, entertained the same crowd and were voluble in their gossip.

"That's Dr. Bouzet," she told him. "He's a dentist, and an alcoholic. His wife died three years ago and he drinks more and more." Jeanot knew Dr. Bouzet as a dentist who had pulled the teeth of three generations of Févriers and as a builder of wooden model ships in bottles. Babette said, "Those are the Dumas. They tell everyone they're related to The Three Musketeer Dumas, but my mother said that's nonsense. They're *nouveau-riches* and stuffy and their parents owned a *boulangerie.*"

A little later, she added, "Oh, look, the man in the wheelchair, the one being pushed by the lady with blue hair? Those are Maître and Madame Gaspard Vincent." She mock-shivered in revulsion. "He helped prosecute Dreyfus." Jeanot shivered too. He didn't know what a Dreyfus was, but if Babette disliked the Vincents, he would too.

A few minutes after that, he said, "That's Captain Walker and Mrs Walker. They rent rooms down the hall."

Babette squinted at them. "Trudy's parents?"

Jeanot nodded. Babette made a snuffling sound of disdain. There had been a minor fashion incident when Trudy had been seen in the hallway by Babette, who swore the American girl was wearing diapers under her dress.

Hervé Bourrillot, a journalist for *Le Figaro*, had brought his son Dédé, a shifty-eyed and slightly hunch-backed kid Jeanot didn't care for. Dédé, in turn, brought two potato guns, the novelty of the month, which his father had received free for plugging the item in his newspaper. Dédé, who smelled strongly of onions, gave Jeanot one of the weapons as a goodwill gesture, sealing a friendship that would last most of the evening.

The tip of the gun's barrel was dug into a potato (or carrot, turnip or radish) to make a vegetable bullet. Dédé operated it by squeezing a rubber pump built into the gun's grip. When fired, the bullet traveled both very fast and very far before splattering on its target. Jeanot thought it was the most splendid thing he'd ever seen.

Each armed with a medium-sized potato stolen from the kitchen, Jeanot and Dédé practiced their aim in the boy's room, leaving large, wet marks on the wallpaper. Dédé shot Jeanot in the butt. It stung! Jeanot retaliated, leaving a sizeable red welt on Dédé's forehead. They sprayed the mirror and windows, defaced one of Maman's better aquarelle, and took pot shots at the light bulbs. This was particularly satisfying since the load sizzled and steamed when it hit the bulbs and the room was filled with the aroma of potato bread.

When Mathilde called them to dinner, she shook her head in disgust. "A waste of good food," she said. Then, looking at the potato guns, she added, "Besides, I imagine there are better and bigger targets in the living room."

Oncle Yves and his celebrities arrived around ten; a noisy, argumentative group that stuck together in a nucleus of fame. They were polite yet distant, drinking a great deal, eating messily from the buffet table and pointedly not mingling with the less stellar guests. Conversation stalled; Maman's friends suddenly seemed uncomfortable. Jeanot felt awkward in the heavy atmosphere; Dédé began yawning and even Babette was uncharacteristically quiet. It seemed that Oncle Yves' famous friends had only ended what had started off as a rather amusing party. Jeanot was disappointed. He was concerned that if the guests began to leave, the gift of the potato gun might be untimely revoked.

It was at that moment that Oncle Yves suggested a leg contest; a party game all the rage some years before among "balletomanes," he assured the group.

"In the old days, Nijinsky won the contests so often," said Oncle Yves, "that after a while, Diaghilev refused to let him participate."

He undid his belt and let his trousers fall to the ground. Babette gasped, covered Dédé's eyes and had her hands batted away. Jeanot noticed that Babette didn't think to cover her own eyes.

Hortense and Violette Beaumarchais, the 60-ish twins from the fifth floor, shrieked in unison. Oncle Yves shot them a withering look and extended a leg clad in flesh-colored ballet tights.

"What we need," he said, "are bed sheets." He looked around, "Where is the housekeeper… Mathilde!"

Mathilde had confessed to Jeanot once that she had never liked Oncle Yves. A man "without an honest means of employ, who slept late, loafed at home and went to the toilet while talking on the telephone," was not a man she could respect.

"Get sheets, Mathilde. Three of them. The large ones."

When she returned, Oncle Yves directed the sheets be tied together lengthwise to make a thin curtain which could shield people from mid-thigh to above the head. The women were gathered on one side of the curtain, the men on the other. Oncle Yves told them to remove their pants, socks and shoes.

"Now," said Oncle Yves, "each man walks the length of the curtain so that his legs—and only his legs—are visible to our friends of the opposite sex. They may ask an individual to demonstrate some skill—a jump, a hop, an *entrechat*—to best reveal his attributes. Applause shall select the winner."

Captain Walker looked shocked and chose to quietly fade away but most of the other men—save Dr. Bouzet who pleaded psoriasis, and the wheel-chair bound Gaspard Vincent—doffed their trousers. Dédé looked for a moment as though he might do the same, but a withering glare from Babette forestalled him. Jeanot had no interest in removing his own trousers, but he found himself fascinated by the ridiculous display.

The collection of legs revealed an amazing array of morphologies. There were fat ones, skinny ones, tendons and muscles displayed or swathed in rolls of lard, some hairy, some hairless, all a milky pallor.

The men capered behind the sheets, not at all like the gazelles in Jeanot's bedroom; the women laughed, booed, cheered, called out orders and applauded. Monsieur Dumas' turn to parade was met with an audible gasp, and whispers of "here, now, is a pair of worthy legs!" Monsieur Dumas, Jeanot had overheard during the party, played tennis, swam and was an avid collector of butterflies. He had been known to chase into exhaustion evasive species in order to pin them in his display cases.

Monsieur Dumas was asked to kick right, then left. He was told to stand on tip-toes, to turn this way and that, to bring his heels together, apart and together again. Piaf whistled loudly and Chagall whipped out his sketchpad. Oncle Yves stared shamelessly, leading Jeanot to wonder, for an uncomfortable moment, remembering what Mathilde had said about hisOncle Yves being "smitten" with Papa.

Dédé and Jeanot opened fire with the potato guns just as Monsieur Dumas attempted a plié.

Later, much later, Dédé Bourillot burst into tears when accused of vandalism and pointed a finger at Jeanot, sobbing, "*C'est sa faute! Il m'a forcé!*" After all the guests had left, Papa smashed the toy guns with a mallet and cursed the reporter for being such a thoughtless oaf. Mathilde had left, promising to return in the morning to clean up (while wearing a smile inappropriate to the situation). Jeanot, all four cheeks afire, was sentenced to the hallway closet—the direst of punishments.

It was totally, completely, irremediably dark in there and smelled of mothballs. He sat on a pair of Papa's winter boots and played with the laces. He mourned the potato gun, now in several pieces, its rubber pear cut into thin strips by his mother. Dédé, that spoiled baby, had sold him out without a moment's thought. Now Jeanot would never get a *real* gun, or even one that shot caps; certainly not before next Christmas, an eternity away. It was all very unfair, and for the longest time, surrounded by shoe smells and drowned in darkness, he wondered if for the rest of his life all the good moments would merit bad ones.

While Jeanot sat in the closet, he listened to his parents having a violent argument, each accusing the other of inviting the Figaro reporter. The words were unclear but the boy could hear the rise and fall of voices and, finally, the slamming of doors. He waited a half-an-hour until everything was quiet, then let himself out. The apartment was still lit, the two large chandeliers in the party room ablaze. He could hear his mother's soft snores coming from the master bedroom. He tip-toed into the living room that smelled of cigarette smoke, perfumed sweat and spent champagne. The place was a welter of overflowing ashtrays and half-empty glasses. Maman never cleaned up right after a party; she preferred to wait until the next morning, declaring that a good evening should not end in drudgery.

Jeanot was thirsty. He surveyed the surroundings, found a glass almost full of amber liquid and drank five large mouthfuls while holding his breath. The stuff fired his throat and hit his stomach like a depth-charge. For a moment, he thought he might vomit his supper on the floor, but he didn't.

There were other glasses, different colors. Wine, he could recognize and stayed away from. His parents often served him *abondance* with his meals, mixing a centimeter of wine into a large tumbler of water, but he didn't like the stuff's coppery flavor.

He sniffed a few more glasses, and settled on one shaped like a balloon and smelling like *baba au rum*. He swallowed its contents without gagging. A third glass, he knew, contained Pernod. He liked the ornate blue, green and silver label on the bottle and always watched when his father fixed one. The distinctive anisette aroma filled his nose, so he drank three large swallows of that too.

He slid under the big Napoleon III couch, then stretched out. The ceiling panels swayed slightly like gentle waves, and that was very restful. He stared at them for a while, decided he was still thirsty and finished the Pernod. He thought a big chunk of dark chocolate might go well with the anisette so he found the box from Belgium his mother kept on the piano and ate a few of those. Soon he was thirsty again.

Now the choice of beverages appeared limitless, so he sampled one, grimaced, and spit it back into the glass. Something honey-colored caught his eye. It smelled vaguely of oranges, which tasted good with chocolate. It was smooth and the tang filled all the spaces beneath his tongue and between his teeth. He got drowsy and knew he should go to bed but his legs were thick and rubbery and he decided it would be a lot of trouble to take his clothes off, so he didn't. He curled up on the couch. He thought again about the potato gun and giggled at the remembered image of Oncle Yves jumping at least a foot off the floor when the potato bullets hit him in the back of the thighs. He fell asleep in mid-laugh, trying to stifle the sound so he wouldn't wake his parents.

In the morning, Maman found him. She was not angry and she didn't preach. She had Mathilde fix him tea with a dash of rum, which he drank happily—three cups—before falling asleep again. Mathilde offered to make tea for Maman as well, but Maman said she preferred a glass of water with her morning pills.

Papa was more worried and didn't seem to care much for Maman's remedy. There'd been drinkers in his family, he told Jeanot with a serious look in his eyes. His older sister was a sequestered drunk. He'd dealt with intoxicated soldiers during the war, and had come to realize there was no greater danger to groups or individuals than someone incapable of holding his liquor.

Jeanot listened, but his head hurt and it was hard to pay attention.

There was a lot of whispering back and forth, with Mathilde for once taking Maman's side. "A drink never hurt anyone," she said, though she seldom drank herself. "Where I come from, you start the day with a little white wine, and it carries you through the worst weather. Everyone knows that. Leave the boy alone; there's no harm done."

By the time Jeanot felt well enough to stand, trundle to the bathroom, puke, dress and make his way to the street with Mathilde, it was nearly mid-afternoon. The school day was almost over, and though his eyes hurt from the sunlight, he felt the evening had, all in all, been a success.

Later, he helped his Oncle Répaud walk Soldat, the three-legged dog, ran an errand for his Tante Jacqueline, spent an hour in the cellar rearranging his magazines and covered three sheets of paper with doodles. He started a poem but couldn't quite make it rhyme or move the way he imagined it should, so he gave that up. He wished he could be a poet like Minou Drouet, the 8-year-old genius who had recently been featured in *Paris Match*. It galled him that a girl could get that much recognition doing something he should be able to do. He was, after all, very good at placing words next to one another, not that it impressed anyone. When Minou Drouet did it, everybody noticed. Even his teacher at the école maternelle had said Minou was an *enfant-prodige*, a one-of-a-kind and didn't she wish she had students like Minou instead of a bunch of slow-witted children who couldn't remember how to spell 'Napoléon?'

Chapter 3

A dark intimidating corridor led to the kitchen and toilet. Often, Jeanot secretly peed in the bathtub to avoid going into that corridor, or he crossed his legs and held his breath.

At one end of the apartment were three rooms rented to Captain Walker, his pregnant wife, and their daughter, Trudy. They'd moved in after the end of the war. Grand-père Leopold had loaned the apartment to Jeanot's parents shortly after their son's birth, and thought the modest rent the American family paid might help Jeanot's family make ends meet. The Americans' rooms were furnished with a mad mix of Grand-père's most worn antiques: Louis XVI Bergères chairs painted red with scarlet upholstery, a sagging Art Nouveau sofa upholstered in fading velvet, and upright gas lamps poorly converted to provide electrical lighting.

Trudy fascinated Jeanot. She was six and he'd never seen a girl that looked even remotely like her. For one thing, she took a bath every single night, and the thought of that much hot water devoted to one small body boggled his mind. *He* took a bath twice a week usually following his two sisters, Madeleine and Françoise, when they came to spend the day and use the facilities. When it was his turn, the water was already grey and mucky with a ring of spent soap and grime around the tub.

Also, Trudy was blond. She was *really, really* blond, as if someone had painted her hair bright gold and the paint hadn't dried yet. She always wore white, spoke only English and was a snob, ignoring him with studied disdain whenever he happened to be standing by the bathroom door as she came from her bath wrapped in a fluffy pink towel.

Once, he asked his Maman, whom he knew dyed her hair from mousy brown to Hollywood blonde, if Trudy dyed her hair too.

"Nobody in Paris has hair that yellow! It can't be real!"

The announcement seemed to perplex his mother. "*Vraiment?* I don't know. Maybe in America the sun is different. It does things to children's hair. Ask your Papa."

Jeanot never did. Hair dying, he was certain, was not a subject on which his Papa would have extensive knowledge.

Trudy's father, the Captain, was a pale stout man with close set squinty eyes. Jeanot rarely saw Trudy's mother. According to Papa, she was adjusting poorly to foreign lands, their people, foods, languages, and habits. Whenever Jeanot caught a glimpse of her, she looked feral and frightened. Once, turning a corner, Jeanot surprised her as she carried a load of hand laundry back to their rooms. The woman yelped something incomprehensible and dropped everything on the floor. Jeanot helped her gather the clothing and sheets, taking the opportunity to pocket a pair of Trudy's panties for later inspection.

The American couple paid part of their rent by buying goods at the American PX for Jeanot's parents. There were things at the PX rarely found in French stores or, if available, so expensive they belonged to the world of fantasy. Papa got shoes, big black squashers he kept meticulously shined, and Maman had a steady supply of Pall Mall cigarettes in royal red packs. There were boxes of Tide, Johnny Walker whiskey, Ivory soap, pancake mix that, water added, made somewhat edible *crêpes*, potatoes the size of small dogs and strange, tasteless red sausages served on buns so soft they might be cake. Jeanot got underwear with a slot to pee through and a toy Colt 45 with a black plastic belt and holster. Even Madeleine and Françoise got stuff from the PX: bras with reinforced cups, an accurate-to-the-nanosecond metronome for Madeleine, an Olivetti portable typewriter for

Françoise who, barely seventeen, was heading off to England to train as a "bilingual secretary." Jeanot understood that meant she could perform boring menial tasks in both French and English. The culture in Grande Bretagne was nothing like American culture, he'd been told, and didn't interest Jeanot at all.

Jeanot had never actually been to the PX, so the mysterious market open only to US citizens became in his imagination everything France was not and America was—rich, modern, plentiful and inaccessible.

The family's other major American connection was Papa's automobile, an olive green 1941 DeSoto Series S-8 Custom Coupe that Papa bragged had once belonged to the cultural attaché of the Canadian Embassy.

The car dwarfed its Parisian counterparts, belched clouds of blue smoke, stank of gasoline, ran only on moderately sunny days, and menaced the rest of traffic. The brakes worked when pumped *precisely* four times in rapid succession. The blinkers did not blink, the tires were bald, and the clutch was worn and wheezed. To start the DeSoto in the winter, Papa would light a newspaper fire beneath the hood to warm the carburetor. The car was his joy and, by osmosis, that of Sergei Kharkov, the concierge.

Kharkov washed the car every Friday. Jeanot once helped him, lugging buckets of soapy water from the courtyard to the street.

"A magnificent car," Kharkov told him as they were cleaning the wheels with soap and a stiff brush.

"Papa sometimes curses when he tries to start it, especially when it's cold. He says bad words in English.".

The concierge nodded. "Well now, that makes perfect sense. Cursing in French at an English-speaking car serves no purpose at all."

Jeanot thought Kharkov was pretty sharp. "Do you speak English, Monsieur Kharkov?"

"Of course," said the concierge, and recited his favorite words. "Beaver coat, amber waves of grain, special skies, to be or not to be." He paused, scrubbed. "I know a lot more, of course. But those are the words everyone must know in America."

"Papa says you should also know, 'Hello, I am lost, my name is Jeanot.' But not in your case. You'd have to say, 'My name is Monsieur Kharkov.'"

Then they dried the DeSoto's hood and sides with a chamois cloth, scrubbed the bald tires, swept out the inside with a straw broom, polished the chrome and cleaned the windshield with a mixture of ammonia and soap.

In exchange for these services, Papa allowed the Russian to sit in the passenger seat while the car was parked, looking like a man impatiently waiting for something or someone important. Kharkov was not allowed to smoke his cigarettes in the car. It was a small sacrifice. Kharkov ate his lunch in the DeSoto, gossiped with his Russian friends who knew where to find him every day from noon to two, ogled girls who passed by, and if he noticed that Jeanot was around, entertained him with his deep knowledge of America.

"They all wear hats. Except the Indians, of course, who wear feathers and mink tails in their hair," he assured the boy. That sounded good. Jeanot saw himself in a hat like Gene Autry's, or wearing a Blackfoot headdress made of eagle and pigeon feathers. He wasn't sure about the mink tails. Tatie, his great aunt who lived in St. Germain and visited twice a month, wore a ratty fox collar with tails *and* heads attached and he wouldn't be caught dead in that.

"And they're all rich," said the Russian. "But then," he made a face the boy had seen whenever France was mentioned, "it's easy to get rich over there. Not like this damned shitty hell hole of a country."

Kharkov had a wide-ranging collection of books, magazines, photographs and records dedicated to America, which he allowed Jeanot to inspect.

He referred to these often when declaring his expansive knowledge of the United States. Thoughts of that almost mythical nation—he sometimes called his library "The Church of America"—softened his usually harsh features. He smoked American-made Camel cigarettes when he could afford them and when he couldn't, filled empty Camel packs with hand-rolled mixtures of Turkish, Algerian and

Gitane tobacco. He field-stripped the butts, kept what was smokable and re-rolled it so that he gave off a smell Oncle Répaud likened to a barnyard on fire after a rainstorm.

Back in the concierge loge, Jeanot hung onto the Russian's every word about America. Kharkov looked around as if making sure no one could overhear him and whispered, "But the great secret of Americans is that they have very tiny *zizis*. It's a fact; one centimeter, maybe two if they're fortunate. And that," he paused for emphasis, illustrating a two centimeter span with his thumb and forefinger, "is why American women always want to come to Europe."

This made no sense to Jeanot, who nodded his head anyway. He knew what a *zizi* was, but the relationship between *zizis* and women was unclear. As far as Jeanot was aware, *zizis* were the province of men only, although in America, of course, things might be different.

"A lot of Americans have six toes," the Russian concierge continued, "which is why they so run fast. The extra toe makes them more stable. Jesse Owens has *seven* toes on his right foot; that's how he won the Olympics. It is also why Hitler hated him. Hitler only had four, and one tiny ball that according to what I've heard, never worked at all."

Now *that* made perfect sense. There was a kid in Jeanot's class who was thumbless and had the devil of a time writing without making huge ink spots all over his notebook. The kid shook so much no one wanted to sit next to him; he sprayed ink in all directions. It was said his palsy came from mono-ballism.

"The Americans come from all over the world," said the concierge. "But it's easy to tell them apart. The short ones who smell bad are either Italian or Greek, though sometimes they're Irish. If they smell bad and work in a restaurant, they're Italian. Most Russians are teachers or musicians, unless they're Jews, in which case they sell clothing in the streets. I have photos of this. Generally, it's very cheap clothing, nothing a civilized man would wear so they sell them to the Chinese and to the Africans. In any case, the Russian Jews are very good business people, so watch your pockets. There are a lot of Africans and Chinese, but not in the big cities."

"And the French?" asked the boy. "What do they do in America?"

The Russian shrugged his shoulders. "The same as they do here. Next to nothing, the lazy bastards. *Des bons à rien.*"

Jeanot felt he had to defend his countrymen, an easy task since that week's *Tintin* had been devoted to the greatness of French inventions. "But we invented the airplane, and the telephone, and radium, and cheese."

The Russian scoffed. "All those are Russian, except maybe the cheese."

Kharkov apparently knew everything there was to know about America, France *and* Russia.

Once a month or so, Papa drove Kharkov around to impress the less affluent *emigrés*, and on two or three occasions Jeanot was permitted to ride along, provided he kept his mouth shut. Dressed in his best clothes and topped with a faded black homburg that gave him a sinister look, Kharkov would treat Papa like a chauffeur, projecting so much *hauteur* that Jeanot pictured him as a Russian Czar. Papa drove to the Russian épicerie, where Kharkov gossiped with the owner and bought a small bottle of cheap vodka, to the *pharmacie* for pills that promised eyesight improvements, and slowly past the Russian tea room on Avenue Foche.

One time, a few days after the spud gun party, Papa and Kharkov took Jeanot along and the Russian gave the boy a swig from the vodka bottle. Papa stopped the car with a squeal of tires, opened the passenger door and shoved the Russian out. It was many months before the Russian was allowed in the DeSoto again.

Chapter 4

Jeanot's great aunt Tatie owned a house in St. Germain en Laye near a large public park abutting a *château.*

It was called the *Château de Neuilly,* and its surrounding grounds were a maze of wide yellow gravel-covered avenues that crisscrossed 170 acres of grass, trees, streams and ponds. Jeanot had been there dozens of times, once to model children's outfits for a fashion magazine.

That had been in 1951 when Maman had answered an ad in *France-Soir* seeking four, five, and six-year-old children for a day's work. The parents, she assured Papa, would be paid a massive sum; the equivalent to two months' salary for an entry-level government worker if the photos were published.

Ever since she'd seen an advertisement for a little girl's mink coat costing 300 francs, Maman had been talking to her family about opening a dressmaking shop. She had a good eye for fashion, was nimble with a needle, and had been given a non-functional Singer electric sewing machine by the American Captain's wife. Papa had fixed the machine by resoldering a loose wire, and he and Maman had calculated the startup costs of *Créations St. Paul.* They would produce expensive children's clothing for those Papa referred to as "the stupidly wealthy." Jeanot's modeling debut, his parents assured him, would be the perfect entrée to a *haute couture* career.

Maman had a photographer friend take a few shots of Jeanot and sent them to the advertising agency. To her delight and amazement, and to Jeanot's chagrin, he was one of twelve children selected.

That morning was not a good one for him. Earlier, the American girl, Trudy, had snubbed him, calling him something vile in English— he hadn't understood the word but the meaning was unmistakable— and Mathilde had swatted him for being underfoot. Either at the Gare St. Lazare or in the train to St. Germain, he had lost the tin cowboy he most treasured. Fifteen minutes before the modeling session, Jeanot was in tears, his nose bathed in snot and his eyes red.

Maman wrestled him into the first outfit, a smart if scratchy flannel suit with short pants, an Eton jacket and a matching cap. She won his cooperation only by promising he would get to keep the cap. Based on this vow, Jeanot behaved through three hours of posing and changing outfits, and only when it was all over did he notice the cap was gone, packed up in a cardboard suitcase with the other fashionable items. Furious, he unlatched the suitcase when no one was looking, peed in it, ran away and hid in the woods. Maman, panicked, called the local police which sent two young gendarmes on bicycles. They found Jeanot asleep under a tree sucking his thumb.

In the café where they later ate lunch, he sat up very straight even though his butt hurt from the spanking, but it was well worth it. The gray flannel cap hidden in the crotch of his pants itched only slightly. Then it struck him on the way to his Tatie's home that he would never be able to wear the thing in public. That made the punishment costly, cheeks-wise.

Weeks later, Mathilde found the cap and, not knowing its significance, donated it with a bag of old clothes to the Algerian Children's Relief Fund. She mentioned the donation to Maman, and Jeanot had to pretend complete disinterest until he could retreat to his room and shed a few frustrated tears.

Maman returned to Paris and Jeanot spent the night and the following day at Tatie's and thought for the very first time that perhaps crime did not pay.

Tatie slept with her hat on, the veil covering her face down to the nose. Her house smelled of lavender and animal skins, boiled potatoes, hard-boiled eggs and dog. The mutt, Mathurin, lay like a dead beast on Tatie's zebra rug and farted quietly in its sleep. He was, thought Jeanot, about the least interesting animal ever created. Tatie's maid, Guénolé, detested Mathurin, and she abused the beast whenever Tatie was not around, dragging him by his leashed neck for forced walks. Mathurin endured the maltreatment and kicks stoically, and Jeanot decided the animal was so uninteresting as to merit the abuse. The dog's revenge lacked subtlety. Every once in a while, Mathurin would sneak up on Guénolé, get up on his hind legs and hump her left thigh. This so repulsed the old woman she would be unable to eat for a day or so, and Tatie would feed the table's leftovers to the dog instead of to the maid.

Jeanot had once asked Guénolé, "Why don't you like Mathurin?"

The maid had made a spitting sound, even though they were indoors. "That's not a dog," she said. "It is a *sac de merde.*"

Jeanot more or less agreed.

Tatie's house was filthy. There were large balls of dust, dog hair and stuff Jeanot couldn't identify on the floor and caught in cobwebs on the ceiling. Guénolé never cleaned. A woman came twice a month to dust and push a wheezing vacuum cleaner across the threadbare rugs, but it didn't make much difference. Papa and Maman brought their own bread when they visited and refused everything but sardines from cans and hard-boiled eggs from which they peeled the shells themselves. Papa said it was the only way to make sure Guénolé didn't actually touch what they were going to eat.

Tatie herself survived mostly on white chicken meat smothered in mayonnaise, so that's what Jeanot ate too when he visited, though the mayonnaise always made him queasy. Sometimes there were croissants, occasionally a piece of cheese and some carrots. Jeanot didn't come for the food, he came for the adventure.

Tatie's house was a museum, a repository of ancient military uniforms and kepis, ceremonial swords, single-shot infantry rifles, the leg of an elephant, and a large rug made of jaguar skins stitched together with three heads on it. There were African spears mounted on one wall, a harpsichord that made dainty sounds, medals and certificates, a full suit of armor so delicate Jeanot thought it must have belonged to a child, an elk antler coat rack with burnooses and *ao dais* from French Indochina.

Outside under an oil cloth was an old motorcycle with "Vincent" in faded gold on the gas tank. Jeanot wondered who Vincent was but was afraid to ask. Tatie, he knew, had lost someone—either a son or a husband, he wasn't sure—to a horrible illness contracted in Madagascar; a French colony, he knew, and an island as well. No one was allowed to talk about it. He hoped Vincent wouldn't come back and claim the machine so maybe *he* could have it when he was older. He'd ridden on the pillion of a motorcycle just a year earlier and it had been the most exciting thing ever. The thing roared like a lion, accelerated like a dragonfly, vibrated in such a way it made his crotch feel good.

He liked to accompany Tatie when she went shopping. Guénolé no longer went to the market daily since she'd lost her teeth there sampling a peach. Jeanot had been there when it had happened. The dentures had popped out of the maid's mouth with the peach and fallen to the ground. They were then kicked into the storm drain by a passerby. Guénolé made such a scene that the firemen came and lifted the nearest manhole cover to see if the teeth had survived but of course they hadn't. The maid returned to Tatie's house and locked herself in her room. Tatie didn't seem to care. Guénolé, Jeanot knew, was a moody creature known to not speak for days and who often cursed and attacked the carrots and celery she was peeling with a butcher knife. This self-imposed solitude was nothing remarkable in comparison.

The next day, however, Guénolé and Jeanot went to the market, and the maid spied a pair of eyeglasses on the offending peach seller's stand. She stole them. She wore them around the house for a week though they made her blind and she bumped into the furniture, but as she explained to the boy, this was an honest exchange. "They took my teeth, I took their eyes. This is how the world works, boy, and you'd better get used to it."

Jeanot said, "Really? Papa says you should never steal. It's wrong."

The maid replied, "I didn't steal, I borrowed. When they return my teeth, they can have their glasses back."

When Tatie shopped, she never bought one or two, she bought six or eight. The merchants all knew this and greeted her effusively; very few people, Jeanot thought, bought a half-dozen *saucissons* or eight wedges of Camembert cheese at once, or, for that matter, six baguettes. It never seemed to bother Tatie that no sooner did the supplies come through the front door than they went out the rear, hidden, Jeanot suspected, under Guénolé's capacious skirts. He'd caught the maid exchanging them at the local café for two early morning shots of Cointreau.

Tatie only disliked one person as far as Jeanot knew, and that was her own nephew, Yves. Tatie knew, of course, that Oncle Yves was an accomplished pianist, friends with Ravel and Poulenc, that his fame reflected well on the family and by association on Tatie herself. Maman had said as much. None of these things mattered, however. Oncle Yves was a *grande tapette*, Guénolé once explained gleefully to Jeanot. He was a "sinful homosexual" whose mores were shameful, indecent, and unworthy of French citizenship.

Later, when Jeanot hesitantly asked Babette what the maid had meant by "homosexual," he was shocked by her explanation. He was also reminded of the remark he'd once heard at home, when Mathilde had mentioned Oncle Yves' attraction to Jeanot's own Papa. Jeanot considered mentioning that episode to Babette, but ultimately he decided Papa would probably not have approved of the gossip, and that Maman would have been horrified if indeed this behavior was as "sinful" as Guénolé led Jeanot to believe. No, she wouldn't have liked anyone outside of the family to know about it, and so Jeanot kept it to himself, for the time being at least.

Tatie once said that she believed Oncle Yves's preferences stemmed from an incident dating back to the 20's when her brother, Jeanot's Grand-père Léopold, trying to impress a billiard-playing crony, bought an expensive Brunswick & Balke table and had it installed in its own room in the rear of the apartment. The table had to be craned in, windows removed from their frames, and reinforcing steel bars inserted into the floor to ensure the table's level.

Oncle Yves was 12 at the time, already acknowledged as a prodigy. He was forbidden from entering the billiard room, nor was he allowed to touch the cues or the ivory balls. One day, however, he did. When Grand-père and his second wife Emma (to whom Jeanot had never once spoken) were attending the matinee premiere of Léopold's long-awaited opera *Mona Vanna*, Oncle Yves racked the balls, chalked and tested a cue as he had seen his father do, drew back and hit the cue ball with force. The shot was low and the stick's tip ripped through the green felt with a rending sound, exposing the polished slate bed.

Oncle Yves, immediately aware of the catastrophe's immensity, stared at the split fabric for a moment before surrendering to terror.

Then and there he decided to run away. In minutes he had packed a change of trousers, underwear, shirt and socks, and a pair of black deerskin gloves in the small rattan suitcase used for vacation travel. He also took with him an unfinished symphony he had been composing since age eight. He bolted out the door, down the stairs and into the street at the very instant that Grand-père and Emma, back from a hostile audience's reception of *Mona Vanna*, alit from a cab. He was carried sobbing back into the apartment where Grand-père, already staggering under the weight of his failed musical efforts, went straight to the billiard room.

The next day a tailor came to strip the felt from the table. A week later, the bright green cloth was a three piece suit that Oncle Yves was to wear at every social occasion until he outgrew it two years later.

Tatie was convinced the fabric's color had somehow warped Yves's sensitivities. *"J'en suis persuadé,"* she would tell Guénolé who paid scant attention, or Jeanot, who wasn't sure he understood.

Over the years, Tatie became certain Oncle Yves's proclivity was the wellspring of everything that was and could go wrong with the family. When Grand-père's very last opera, *L'Oiseau Bleu* was booed even before the intermission, Tatie assured Jeanot that it was Oncle Yves' fault. When the writer Gustave Cassier choked on an asparagus and died while dining at Grand-père's table, it was, of course, Oncle Yves's fault.

Oncle Yves, one day, finally grasping the depth of Tatie's dislike, took to calling her "the leprous bat," even in front of his own family. He announced that he wouldn't be caught wasting his time with her; that when she someday, mercifully passed away, he wouldn't even be at her funeral.

Chapter 5

Maman was a painter. She'd dabbled in other media, had written and published a children's book, and played both the piano and accordion. Jeanot harbored a small resentment when it came to the book, since it had been written specifically about and for his two sisters. He was waiting for his Maman to announce that there was another book written, one dealing with the adventures of Jeanot. He had been waiting a couple of years and come to the conclusion that writing a book might be very time consuming.

Maman's paintings were drawn largely from old family photographs. She wanted to paint a dozen or so oils before she and Papa opened *Créations St. Paul,* the dressmaking shop made possible by a loan from Grand-père.

She painted colorful, confusing scenes; people in wedding clothes, surrounded by beaming armed Swiss guards. Jeanot had asked why guards were needed at weddings, and had gotten back a nonsensical, unsatisfactory answer that involved the Pope. Maman's paintings reminded him of the *contes de fées* that Jeanot knew he should have outgrown years ago; there were flowers in full bloom and beautiful if slightly too-small horses who never pooped, pulling carriages of happy people. Everything Maman painted, in fact, was happy. There were never any old people, never anyone who was sick or injured. The soldiers never bled, or fought, which was jarring, though not really unpleasant. Maman told Jeanot that the style in which she painted was called neo-naif.

He had noted early that her people varied in height and sometimes were outsize standing next to their horses, or small when with their dogs. Jeanot concluded that in the Old Days most people were short and owned ponies and Great Danes. When he asked Maman about that at the dining table one night, she got mad, but his father laughed so hard red wine came out of his nose.

Painting was a family affair. When Maman decided to unfold her easel, Papa and Jeanot would drive to a dealer outside Amiens for the correct *bois d'épicéa* to build the canvas armatures. Then Papa would bring out the canvas stretchers, mallet, tacks and pliers he had bought at the flea market near Notre Dame. Maman shopped for new brushes, paints and old photographs. She always used the same palette and claimed it had once belonged to Auguste Renoir. The trash gatherer, she assured anyone who would listen, in Renoir's Paris neighborhood had found it in the dustbin shortly after the painter's death, sold it to a local antique dealer along with other items from the painter's studio, and Maman had purchased it on a whim, spending that week's food money.

Jeanot's main responsibility was to stay out of the way, for in the week before Maman actually began painting, life in the apartment assumed a fevered pace. The easel was installed in a vacant maid's room on the top floor, and a gypsy was hired to clamber across the roof and clean the skylight with soap and ammonia. When the man claimed to have hurt himself working at such heights, Maman called Kharkov, who professed a deep hatred and distrust for all Romani. Kharkov and the cleaner argued in the courtyard, their voices echoing off the walls with increasing velocity. Jeanot watched with some interest as they traded insults, then slaps to the face that made cracking sounds. Eventually, the gypsy dropped his hands and left the courtyard with one last over-the-shoulder curse. Maman paid Kharkov a few Francs for the service. The Russian, his cheeks glowing bright red, considered the payment unnecessary and the day well begun. He liked, he said, hitting gypsies early in the morning.

When all was in place for her to begin painting, Maman brought from her bedroom armoire a tiny matador's suit of light she had purchased years before in Spain. It fit Jeanot well after minor alterations, and the boy became her model for several canvases.

He liked the costume; the cape that swirled, the odd sideways hat held on by a chinstrap, the small brass-handled metal sword with a dull blade and a sharp tip. He tried parries and thrusts, parading in front of Trudy's door. She was impressed, he could tell. She touched his shoulder, stroked the sequins enviously. She wanted to try the jacket on but he wouldn't let her. These were *men* clothes that should never adorn a woman's frail figure. Trudy pouted, cried, stomped her foot, and called for her mother who didn't come. Then she tried bribery. She pulled up her skirt and showed him her panties. They were pink and very full and Jeanot wondered if Trudy still indeed wore diapers, as Babette claimed. He found that disquieting, turned his back and practiced his swordplay.

The suit of light, for all its elegance, was troublesome to put on and take off. The jacket alone was held in place with six small hooks that fit into eyelets sewn into the trousers' waistband. Halfway through a graceful series of sword and cape maneuvers, Jeanot realized why Maman had asked him if he needed to go to the bathroom before strapping him into the pants and adjusting the belt and suspenders.

Now he needed. There were no adults in sight. Jeanot ran to the kitchen looking for Mathilde but she was buying that day's food. Maman was in the upstairs studio; Papa was out. Jeanot held his breath, cinched in his bladder, knocked on Trudy's door. No response. He pounded harder, feeling a small leakage run down his leg. The dampness along his thigh made things worse. He tried not to think about it, was inundated with visions of hoses, faucets, streams and waterfalls. He charged to the bathroom, inserted the sword into his pants and sawed up and down. Threads gave, the seams, basted but never sown, split; sequins exploded and fell into the toilet. Jeanot, bladder bursting, wiggled out of the pants, peed, and in a moment of utter thoughtlessness, balled up the gold trousers and shoved them into the toilet bowl. He reached his hand into the yellow water, pushed the sodden mass as far down as he could, then even farther with the point of the sword. He pulled the chain on the overhead tank. The water cascaded down, rose slightly as if uncertain, then edged its way to the lip of the bowl and overflowed. Jeanot flushed again, certain another rush of water would send the offending garment down the pipe and into the sewers. It didn't and the floor was suddenly awash, sequins glinting like gold in a Yukon riverbed. He ran to his room, climbed into bed and pulled the cover over his head. He resolved to breathe deeply and evenly, as possible excuses caromed through his mind.

It took only five minutes for Mathilde, back from the market, to find him, whip the cover off the bed and, holding the ruined pants between index and thumb, march him up the stairs to the studio where Maman was sketching. His mother helped him into the sodden trousers of light, held them in place with safety pins and stood him on a stool. He remained there unmoving for an hour as she outlined the first sketches in charcoal.

Chapter 6

Babette Bonjean was two years older and two inches taller than Jeanot, and infinitely wise. In a matter of minutes she pushed Trudy out of his heart and mind.

Dr. Bonjean was a dentist from a well-off family. Mathilde was adamant that Dr. Bonjean had made good money drilling out the cavities of occupying German officers, but both Papa and Maman liked him. He was a genial man who had lost two brothers in the war and donated heavily to the Jewish orphan and widow relief programs. He had bought one of Maman's paintings and always came bearing large picnic baskets full of butter, cheese, ham, wine, fresh fruit and still-warm breads. Jeanot liked him because he brought Babette.

Babette was worldly. She read aloud from adult books although Jeanot suspected she only pretended to read, and just told made-up stories. He noticed she sometimes turned the pages quickly, sometimes lingered. Occasionally, she looked at him while reading. She also told him she read newspapers daily: *France-Soir,* which Jeanot liked because of the comic strips, and *Le Monde,* a daunting daily with no pictures at all. Jeanot thought she was lying about the newspapers, but it didn't matter. She was the most fascinating creature in his world, and to his delight, she was fond of raising her skirt, pulling down her panties, and explaining to him the basic differences between a boy and a girl.

"Tu vois?" She pointed to the small slit five inches beneath her belly button. *"C'est là que je fais pipi..."* She undid the three buttons

holding his pants up, lowered them and his underwear, took his penis between thumb and forefinger. "*Toi, c'est avec ça.*"

He knew instantly this could be trouble. He glanced at the door. The parents were finishing dinner two rooms away; Dr. Bonjean's sonorous laugh echoed down the hall, and Maman's snorty giggles followed it. Mathilde was in the kitchen aligning wedges of cheese on a flat wooden board and helping herself to slices of Saint Paulin from Brittany, as she usually did. Babette squeezed his penis. Jeanot yelped. She said, "*Quoi?* Does it hurt? Hubert really likes it when I do this." Hubert was Babette's twelve-year-old cousin who was away at boarding school in the Pyrenées. "He likes it a *lot!*" She curled her hand around him, squeezed rhythmically. Jeanot felt a hint of pleasure rise, hidden among the panic.

Maman liked to check on him every twenty-or-so minutes when she entertained. She could be at the door any moment. He peered at Babette who was now concentrating on squeezing and moving her hand back and forth. She was looking down at her work, biting her lower lip. Jeanot sensed imminent disaster but couldn't pull away. Then Babette stopped, shook her head. "You're not old enough. *T'es trops petit...* Hubert is much bigger and more fun to be with." She wiped her hands on her skirt, took her panties off and threw them on the bed. Then she raised her skirt to her hips, lay back on the floor. She opened her legs. "*Touches-moi.*" She took his right hand, placed it over her juncture, pushed his small middle finger down. "*Comme ça. Doucement...*" Jeanot held his breath, listened for footsteps. She slapped his arm. "*Concentres toi!*" So he did, moving his finger here and there. Babette's hand relaxed on his. She smiled slightly, opened her mouth, licked her lips. After an eternity she sat up, pushed him away. "*Assez.*"

Jeanot removed his finger, disappointment and relief sharing space. She retrieved her panties, he buttoned his pants. A minute later, Maman cracked open the door. Jeanot and Babette were sprawled on the floor looking at an illustrated fairytale book. Maman smiled, closed the door. Jeanot exhaled like a cannon shot.

Chapter 7

A month later, Jeanot prepared for his birthday party aware something was afoot. He first became suspicious when Maman came up with an American theme for the party. Jeanot was as fascinated with *les États Unis* as any ten-year-old French boy might have been; he believed cowboys and Indians were in constant battle and that all Negroes played the banjo, an instrument for which Jeanot discovered he had an odd liking. His Maman laughed, but maybe it was true. Maybe they were like gypsies who all played guitars, or Africans with their jungle drums. For all Jeanot knew, the streets of America were peopled with banjo-plucking Negroes.

He'd read that one state, Texas, was the size of France. His mother had doubts, but Jeanot was adamant. "There are three cities there that are each bigger than *Paris!*" That, in itself, was amazing. He'd thought Paris was the biggest city in the world. "And," he added, "There's even a Paris in Texas. I don't think they speak French there, though, or at least not French like us."

There would be flags, costumes, American foods and music at the party. Maman would show a Disney film—an amateur cinematographer friend of hers had several—and she assured Jeanot this would be an event remembered by all.

Jeanot paid little attention. He had found his life's calling in the latest *Tintin* magazine. Like Albert Schweitzer, Jeanot was going to go to Africa to cure the leopards. The illness sounded dreadful and it was not fair that the sick leopards weren't allowed to mix with others of their kinds. There was a picture in the magazine of Schweitzer wearing an explorer hat and looking both kindly and sad, with skinny natives surrounding him; hired help, Jeanot figured, to catch the leopards. The sky was cloudless, it looked warm, and the black people were obviously friendly if very, very thin. Maybe working with leopards had its difficulties.

Jeanot had met a few black people in Paris. They were always pleasant with their strange accents and startling white eyes, and they looked nothing like the ones in the photo with Dr. Schweitzer. Obviously coming to France from Africa was a beneficial experience—maybe it was the weather, Jeanot thought, or the air in Africa was somehow *different*. Certainly, the air in Benodet near the sea had little in common with the sooty-smelling stuff in Paris, and Jeanot noticed that whenever he left town for a day or two, the bothersome scratch at the back of his throat vanished. Maybe the air in Africa was worse, which would explain why the people helping Schweitzer with the leopards all looked skinny and ill.

Jeanot told his father about the leopards. "Look, Papa!" He opened the *Tintin* to the center pages and pointed to a photo. "I want to work with the leopards too, just like Doctor Schwe—" He had a hard time pronouncing the string of consonants.

Papa said, "Schweitzer," and then laughed so hard he made choking sounds. He swept up his son and carried him to Maman, where he told him to repeat the story. Jeanot did so with a little less confidence.

"I want to be like Doctor Schweitzer." He pronounced the name right this time. Papa was still smiling. Jeanot shot him an arch look. "Why are you laughing? There are very sick leopards in Africa!" He didn't think ailing leopards was a funny subject at all, and when Maman tried to explain the leopards were fine, it was the people—*lepers*—that the good Dr. Schweitzer tried to heal, Jeanot was certain his mother was wrong. The people didn't have spots on them and looked fit if a little thin, but he chose not to argue the point. He did, though, ask about the African air. Both his parents had been in North Africa during the war. "Do you think people breathe differently in Africa? Is the air bad there?"

Papa, who'd contracted malaria while serving with the Free French in Algeria, thought about it for a moment. "I think, maybe yes, Jeanot. I think there are little animals and bugs there that we don't have here."

"And we breathe them in?"

"Yes. Or maybe you eat without washing your hands, or the little bugs get into a cut…"

"Really?" Jeanot always had some sort of scrape or cut and he wasn't that good about handwashing. After the leopard discussion, he went to the bathroom and scrubbed himself pink, including under the fingernails. No African bugs were going to get him.

There were fifteen children at the party, including Babette and Dédé Bourillot who, as always, smelled like raw onions. Papa glared every time Dédé or his parents passed by, but Maman seemed unperturbed. Babette was unexpectedly friendly with Dédé, and Jeanot, although uncomfortable with this new development, was confident that of the two of them, he was the more mature. Babette quickly tired of anything she considered childish; Jeanot had nothing to fear.

Papa had removed all the paintings from one wall of the sitting room and the cinematographer friend set up his projector on a high table. He was a fat man with a mustache and he laughed a lot; too much, Jeanot thought, since they hadn't seen anything amusing yet. He kept promising the children a wonderful time—he would be showing Disney's *Fantasia*—and there would be ice-cream and candy during the intermission, just like at a real movie house.

Dédé whispèred, "We went and saw it a week ago! Wait until the dancing mushrooms come out!"

Babette, who'd also seen the movie, made a face.

Jeanot looked at her. How silly was that? Dancing mushrooms, really. He didn't like mushrooms; they tasted like dirt. "I read that they have dancing hippos," he said, throwing his two centimes into the conversation. He'd seen photos of the hippos in another magazine, the weekly *Mickey*. It irked him that Dédé, whom he really didn't much like, had already seen *Fantasia*.

Babette said, "Shhh." The fat man turned off the light, started the projector and, satisfied the reels were rolling smoothly, left the room to rejoin the adults. A six-foot rectangle of light appeared on the wall, thin black lines running through the middle like animated snakes.

With no warning, a woman wearing a Nazi uniform strode onto the screen, whipping a riding crop against her booted leg. There was no sound save for the projector's fan. Dédé said aloud, "I don't remember this part," and was shushed by Babette.

Jeanot whispèred, "Germans! Why are there Germans? Papa's going to get angry." He knew what Germans were and what a swastika was; everyone in France knew that.

Babette nudged him and said, "Shhh!" again.

The woman faced the camera, slowly unbuttoned her blouse, and dropped it to the ground. Her breasts hung loosely, large brown nipples pointing to her navel, and Dédé, now with certainty, said, "This is NOT *Fantasia!*"

Babette giggled, elbowed Jeanot in the ribs. The audience was transfixed. The now half-naked Boche, still whipping her leg with the riding crop, turned around and wiggled her rear.

Jeanot leaned to Babette and whispered, "Why is she doing that?"

Before Babette could answer, the woman dropped her skirt. Now she was totally naked save for boots, a German military cap, and the riding crop. She stepped off screen for a moment and returned leading a large man wearing black pants, a striped shirt and a beret. There was no mistaking the nationality. One of the boys hissed, "*Salle Boche,*" dirty Hun, and Babette nodded.

The booted woman unclasped the man's belt and lowered his trousers. Jeanot saw the man had no underwear and wondered if perhaps he couldn't afford them. The woman dropped to her knees and placed the man's *zizi* in her mouth. Even Babette gasped. There was embarrassed laughter from the boys; all the girls—except for Babette—hid their eyes behind their hands.

Jeanot stared, mesmerized. Babette, in a rare show of modesty, tried to cover his eyes with a hand. He batted it away. "Don't! I want to see!"

After a while the woman got on her back and spread her legs. The man lay on her gracelessly, his white pimply rump bobbing up and down. Then he turned the woman around and thrust at her from the rear. A brief view of her face showed boredom and endurance before she turned and smiled for the camera. At this precise moment, the living room door opened. Maman peeked in, asked, "Are you enjoy-ing… *Mon Dieu!*"

She rushed and pulled the projector's plug out of the wall. The projector fell to the ground with a thud and Babette laughed. One of the reels came loose and rolled around the floor, disgorging a tumble of film.

Maman turned the lights on. The girls were still covering their eyes—Babette wasn't—and the boys were open-mouthed. Maman shooed them into another room with promises of chocolate ice cream and cake. She booted the reel across the floor and kicked angrily at the film, then went to find the projectionist.

The children heard yells, curses from both Jeanot's mother and the fat cinematographer. Jeanot peeked back into the sitting room and saw the projectionist attempting unsuccessfully to wind the film back on the reel as Maman pushed him out the door. He protested that it had been an honest mistake: *Fantasia* was next to *Fantaisies Nazies* in his film closet. He and his wife had been running late for the party and he'd grabbed the wrong reel.

Babette appeared beside Jeanot, smiled knowingly and nudged him. "You know what they were doing? They were *screwing…* He put his thing into her and goes in and out and it makes them both feel good, and then he *pees* in her and they make a baby."

Jeanot nodded, not fully understanding but not wanting to appear stupid, either. "They didn't look like they were feeling good. They looked almost sad."

Dédé said, "I *knew* it wasn't *Fantasia!*"

Babette momentarily reigned supreme since she was the only one who understood what they had witnessed. She tried hard to clarify it but her explanations fell short. "Did you see? Did you see what he did?" She whispered again and again to Jeanot. Jeanot simply nodded his head. This was not going to end well, he knew. There would be ramifications, blame assigned, possibly some more yelling and tears.

"We're going to get in trouble," he said. "Just watch."

Babette smirked. "You little kids don't even know what you saw, did you?" She challenged Jeanot and Dédé again. The latter had told Jeanot that he didn't like Babette. That was comforting, in a way. Dédé said she was a know-it-all like his cousin, whom he didn't like either. He professed no interest in naked men and women and said he had come to Jeanot's party strictly for the cake and a movie. The cake was apparently only so-so. His mother, he scoffed, made better, and he was massively disappointed in the film. He left the room, calling to his parents that he wanted to go home.

There was now a dreadful silence emanating from the gathered adults. The projectionist's wife was ashen and weeping quietly, protesting she hadn't known her husband possessed such things; it called into question everything about her marriage. Surely Maman was exaggerating, she insisted. The movie may have been a bit risqué, but pornographic? She pushed past her husband who was still trying to wind the film onto the reel, grabbed a handful of film and held it up to the light. She dropped the offending material as if it were alive. She slapped her husband in the face with a resounding crack, then stumbled out the door gasping apologies.

Parents rushed to their offspring to check on their health. The kids were rounded up and a mother with operatic ambitions led them in song: *Frère Jacques, Au Clair de la Lune,* and *Alouette,* and finally, out of sheer desperation, Edith Piaf's *Rien de Rien,* which they hummed since no one knew the words except Babette. Small voices reached for the high notes and broke, and when the singing was over almost everyone left, some surreptitiously taking back unopened presents. All that remained were cake crumbs on the floor and half-empty glasses of lemonade and Orangina.

Jeanot watched it all happen as from a distance. He hadn't been that interested in a party in the first place but was glad some of the presents were left. He sat on the floor and unwrapped them carefully, Babette squatting at his side.

There was a Jokari; a hard rubber ball attached to a long elastic band that in turn was tied to a heavy stand. The game came with two paddles, and Jeanot thought the courtyard would be big enough but wondered who in the apartment complex would have the time to play with him. There were four lead cowboys, a book on Indians of the Amazon, a box of chocolates that was obviously a hand-me-down gift, a scarf, three pairs of socks and four pairs of cotton underwear.

Babette took the box of chocolates and opened it. Three pieces were missing from the center row.

"Who gave you this?"

Jeanot thought it might have been Dédé. That would explain the missing pieces. "I don't know. Dédé maybe?" He bent down and sniffed the box. It smelled like onions. "*Oui.* Dédé."

Babette made a face, selected a chocolate and popped it onto her mouth. She chewed pensively, then gave Jeanot a hug. "You're going to be much more interesting in a few years, when you understand *things.*"

Jeanot considered the statement and shrugged it off. "That movie wasn't fun at all. It was really dumb, and those naked people...*ils n'étaient pas beaux.* They weren't very pretty. And they didn't say anything, or even smile at each other. What was Maman thinking?"

He opened the book on the Amazon and looked for pictures of shrunken heads. He didn't find any; the photos showed multi-colored birds, men in dirty trousers and raggedy hats, and a lot of green jungle.

He added the new lead cowboys to the Wild West diorama in his room. They were all duplicates and he placed them at opposite ends of the table.

After a while he and Babette took the Jokari to the courtyard. Babette managed to hit the ball repeatedly, sending it speeding until it reached the end of the elastic and came bounding back. Jeanot swatted at it, missed most of the time and then found the rhythm of the game. They exchanged strokes until the concierge told them to stop.

When they returned to the apartment, Jeanot said, "Maman told me that it's storks that bring babies, not naked men and women."

Babette paused in mid-step, gave him a searching look and said, "Your Maman is wrong."

Chapter 8

Jeanot's école maternelle at rue des Epinettes annually put on a show for parents and local dignitaries to involve them in the education of their children. Originally launched by the mayor of the 17th arrondissement as a platform for politicking, over time the show had become a spectacle, with preparations beginning at the start of the school year and involving stage sets, music, sound effects, costumes and special lighting. This year's special guest was Jules Dassin. Jeanot's teacher, Madame Charbonneau explained that Dassin was a director whose 1942 film *Reunion in France* created a stir when it was shown in Paris after the war. Madame Charbonneau was probably, thought Jeanot, somewhere in her thirties. She had a pleasant face, an inviting bosom, and was, according to the whispers of some of the older students, involved with the married school principal.

The school's show, *Les Peaux Rouges,* was a presentation loosely based on the battle of Great Meadows during the French and Indian Wars. There was some confusion regarding historical facts and costuming; cowboys, Indians of many different varieties and tribes, as well as the occasional pilgrim all peopled the stage at the same time.

Jeanot was a Sioux, an unimportant one whose sole function was to be tied to a stake and danced around by other Indians as flames of yellow light devoured his feet and legs. He was to be stoic as he burned; an example of what his teacher referred to as "the noble savage." It was a very small part and Maman confessed to being annoyed that her only son should be relegated to the role of sacrificial Sioux.

Jeanot, on his own, had practiced looking both brave and resigned as the fire devoured him. He wondered if he should writhe and make faces to engage the audience in the drama of the moment, but since he'd been expressly instructed not to utter a word or sound, he decided he would stand as straight as the binding ropes allowed and burn like a man.

Maman rejected this idea. She mentioned the idea of painting Jeanot a glorious shade of red, which, she assured him, would make him stand out among the pale-skinned Parisian urchins. Finally, she hit upon the notion of dipping him in red food coloring to give him an all-over ruddiness truer to the American Indian complexion. Jeanot thought it was a good idea too, and the morning of the performance he climbed into the bathtub and marinated for an hour in the red water. Maman told him to hold his breath as she dunked his head under several times. While he steeped, she also dyed his hair jet black. The transformation was amazing and ghastly, decided Jeanot, gazing at himself in the bathroom mirror. When Papa saw Jeanot, he turned ashen and was speechless during the entire drive to the school.

Maman wrapped Jeanot in a blanket and walked him to the refectory where a complicated multi-platformed stage had been erected. Half-naked children with pastel war paints milled around, as did cowboys in hats with cloth fringes pinned to their sleeves. Inexplicably, one sweating boy was dressed as an Eskimo. There was a teepee made of brown butcher paper, and a stake in the center of the topmost platform. This would be Jeanot's post.

He took a deep breath and dropped his towel.

Madame Charbonneau looked at Jeanot standing redly at attention in his loincloth and her hand flew to her mouth. She turned to Maman, eyes wide.

"Madame, your child is sick. He has *la rougeole*!"

Neither Jeanot nor Maman had considered Jeanot's hue might be mistaken for measles. It took them both a moment to regroup, to react. "*Non, non*, Madame! I assure you our Jeanot is perfectly healthy. He insisted on being as red as a real Indian and there was no arguing with him. I came back from the market and there he was, dyed from head to foot! God knows if he'll ever be pink again!" She laughed, maybe a bit too brightly.

Jeanot kept mum. He was in character and silence was essential. Madame Charbonneau and Maman clucked at each other another minute or two, until Maman took Jeanot by the hand and said, "Now go with Madame. Behave yourself, and after school I'll take you home and we'll wash all this silly red color away!"

"But I want to stay red!" Jeanot had come to this decision minutes earlier. He *liked* being red, was even pleased with the unnatural blackness of his hair. He could see a red future ahead, where people would mistake him for a real Indian child, or maybe Mowgli, the jungle boy from India.

Maman said, "Don't be silly!" She looked at Madame Charbonneau. "Children these days! Don't worry, Madame, he'll be white as snow come Monday!"

"I want to stay red!" This time Jeanot raised his voice a little, edged it with more conviction. It was vitally important that he remain red, crucially important. Staying red would change his life, he knew. People would like him more; his entire future might be altered. His eyes were tearing with the necessity of staying red.

Maman threw up her arms. "Children! *Des petits sauvages!* What can we do?"

Madame Charbonneau, no longer paying attention, was separating little cowboys from little Indians. The Eskimo was stage left, sucking his thumb and crying quietly. Madame Charbonneau called, "Jeanot, *viens içi!*" and Jeanot came, climbed to the sacrificial stake and stood still as the teacher bound him to it loosely.

The lights in the room dimmed and School Director, Monsieur Rampallon, flanked by the mayor and his deputy, made a brief speech on the benefits of education to The Republic. He left the stage to a smattering of applause from parents, teachers, brothers and sisters, and Monsieur Champollion, mayor of the 17em arrondissement, enumerated his accomplishments. Tied to the stake, Jeanot was the image of stoicism.

In time, Indian drums made from cardboard hatboxes, faint ululations and clapping hands beat a haphazard rhythm. A heavily accented voice began reciting Longfellow's *Song of Hiawatha* in French, and as the epic droned on, the room grew summer hot. In time, Puritans and Indians shared a Thanksgiving meal. Sweat formed on Jeanot's chest, forehead and underarms. The beads ran past his red belly button and into his loincloth which soon started itching.

He rubbed his butt against the stake, trying to rearrange the scratchy cloth (a piece of burlap Maman had decided went well with his coloring), and bought a few moments' relief. Then the itching became worse, intolerable, so he gritted his teeth and thought courageous thoughts.

The other Indians danced around Jeanot in a pre-sacrificial frenzy. They whooped, they hollered, they jumped and cavorted; they made terrible, gargoyle faces and rolled their eyes. Among them was the Eskimo, tears forgotten, and one small cowboy who, caught up in the excitement of the moment, had forgotten who he was. The yellow lights focused on Jeanot's feet. He was now officially on fire.

The itch became a torture. He rubbed his butt against the stake again, this time more forcefully. The loincloth, tied with a loose knot, fell about his ankles. Jeanot's triangular, impeccably clean American underwear shone like a beacon on the stage. It radiated white against his red skin, and the first small Indian to notice it stopped dancing, pointed and burst into laughter. The Puritans hooted, the dancing cowboy stood gape-jawed, and from the middle of the audience came a loud guffaw. Jeanot, through his mortification, could see famed director Jules Dassin laughing with his head thrown back. Madame Charbonneau leaped onto the stage and wrapped her shawl about Jeanot's middle, tore him from the stake and whisked him away.

It took more than ten minutes to quiet everyone down, reassemble the players and find another child—the Eskimo—for the stake.

Chapter 9

Créations St. Paul came together quickly. Jeanot and his parents scoured the flea markets and second-hand shops for used sewing machines, mannequins, tailors' tools, and bolts of cloth. Maman hired a designer who could turn her sketches into reality, and found part-time models and a retired seamstress willing to return to work. She transformed one of the apartment's sitting rooms into an *atelier*.

Always good with a needle and thread and even better with the electric Singer, Maman became an able *couturière* in a surprisingly short time. She soon found clients among the *haute bourgeoisie* who demanded the latest from the likes of Chanel and Dior; names which were new to Jeanot, but which carried obvious weight and importance. Papa explained that Maman's friends wanted clothes looking just like those from the famous fashion houses, but that they were too cheap to pay the price, so Maman would make a garment almost exactly like the fancy, expensive ones her friends desired. Maman assured Jeanot that it was almost impossible to tell whether a dress was an original from Coco's seamstresses, or a far less expensive copy fashioned by *Créations St. Paul*. Coco could claim the little black dress, but Maman liked to boast that she herself had invented the little *white* dress.

An elderly maid, Solange, handled the cutting and basting of patterns. She said she had heard through the servants' grapevine about the new *maison de couture* on the third floor of the apartment building, and when the maid demonstrated her sewing skills, Maman hired her on the spot.

The day-to-day workings of the shop were handled by the designer, Jean-Sylvain Biscottin, a small and tidy man with excellent manners. Mathilde whispered gleefully to Jeanot that Jean-Sylvain's former employer, the celebrated *Maison Bellemain*, had summarily dismissed him for "taking advantage" of Madame Bellemain's seventeen-year-old son in a changing booth. When Jeanot asked what it meant to "take advantage," Mathilde informed him that this Jean-Sylvain was like his Oncle Yves; a homosexual, who lusted sinfully after other men. Mathilde was so scandalized by the tale of these men's misdeeds that she couldn't stop herself from grinning.

Jeanot only truly understood what Mathilde had told him when, on Jean-Sylvain's first full day as Maman's employee, Jeanot watched him very obviously and passionately fall in love with Papa, much to Mathilde's amusement and Papa's discomfort. Every time Papa was in the room, Jean-Sylvain seemed drawn to him like a moth to a flame. Jean-Sylvain's eyes lingered wistfully on Papa's retreating back, and he seemed to have a hard time focusing on his work while Papa was nearby. Jeanot knew something of these feelings from his breathtaking, sometimes very confusing moments with Babette, during which his heart would beat at a frankly alarming rate, and funny feelings inside would make him uncomfortable and uncertain. He'd seen movies and had read enough to know that this must, of course, be love, and the way Jean-Sylvain looked at Papa was exactly the way Jeanot felt around Babette.

Jeanot wasn't sure what to think about this. After all, strange though it might have been for a man to love another man, he supposed that if Jean-Sylvain were to fall in love with any man, it at least made sense that it would be Papa. Papa was a remarkable man. Everyone loved him.

For Jeanot, the sewing room was a fascinating playground. There were buttons, endless spools of thread, machines that whirred and clattered, swatches of fabric of every color and feel. Half-naked women, too, on Thursdays, when the models came to try on that week's creations.

Cécile and Fabienne were twenty-year-old cousins who arrived at ten in the morning, stripped to their *soutien-gorges* and *culottes*, garter belts and stockings, and walked about with complete insouciance. No one was shocked but the elderly Solange, who muttered darkly under her breath, but loudly enough for Jeanot to hear. In response, at least once every Thursday, Cécile would shed her brassiere right before Solange's eyes and jump up and down to make her large round breasts bounce.

Jean-Sylvain hardly seemed to look at the girls. Running a *maison de couture* while staring at Papa, Jeanot surmised, must be hard work. Between fitting sessions, Cécile and Fabienne often played cards at one of the cutting tables and invited Jeanot to join them. Whenever she won a hand, Fabienne was fond of hugging the boy and squeezing his skull into her cleavage, which made him light-headed. He lost as often as he could.

Possibly because he had only just become aware of how attractive his Papa was to the world at large, Jeanot noticed when Papa also caught the eye of Cécile the model. Jeanot was sure he didn't approve of that; he had never cared for Cécile, aside from her cleavage. Cécile was boring, unimaginative. She was modeling for *Creations St. Paul,* he'd heard her say, because it was a job and her cousin Fabienne had encouraged her, but she knew the limits of the company. Maman's dresses, she proclaimed, would never make it into the fashion magazines.

Jeanot, certain that Maman's dresses would greatly exceed Cécile's mundane expectations, decided that Cécile was hardly worthy of being in love with his Papa, and dismissed her from further speculation.

The *atelier* provided the boy with endless entertainment. There were always strange yet kind people around and they doted on him.

Pascale, the dwarf accountant struck in childhood by poliomyelitis and now strapped to a wheelchair, had frightened him at first, but won him over with weekly gifts of tin cowboys and Indians. Trudy had become much friendlier when she realized leftover swatches of fabric could be made into fashion accessories. She came by the *atelier* daily, exchanged English lessons for remnants in which she swathed herself and paraded through the apartment.

Pascale the Accountant was joined by Marie-Louise, whose responsibilities within the concern were hazy. Marie-Louise was an artist who specialized in museum copies. An old friend of Maman's from pre-war days, she was often found snoring on the living room divan with a half-empty bottle of Calvados at her side. Marie-Louise always wore the same clothes; a shapeless brown skirt, a white blouse with a frayed collar, and a grey sweater scarred by dozens of cigarette burn marks. One day, Jeanot watched her pass out on the couch with a lit *Gauloise* between her lips. He'd stood ten minutes, immobile, to see the ember reach Marie-Louise's mouth. Just before it did, she spit the *mégot* out. It landed on her sweater in the center of her chest. Marie-Louise licked two fingers and extinguished the glowing ember without opening her eyes.

Kharkov, the Russian concierge, became one of Maman's customers. He came to her with a sketchbook of White Russian Army uniforms, explaining that his sainted father had served under General Drosdowsky's regiment against the Bolsheviks. To honor him, the concierge wanted a white jacket with gold epaulets, buttons and piping, black jodhpurs, and a red, white and gold kepi with a patent leather bill and chinstrap. He already owned the belt and boots which his son shined weekly.

Maman created the uniform but suggested Kharkov find a kepi at a second-hand clothing store, which he did. Within a week the concierge had his first fitting and Jeanot, sitting on the floor of the cutting room as his mother pinned and adjusted, thought Monsieur Kharkov looked very dashing.

From that day on, Kharkov wore his uniform every Sunday when he went to Russian Orthodox mass. Jeanot watched him leave on Sunday mornings, and listened to people whispering about him in the building's lobby. The attire made him celebrated, the subject of much gossip, and he announced some months later that he had been elected president of the Sons of White Russia. He asked Maman to sew a few stripes of rank on his left sleeve. Next, he ordered an aide-de-camp uniform for his adopted son Rémy, a far simpler thing of khaki flannel *sans* piping of any color. Jeanot judged from the boy's expression that it was not a comfortable outfit, so Maman lined the pants and shirt free of charge. Jeanot found the father and son an interesting pair when in uniform, but was glad his own Papa didn't have to dress up in white and gold.

Shortly after this, Jacqueline Répaud, who lived on the *rez de chaussée,* decided she would surprise her ex-husband Clovis with a new uniform as well. Clovis had suffered frostbites during the Great War. Now almost four decades later the uniform he proudly wore on Bastille Day was threadbare and bulging around the middle. Though no longer married to him, Jacqueline still loved Clovis in a motherly way; they were each other's confidants, far better, insisted Papa, as devoted friends than they ever had been as husband and wife.

Maman's staff patterned the new uniform exactly on the original, which Jacqueline had acquired by telling Clovis she was going to have it professionally cleaned. When he saw the finished garment, Oncle Repaud wept, which Jeanot found somewhat embarrassing. Oncle Repaud pinned his medals on, shined his boots, sucked in his stomach and hired a photographer to take a photo of him seated next to Soldat, his three-legged dog.

Jeanot was particularly thrilled by the collection of scissors around the *atelier*. They were everywhere, shiny and sharp, too many pairs for anyone to keep track of. If he sat quietly in a corner of the *atelier,* no one noticed him and he could cut patches of fabric into parachutes to which he tied lead soldiers. These he dropped out of the third floor windows into the courtyard with varying success. Some floated elegantly down, swaying in the breeze. Others' parachutes did not open and they hit the pavement with soft thuds, reducing the tiny figures to shapeless globs of colored metal.

Chapter 10

Papa had found work as a freelance writer for a number of British newspapers. He had what he called "an easy style" and liked human interest stories, though most of what he filed was news. He wrote about the war in Indochina and of the attendant political debate, of the August strikes to protest a change in retirement age, of Charles de Gaulle and the newly formed Republican Union for Social Action, and of the first French airborne attack against Dien Bien Phu in what soon would be known as Vietnam. At the table, he tried explaining all of these varied interests and stories to Maman and Jeanot, and Jeanot, determined to be a man of the world like his magnificent Papa, pretended to be interested, but could never manage it for very long.

While Papa wrote and Maman sewed, both mostly oblivious to the complicated emotions of their employees, Jeanot watched as both Jean-Sylvain and Cécile vied for his Papa's attention.

Jean-Sylvain's tactics relied on appealing to Papa's pride. Papa was a handsome man; inches taller than the average Frenchman, and he knew it. He didn't smoke and his clothes never smelled like *Gauloise* butts, like so many of the fathers of Jeanot's friends. Papa had a marvelous speaking voice, an easy gait and a winner's Yankee smile. He'd been in the war, too; a Free French who actually knew *Le General*, a decorated fighter too modest to ever mention his medals. Papa was close to being the perfect man, thought Jeanot, and Jean-Sylvain obviously agreed.

Under the pretext of designing some new men's apparel, Jean-Sylvain took Papa's measurements efficiently and without any hint of pleasure. He measured Papa's shoulders, his chest, the length of his arms, and with trembling fingers the inseam of his trousers. He casually asked whether Papa dressed left or right, and when Papa admitted that he didn't know what that meant, Jean-Sylvain explained with suspicious airiness that it had to do with Papa's private parts. In which pant leg did Papa put them when he dressed in the morning? "The left," Papa answered. Jean-Sylvain and Jeanot both saw Papa blush and Jeanot wasn't too pleased with that. Jean-Sylvain remained stone-faced.

Cécile took a remarkably similar tack, appealing to Papa's pride as well. Papa, who had visited America before the war, had decided to teach his family basic English. Cécile spoke a smattering of English. She'd spent a week in London before the war, she said, and for three days taken a British lover of little skills. Now, she sought Papa out at every opportunity, asking for the translation of this word or that. Papa said she had a good accent, and soon they were exchanging greetings, jokes and asides in English.

Papa may have been impressed, but Jeanot, who now found Cécile completely unattractive, was not.

Chapter 11

With the *atelier* doing well almost from opening day, Maman decided to accept the invitation to visit the Bonjeans at the château they owned in the Loire Valley.

Jeanot, Papa and Maman cheerfully piled into the DeSoto to spend some time in the country, but even with all the windows open, the aging car's interior was stifling. They'd stopped three times to add water to the leaky radiator. That the automobile had traveled 260 kilometers without a major mishap was a miracle, Papa said. Papa insisted the "American beast" had carried them safely through the sheer force of his will.

The château was the architectural equivalent of the aging car. The circular coachway leading to the front entrance was rutted with missing cobblestones. To Jeanot's horror, in the entranceway, Babette and Dédé Bourillot of the potato gun and naked Nazi fiascos stood holding hands, Babette smiling her welcome.

Jeanot felt as if the DeSoto had run over his chest, as if his guts had been torn out and eaten by a savage cannibal Zhivaro headhunter.

So, apparently, did Papa. "*Ah non! Non non non! C'est l'idiot avec le pistolet à patate!*"

The idiot with the potato gun seemed no happier to see the St. Paul family. Dédé scowled, whispered something in Babette's ear. She giggled and the sound further bruised Jeanot's heart. They turned and skipped away, still holding hands. Jeanot let himself slide to the floor of the DeSoto.

He moped through the afternoon and in the evening decided to go catch frogs at the estate's étang, a walled pond that in earlier times had been the chateau's water supply. Maman equipped him with a swatch of red felt tied at the end of long piece of string. The idea, she said, was to fool the frogs into believing the cloth was a piece of meat. Frogs, being both stupid and carnivorous, would take the bait, swallow it, and Jeanot would reel the string in with an amphibian at the end. It made sense in a strange way so he spent forty-five minutes being ignored by frogs too numerous to count. He caught one with his bare hands, tried to feed it a morsel of the cloth but the beast was adamantly anti-felt. He was about to shove the offended animal in his pocket when a pair of soft arms enveloped him from behind.

Babette.

He dropped the frog, tried to slither away from the two-timing hussy but she refused to let him go. She whispered, "I'm so glad you're here," and then, "Dédé smells like onions. It's really *dégoutant.*"

Monsieur Bourillot, Dédé's journalist father, had once written a long article for *Le Figaro* about the benefits of healthy eating. Papa had read it aloud at the table with great distaste. Monsieur Bourillot had propounded the theory that onions were beneficial to dental hygiene. The Bourillot family, father, mother and son, he wrote, each ate an onion a day. Their splendid teeth were the pride of their dentist, but the entire family emanated an onion soup smell that Jeanot and his family found disturbing.

Babette said, "*Il sent vraiment mauvais...* But you smell good, Jeanot, like soap and American shampoo!"

In fact Jeanot did use Procter & Gamble's Prell twice a week. Trudy's American family bought it at the PX, and it did indeed smell good, though his mother accused it of fading her dyed blonde hair.

"Are you trying to catch frogs?" Babette pulled in the line with the soggy cloth attached. "That won't work, you know, the red bait. That's something grown-ups tell little kids to get them to go somewhere.

Then the grown-ups have fun and drink a lot and they don't have to worry about the children." She shrugged. "It's an old, old trick."

With that she let go and ran off. Jeanot was tempted to go after her but didn't; it was a question of pride. In the evening when everyone had dinner and the children sat at their own, smaller table, it appeared to him that Babette and Dédé were very friendly again, onion breath or not.

Dédé was not a good soup eater. He slopped it over the side of his bowl, left a lot on his chin, and dropped globs in his lap. Jeanot sat ramrod straight, placed his non-ladling hand smartly on the table next to the place setting, and carefully spooned the thick liquid into his mouth. He did not smack his lips or make a face despite the fact that he disliked soup (potato leek in particular), and when Dédé dunked large chunks of hard brown bread into his bowl, Jeanot pretended not to notice. He refrained from talking with Babette, focused his attention instead on what the adults at the big table were saying. He could tell Babette was being stoic regarding Dédé's table manners. He chose the high road and stared straight ahead. When he was through with his soup, he carefully placed the spoon next to the other utensils.

Dédé licked the inside of the bowl and struggled with the next course. He manhandled the asparagus, broke a chicken bone in his mouth and started crying, then picked up the drumstick with his hands and gnawed at it. His father, seeing this, rose from the big people table and swatted the back of his head, causing him to tip over the water glass. He said, "*Merde!*" and his dad whacked him again, this time a bit harder.

For dessert they had flan in small glass bowls. Dédé fell on his with gusto; Babette nibbled, sucking on her spoon. Jeanot used his fruit knife to surgically remove the skin from the top of his custard. He folded it upon itself twice so it resembled a tiny slice of pie and offered it to Babette who was very impressed. He ate the rest with delicacy, leaving a small amount at the bottom as he'd been told to show his appreciation for a wonderful meal.

Afterwards, as the adults were having coffee and liqueurs, Dédé crunched into his onion with a large smile on his face. He really *liked* onions.

Things got better. Babette soon realized Jeanot's true worth, though she steadfastly refused to abandon Dédé. "It would not be elegant," she said. "He's just a poor child who eats onions, and even that isn't really his fault. If your parents told you to eat onions, you'd do it too!"

Actually, Jeanot was reasonably sure he would not. Beets, perhaps, or Brussels sprouts, but not onions. He didn't argue—Babette was all but his; the battle had been won.

For the children, boredom soon set in. The parents ate, drank, played cards, had lively but unintelligible discussions about the state of the nation and politics, went for walks and talked history. At night, they danced and sang, Maman on the piano and the dentist's wife accompanying her badly on the cello. Babette, Dédé and Jeanot played endless card games, war, hearts and 21, though Dédé, whose consumption of onions did not improve his numbers skills, was a poor player who often cheated. They also played Monopoly but the notion of sales and rents eluded him. Babette was always the banker and Jeanot suspected her of stealing money.

When the children began to complain, the adults set up races, contests of strength and wit (there, too, Dédé suffered), and sent them out to find acorns, hazelnuts, bird eggs, variegated leaves, mushrooms and snails.

That night Jeanot was awakened by a scrabbling noise in the bedroom he shared with Dédé. He opened his eyes to see the other child on all four, making his way to the bedroom door. Jeanot got up, waited for Dédé to leave and quietly followed him. It was past three in the morning and the dining room had not been cleared of that night's meal. Jeanot found Dédé eating leftovers from the diners' dirty plates, stuffing himself with cake, cheese, asparagus and cold mashed potatoes, gnawing at pork chops bones. The boy looked up as Jeanot entered but didn't miss a bite. "*C'est les onions...* I wake up in the night and I'm starving!" He swallowed a chunk of bread without chewing. "Don't tell anyone; I'll get in trouble."

Jeanot nodded, saw a half-empty wine glass, drained it. There were a lot of glasses and suddenly he was dying of thirst.

Dédé made snuffling noises as he ate, like the horses Jeanot had seen once at the Bois de Boulogne.

There was more wine and a glass of flat Vichy water simply because it was there. He burped, giggled. Then Dédé farted and they both thought that was the funniest thing either had ever heard so Dédé did it again, straining a little. Jeanot tried but couldn't.

Dédé left, rubbing his stomach through his pajama top, and a moment later Jeanot realized he had no idea where his room might be, so he made a little pillow out of all the dinner napkins, lay down on the floor and fell asleep.

Maman found him there in the morning and swept him off to his own bed where he slept three more hours. She announced Dédé's bad influence had once again led her boy astray and told Papa they would not entertain the Bourillot family after the vacation was over. Neither she nor Papa, Maman told Jeanot, had liked the Bourillots in the first place, though Madame B. had some good entrées in Parisian middle society. Maman warned him against drinking at such an early age. Alcohol, she explained, was for adults, and even then, some people had bad reactions. She spoke of a family Jeanot had never met, of the travails of the mother and father whose son had fallen under the influence, of the pain it had caused them, and of the eventual illness and death of the son in an automobile accident. Jeanot listened to the story with limited interest, glad that his conduct merited no more than a boring tale. He was tempted to rat out Dédé, who had vomited during the night, seriously soiling his sheets, mattress and a nearby throw-rug, but he kept his peace. Dédé, Jeanot realized, was one of those unfortunates who could not handle his food.

Later that day Babette gave Jeanot a talking-to. She compared him to her Oncle Albertin, who was no longer welcome in their home because he always drank too much, said mean things to her mother and, like Dédé, threw up. Oncle Albertin was also a thief who had stolen money from her mother's purse and done something nasty—she wasn't sure what—to the maid.

Jeanot, penitent, agreed such behavior was indeed very rude. "But I didn't throw up, and I promise I'll never, ever drink again," he told Babette.

Babette stared him in the eyes and replied, "That's what Oncle Albertin always says."

"But," Jeanot insisted, "*I* didn't throw up."

In the morning the parents organized a grand snail hunt, with prizes for the biggest, best-looking, most fearsome snail, as well as the escargot-with-the-sweetest-disposition. The children were sent out, each with a shoebox, a sandwich and a bottle of lemonade, and told they could not return before lunchtime.

In minutes, Dédé proved his worth with his unerring ability to spot snails from yards away. As Babette and Jeanot lifted leaves, studied branches and crawled through shrubbery, Dédé scooped snails from the dewy grass as if drawn to them by a magnet. Some he picked up, glanced at, and discarded—too small, broken shell, unappealing color.

"*Il est incroyable,*" Babette whispered, and Jeanot felt a stab of jealousy. He didn't think Dédé was incredible at all, merely lucky. Besides, how far could such a skill take you in life? He, Jeanot, had been an Indian, and if that wasn't meaningful, what was?

Dédé was inspecting a smallish specimen with a bright grey and yellow shell when Babette found the monster.

The snail was so big she refused to touch it. It was as large as her fist, and its antennaed head was thrust forward in unmistakable aggression. Its slime trail was an inch-wide rainbow, and Jeanot could have sworn the beast hissed when he approached it. "*Escargotus Monstrogamus,*" intoned Babette. "I'll call him Goliath!"

Jeanot poked it with a small stick and Goliath retreated into its shell, but barely. When Jeanot picked it up, the shell seemed to vibrate. He cleared a corner of the shoebox and deposited the beast.

"Do you think he'll eat the others?" asked Jeanot.

Dédé ran back to the château and returned minutes later with a bucket. He added leaves, torn grass, a twig or two and a couple of stones. He picked up the large snail gingerly and put it in the bucket.

Babette sniffed, "He'll get out, stupid!" but Dédé shook his head, led the two children to a crumbling outbuilding and pried a square of glass from a window. The pane fit neatly over the bucket.

"Now we can watch what he does," he said, "and he won't escape! Come on, there have to be more like him!"

There weren't. Goliath was a one-of-a-kind, a true freak of French nature.

They took their prizes back to the château and showed them to the adults who marveled at the colors and were properly awed by Goliath's size. The dentist weighed it; Goliath tipped the postal scale at 40 grams.

That evening, the cook took the children to the movies. It was a small theater seating no more than 100 spectators, and the featured film was Walt Disney's *Living Desert*. The room was stifling, redolent of cigarettes, and the floor was sticky from a season of chewed gum, ice cream drippings and spilled Coca Cola. The children gasped at rattlesnakes, moving rocks that traveled kilometers, scorpions and shifting dunes. The cook seemed particularly taken by a flower that bloomed only once every decade, and she spoke of this miracle all the way home.

In the château's dining room the grown-ups were finishing dessert and fell silent when the children walked in. It smelled like butter and garlic.

Dédé emitted a frightened sound and moaned, "Goliath!" Jeanot spotted the pile of empty snail shells on a side table.

Babette turned white. *"Vous les avez mangé? Nos beaux escargots?"* They had. The little ones, the big ones, the giant one, all the snails were gone, devoured by the grown-ups.

Babette yelled, *"Vous êtes tous des horribles cons!!* Horrible, horrible people!"* She ran from the room with Dédé and Jeanot trailing and screaming, crying, noses running like faucets, stamping their feet on the ancient floors.

Dédé ran away that night. Jeanot watched him go. Dèdè emptied his schoolbag of all the books he was supposed to be reading during the holidays but hadn't, replaced them with two apples, a liter bottle of lemonade and a small bag of red onions. He also took a handful of toilet paper sheets, some matches from the kitchen and Jeanot's latest *Mickey* magazine. Jeanot, too miserable to argue, let him have it.

It was mid-morning before anyone realized Dédé was missing. His father refused to worry. "He's always doing that," said Monsieur Bourillot to Maman. "Every time he's unhappy about something, he runs away. He won't go far. The last time he ended up at the patisserie down the street and cost us a small fortune in *choux à la crème.* He'll be back as soon as he gets hungry."

Madame Bourillot was less cavalier. "I don't know… the cook says he took some onions," she shook her head, "and he can last a long time with onions…"

Maman and Papa were all for calling the gendarmes. They both grilled Jeanot. Did Dédé mention his plans? Was he really that upset about the snails? Jeanot pleaded guilty ignorance, but he wasn't particularly impressed with Dédé's chosen course. Jeanot thought if anyone should be upset about the snails, it ought to be Babette who had first discovered Goliath.

Babette bawled more over the loss of the snail, with whom she had bonded, than over Dédé's predicament. She did sniffle that Dédé was a *pauvre gosse,* a poor misunderstood kid whose mother and father should have known better than to behave as they did. She added that anyone who would consume a household pet was *a priori* and *sine qua non* monstrous and *ipso facto* unfit to have children. The vacation was turning into a good occasion for Latin.

Dédé was gone the better part of the day before Monsieur Bourillot acceded to his wife's demands and called the police. Within the hour, Jeanot watched two unshaven gendarmes arrive on bicycles. "Peasants in uniforms," muttered Monsieur Bourillot, before giving an acceptable description of his vanished son. When asked why Dédé ran away, Madame Bourillot explained the snail situation and this seemed of great interest to the policemen. "Lots of snails here," said the thinner of the two. "The wife and me, we go out in the morning after a rain or heavy dew, find a dozen or two and cook them in butter and chives,,," Monsieur Bourillot nodded, adding that in his family, garlic, parsley and tarragon were the preferred recipe, to which the fatter of the two lawmen agreed that chives were wasted on snails, but garlic was exactly right.

The men discussed this for a moment before returning to the subject of the missing child. Jeanot watched all this with interest and thought an important piece of information was missing. "He has onions," he said. "A little bag of them."

The gendarmes looked at one another and the thin one wordlessly mounted his bike and pedaled away. The other rolled a cigarette using yellow corn paper, puffed hard and addressed the children. "Where did you find the snails?"

Jeanot and Babette led the gendarme to the exact spot where she'd come upon Goliath. The policeman squatted to touch the grass, pronounced it too dry now for gathering anything but chiggers. Within fifteen minutes, the other gendarme returned with Dédé riding the handlebars of the bicycle and looking abashed.

His mother hugged him and his father cuffed him on the back of the head.

"It was the onions, you see," the thin gendarme said. "I saw your boy with some other children, they were cheering him on, and it's an unusual sight, a boy eating onions; not something you see very often around here. Boys eat pears, cherries, apples…" He looked thoughtful, added, "The shoemaker's son eats raw potatoes from time to time, and sometimes wanders the village with a leather lace dangling from his mouth," he pointed to his head and made a whirling motion with an index finger. "But no onions. So, I knew it had to be your child." He looked pleased.

Monsieur Bourillot gave him a fifty Franc bill which the policeman refused, though he allowed that bicycling was thirsty work, particularly with a passenger on the handlebars. "A glass of wine," he said, "would not be frowned upon."

Dédé, it turned out, had not gone very far. Jeanot and Babette had the whole story from his own lips as they sat together in the kitchen, bemoaning the loss of the snails and of freedom. He'd walked to the village, eaten the apples and drank the lemonade while sitting on the empty fountain commemorating the local dead from four wars. He'd played with the *boulanger's* kids and was fed a ham sandwich by the *boulanger's* wife, had gotten into a shoving match with the nine-year-old son of the bistro owner, had eaten the rest of his onions one after the other on a bet and with the money he'd won, had bought himself a bottle of *diabolo menthe* and some nougat.

"He struck a blow for the *escargots*," proclaimed Babette as she hugged him. "He's like Spartacus in the movie! *Sic Semper Tyrannis!* Right, Dédé?"

Dédé grinned happily, his father's backhanded cuff apparently forgotten. Jeanot thought kids who eat onions probably didn't get that many brushes with fame and so was only mildly resentful.

Two days later using a clear glass jar the boys caught a frog and, of course, dropped it in the small leather purse Babette carried everywhere. She screamed and threw the purse in the air spilling its contents; a brush, a stick of Beechman chewing gum, a pencil with no eraser at the tip, a lace handkerchief, some copper *centimes* coins, a tube of lipstick taken from her mother's dresser, a tattered picture of the Holy Virgin blessing a crowd of children as she ascended to Heaven, and the surprised frog. She chased Jeanot, who evaded her, then Dédé who was slower. She caught him, slapped him *hard* once, twice, then a third time and called him a *pauvre crétin.* Jeanot watched her fury with amazement. This was a Babette he did not know.

She didn't talk to them the rest of the day, ate dinner in the kitchen, stayed with the adults until bedtime and retired to her room without a word. In the middle of the night she snuck into the boys' room and poured a glass of warm water over Dèdè's midsection while he was sleeping. Jeanot watched in silence. Dédé woke up the next morning, horrified to have wet his bed during the night and made Jeanot solemnly swear not to mention it to anyone. Of course, Babette knew.

In the morning of a day that looked harmless, they went to mass. The château-owner wanted to show his guests the medieval chapel, a structure with a failing belfry and no stained glass. There were a dozen or so villagers attending, mostly shrunken women in black, made even smaller by their lowered, shawled heads. Babette echoed the priest's mutterings: "*Gukka tamen orifice dayo. In spiritutuem nabisco.*" Latin, she told Jeanot, would become her mother tongue.

That afternoon Dédé drowned in the pond. He did it quietly, without a fuss, holding a butterfly net made from a broomstick, a length of fence wire and a large square of cheese cloth the cook used in the kitchen to make *fromage blanc*.

Dédé had built the net himself after seeing swallowtails flitting near the pond. He and Jeanot had also spied a large frog, and Dédé was torn between which one he should chase. A butterfly, he told Jeanot, would please Babette to no end, particularly if he did not harm it and simply gave it to her intact. She would let it fly away, and Dédé thought that would be nice. The frog—the amphibian equal to Goliath—could have numerous uses, including being set free during dinner. Dédé giggled to himself imagining the fracas. His Papa, he announced, would cuff him again but the blows mostly just glanced off his head. The frog was worth the blow. Graciously, he allowed Jeanot to chase the butterfly.

Jeanot watched from the bank as Dédé neared the pond, held his breath, got on his hands and knees and crawled towards the water. The frog had its rear to him, fat purply green frog haunches resting on a lily pad not ten feet away. Jeanot could see its sides moving in and out as the animal breathed.

Then the swallowtail got close enough for Jeanot to make his move.

While Jeanot swatted for the butterfly, Dédé lunged, and the frog hopped out of his reach. Dédé gave chase. The frog disappeared in the dark waters. With one quarry gone, Dédé concentrated on the other. He stood and hopped onto a stone that broke the water's surface, then onto another a few feet away. The butterfly alit on a cattail, its wings moving nervously. Dédé balanced on the stone, stretched out and swung the net which caught the butterfly just as it was escaping. He laughed, jumped in the air, lost his footing, and dropped the net.

The rock where he was perched was algae-slick and he slipped, flailing his arms as he went down. The back of his head hit the stone hard exactly where his father cuffed him whenever he did something wrong. Dédé stopped moving or screaming before his face slid under-water. The net remained afloat, its captive's wings beating weakly before it succumbed.

Jeanot sat, frozen with horror, for a long moment. He took several steps towards the pond, and then panicked, dropping his own butter-fly net and went running as fast as he could back towards the chateau. There, he found the cook, and managed to tearfully tell her as much as he could. Then Jeanot and the cook returned together to the pond.

The cook found Dédé floating where Jeanot had left him. She didn't panic. She waded in, grabbed the small boy's left foot and dragged him to shore. Jeanot knew without asking that Dédé was dead, but the cook told him anyway. Her father had been a part-time *croque-mort*, she informed him, and as the village undertaker's daugh-ter, she had often seen bodies laid out in the barn prior to burial; at the family farm, death had been commonplace.

She picked up Dédé and cradled him in her arms. Water from his body soaked her bust and apron. Jeanot avoided looking at Dédé's face, though he'd noticed when the cook first pulled him out that Dédé wore a small smile, the briefest of curls at the ends of his mouth.

The cook returned to the kitchen, and Jeanot followed. She laid Dédé carefully on the big butcher block table that smelled of onions. She washed her hands, arranged her hair, straightened her skirt and made sure her shoes were tied while Jeanot stood and stared. Then she went calling for Dédé's father.

When Monsieur Bourillot came into the kitchen the cook merely pointed him in.

She put her coat on and looked as if she was pretending not to hear Monsieur Bourillot's keening.

Jeanot heard.

Chapter 12

Of course, the family canceled the rest of their vacation. It would have been unseemly, said Maman, to continue their drive to the Côte d'Azure as if nothing had happened. Instead, they returned to Paris and Jeanot and the family went to Dédé's funeral at a small church not far from their apartment. There had been some argument about letting Jeanot attend. Maman said she thought it a bad idea for someone so young, but Papa insisted. Jeanot, he said, must know tragedy could strike any time, and that children were not immune.

"It was a tragedy," he told Maman, as though Jeanot was not present. "*Une terrible chose...* Jeanot has to put all this behind him." Then he turned and put a large hand on top of Jeanot's head. "*Il est un grand garçon.*"

It was the first time his Papa had called Jeanot a big boy. He wondered if the promotion had been caused by Dédé's death, but he had no particular interest in attending the funeral. He'd seen enough, he thought, of tragedy.

Jeanot already knew about death. The mother of a schoolmate had passed away and the entire class had gone to the funeral, but the concept of Dédé simply no longer *being* was hard to understand. Dédé was with the angels and that seemed right because in the end Dédé had been a pretty nice kid, certainly not the brightest, and the onions were a strange habit, but a kid with a natural joy to him in spite of being regularly cuffed by his father. Dédé had laughed a lot, sometimes at nothing at all, and in retrospect, even his closeness to Babette was excusable. Babette was a hard girl to resist.

It made Jeanot wonder about God, too, and about things right and things wrong. Maman had given a long explication about heaven and angels, and that Dédé was in a happier place where he didn't have to eat onions, which made no sense, since Jeanot knew Dédé *liked* onions. Papa's attempt was as fruitless though more down-to-earth. Bad things happen, he told Jeanot; they simply *did,* without reason or justification, and it was right to be sad but that would go away and life would continue.

Babette was at the funeral muttering in Latin. She had refused to speak in any other language since the accident. She wore a black dress with a black veil of her own making and her eyes were red. She took Jeanot's hand as he walked past her, forced him to sit with her and her parents. During the mass she knew exactly when to kneel and when to stand, how to respond to the priest's incantations. She cried throughout and at the end hugged Jeanot hard.

After the calamity, Babette had taken Dédé's linen pillowcase and hidden it in her bag. She showed it to Jeanot, making him swear not to tell anyone. Once home, she said, she'd cut the fabric into small squares, drawn hearts on each with a fountain pen, and now she always carried one square wherever she went. At the end of the mass, she pressed a cloth square into Jeanot's hand and closed her own hands around his. The relic smelled faintly of onions.

Later that day in the bathtub, Jeanot held his breath and dunked his head under to feel what it was like to drown and when he came up gasping for breath he wondered for the first time how Dédé must have felt down there, with the air exploding out of his lungs and not able to come to the surface. It scared him, just as he thought it must have scared poor Dédé.

Jeanot kept the pillowcase square in an old shoebox with the rest of his treasures. If he felt any foreboding, he would get the square from the treasure box and keep it in his pocket for a day or two. Sometimes he took it out, acting as if Dédé were with him and sometimes he tried to ask Dédé how it was up there in the sky.

Once when he had a cold he accidentally blew his nose into it. That was so sinful he spent ten minutes washing the cloth in the bathroom sink with Maman's lavender soap. The heart Babette had drawn on the cloth faded, but now the rag smelled better than Dédé ever had.

Three months after the funeral, Babette told Jeanot she was dropping Latin in favor of English, a language she felt was better able to express sorrow. She memorized *The Ballad of Reading Gaol* because Oscar Wilde, like Dédé, had been a young man traumatized by society. When she recited the poem in its entirety, Jeanot thought it sounded very pretty but he didn't understand a word or see what it had to do with Dédé's death. When he told Babette, she gave him a distressed look and said, in English, "You are such a baby."

Chapter 13

In the weeks following Dédé's death and burial, Maman had thought it wise to enroll Jeanot in the Louveteaux, the Little Wolves, an organization, she said, patterned after the British and American Boy Scouts. The Louveteaux claimed to foster honesty, health, and a respect for the Republic and its outdoors. Maman said the group would introduce Jeanot to other boys. He would learn that friendship need not end in calamity, and that nature was not necessarily a dangerous, even deadly, place, despite Dédé 's recent watery end.

She bought Jeanot an official uniform; navy blue short pants and short-sleeved shirt, white socks, a leather belt, a beret and a red and yellow foulard that technically he should not wear before his formal induction into the ranks. Then she altered the shirt and shorts subtly to give her boy a more distinguished look.

The scouting experience did not turn out as beneficial as Maman had hoped. Jeanot thoroughly disliked just about everything involving the Louveteaux and their outings. The group of children, some thirty0 in all, met on Saturday afternoons in the courtyard of Jeanot's school. Not much excitement was to be found there; the yard's only tree had died years earlier and now only a stump remained. Bored teachers monitoring recess stubbed their cigarette butts there, and now the stump looked like an empty and wounded pedestal.

The Louveteaux sang the *Marseillaise* at every opportunity. None of them knew more than the first verse, but they all shouted with gusto the part about impure enemy blood flowing in the furrowed fields. The scoutmaster, who, Papa told Jeanot, had never fought and indeed spent his war as a minor functionary with the Vichy government, puffed his chest out and saluted sharply. The Louveteaux returned the salute with two fingers aimed like a small double-barreled gun at the temple, then tromped into the school for a movie about France's natural bounties. Later, Jeanot practiced helping an old lady across the street. The old lady was played by another Louveteau with sharp body odor. The street was the courtyard.

Three weeks after that the newest Louveteaux ceremoniously jumped over a rope to earn their red and yellow scarves. His altered shorts restricting movement, Jeanot tripped and skinned his knee. Another scout, a 12-year-old polio victim did not have to jump but was made to wheel his chair four times around the yard. He was a nasty kid, the only one who laughed when Jeanot tripped.

One time, the entire troop boarded a wheezing bus and drove an hour out of Paris to a forest devoid of wildlife. Jeanot thought it interesting that there were more birds in his apartment building's courtyard than in all the trees surrounding him. They learned how to make fire by rubbing sticks together; a tiresome procedure that so frustrated the scoutmaster that after a few minutes' frantic friction, the man took out a lighter and a small piece of paper that he crumpled, lit, and placed carefully under the pyramid of twigs. The wood was damp and smoked and two of the asthmatic Louveteaux coughed and cried, which the rest of the group found mildly amusing.

They tromped a well-worn path through the woods. Suddenly, the scoutmaster froze, raised an arm to stop the boys while simultaneously holding a finger to his lips for quiet. He pointed to the path a hundred feet ahead. There, sitting on its haunches and chattering, was a small red squirrel; an untamed wood denizen unlike anything the Parisian boys had ever seen. It looked up and instead of running away came closer to the group. The boys held their breath; all but Eddie Simenon, a slow-witted kid far too old for the Louveteaux. Eddie Simenon picked up a stone and whizzed it at the squirrel, hitting the animal hard on its side. The squirrel jumped straight in the air, landed, and charged the boys who scattered like dandelion dust. The scoutmaster made a bleating sound before grabbing the low hanging branch of a nearby pine tree and hoisting himself up like a rhesus monkey. The squirrel veered left and disappeared into the underbrush.

Later, back on the bus, the Louveteaux were of two minds. Half the group said they thought Eddie should be congratulated for his accurate aim, while half thought he should be condemned for frightening the only uncaged wild beast any of the boys had ever seen. When Jeanot got home and told his parents about the adventure, Maman said she would complain to the scouting authorities and have Eddie Simenon stripped of his Louveteau rank.

Jeanot also disliked the Louveteaux rituals. He understood their importance, but could not appreciate their necessity. After the first gathering, a bunch of the smaller boys had surrounded him, making fun of his shorts and shirt. If he was to be one of them, the group's leader said, he had to do as they did. This consisted of passing a wad of Wrigley's chewing gum from Louveteau to Louveteau, then spitting on the ground. By the time Jeanot got the gum it was flavorless, and someone had supplemented the gob with a thick rubber band for added consistency. Jeanot chewed, spit, and passed it on to the wheelchair kid.

Then there were the *grands garçons,* bigger boys who should have been full-blown scouts by now but had been held back for moral or intellectual shortcomings. The *grands garçons* clumped together in a corner of the schoolyard away from the rest of the boys. One, François, (Franfran to familiars) was taller and heavier than any of the others, and Jeanot learned that he'd once thrown a cobblestone from one end of the yard to the other. Another, the putative squirrel murderer Eddie Simenon, liked to sling stones at the younger boys' legs when no one was looking. The larger boys frightened the scout leader and he gave them a wide berth.

There was a set of identical twins, a perfectly symmetrical pair of pale-faced, blond brothers whose pinched features grew around pointed noses. They seldom spoke and communicated with each other through winks, nods, gestures, and grunts. It was rumored that a few months before they had faced down the *grands garçons* and, though much shorter, had beaten up two of them with a series of coordinated attacks, one boy going low, the other high, employing fists, kicks and head-butts. Jeanot wished he'd been there.

Then there was Stéphane, the Dédé look-alike.

His resemblance to the late Dédé was uncanny—same nose, lips, out-thrust ears, clipped blond hair. For the first three meetings of the Louveteaux, Jeanot stood across the courtyard from Stéphane, and the boy's very presence made him uneasy, infused him with the guilt he had wrestled with ever since Dédé's death.

He had broached the subject with Papa six weeks after the drowning.

"I think it's my fault Dédé died. I should have helped. He wasn't a very smart little boy."

The statement took Papa aback, and he was silent a long time before speaking. "*Non,* Jeanot. You had nothing to do with Dédé's death. Nothing at all. Sometimes things like that just happen, and they're no one's fault, not even Dédé. You couldn't have helped. That's why they're called accidents. Because no one did anything on purpose, and no one could predict something like that would happen."

Jeanot repeated, "He wasn't a very smart little boy."

"Not as smart as you."

"Not as smart as me. I wouldn't have drowned."

"*Grace à Dieu!*"

"There's a boy at the *Louveteaux* and he looks just like him."

"Like Dédé?"

Jeanot nodded. "He scares me. Do you think maybe…?"

Papa interrupted him. "Does this boy smell like onions?"

Jeanot shook his head, no.

Papa smiled slightly. "There. You see? Ghosts don't exist, Jeanot. When people die, they go away for good. Even little boys."

"He looks *a lot* like Dédé. Like his twin brother, almost."

"Have you spoken with him?"

Jeanot shook his head. "No."

"Why?"

Jeanot shrugged, and Papa smiled. "Because you're afraid to?"

Jeanot shrugged again. "What if it *is* Dédé? What if he's mad at me? Tatie's maid, Guénolé, says dead people come back and do nasty things to those who are still around! She says she's seen it!"

Papa took a long look at the ceiling, followed by a deep breath. "*Écoutes moi, Jeanot.* Guénolé is a mean old woman who likes to scare little boys. She's not a very smart old woman either, and the next time we see her I'll tell her so. She's wrong, Jeanot. She shouldn't be saying things like that to you, and when she does you shouldn't listen." He paused, sat, and drew the boy to his lap. "This Stéphane? Next time, speak with him. Ask him what he likes to do, and where he goes to school. I bet if you ask him if he's Dédé, he'll say no."

So Jeanot did, and if the boy was surprised, he didn't show it. "No. I'm Stéphane. I don't know anybody called Dédé."

That was a relief. Jeanot said, "He was my friend. He died."

Stéphane nodded. "I had a little brother. He died too."

"And his name wasn't Dédé?" Jeanot wanted to make sure.

"No. His name was Alain. He was four-and-a-half. He got sick and then he died. He's under the ground now, but actually he's in the sky." He paused. "At least that's what my mother says. I really didn't like him very much. He cried all the time."

Jeanot could understand that. Nobody liked crybabies.

Stéphane and Jeanot didn't become friends, but their mothers did. The two women often lingered and chatted together outside the school after the Louveteaux meetings. Stéphane's mother, Janine, was divorced. His parents' marriage, Stéphane explained, had not survived the death of his little brother. She had mourned so long, so deeply and painfully that Stéphane's papa, a psychologist, had one day packed all his clothes and left, abandoning an apartment, a Citroën car with fewer than 10,000 kilometers, and a Bechstein Boudoir Grand piano upon which Stéphane practiced his scales diligently if without enthusiasm.

Jeanot knew, and Stéphane agreed, that there were reasons for their being thrown together, and that it had something to do with death, and their respective Mamans who had each in their own way lost children.

The boys discussed it casually; each thought it was a special situation where he might do some good, might abet the healing of wounds not fully understood.

Soon Stéphane's mother began dropping him off at the *atelier* after school; there were so many things to do, she was overwhelmed and welcomed the opportunity to spend a little time alone shopping and rebuilding her life. All the friends she and her husband had as a couple had deserted her, incapable of plumbing the depth of her wound, she said. Stéphane's mother was alone; Maman, Jeanot and the *atelier*, she exclaimed, were her saviors.

She was a handsome woman in a hollowed out way; something vital had been taken from her and discarded. *"Elle vit dans sa tristesse,"* sighed Maman.

Jeanot could understand that. The sadness he'd felt after Dédé's drowning still surfaced at odd moments. Try as he might, he could not ignore Stéphane's uncanny resemblance to his drowned friend. Often, when Stéphane had his back turned, Jeanot would stare at the nape of the other boy's neck and think, almost aloud, "I'm so sorry, Dédé, but Papa says it wasn't my fault. It wasn't nice of you to drown like that. It made a lot of people cry. You should have been more careful." Then Stéphane would turn around, aware of Jeanot's gaze but nothing would be said.

Stéphane had been to the United States, he told Jeanot, only months after his brother's death. Stéphane's papa had taken the remnant of his family there because he needed to see some people in America, and so the three of them had spent six days crossing the Atlantic on the French Line ship *Flandre* and then another day traveling by train to Boston.

When Kharkov overheard the boys talking about the trip one day in the courtyard, he invited them to his street-level apartment, sat them down in the living room and gave them each a bar of bitter Russian chocolate that Jeanot found inedible. Then Kharkov started peppering Stéphane with questions. Were the people really tall? Yes, answered the boy, and wide too. The women were all pretty in a common sort of way, like the family's maid from Alsace. Stéphane had been to Germany too and thought a lot of American ladies might actually be German.

Were all the cars new? Yes, said Stéphane, they were, and every color of the rainbow, and very big. Entire families, grandparents and cousins could fit in the cars, and they (the cars) were quiet as well, with very large wheels. The men who drove them all wore hats.

And the buildings? Huge, answered Stéphane, so tall you had to hold your head perpendicular to your neck—he demonstrated—to try to see the tops and even then you couldn't. It was said that a coin dropped from the top of a New York building could kill a man walking in the street below.

What about the food? There Stéphane hesitated, thought for a moment and shrugged "Not very good. They have bread that looks like white sponges but doesn't taste like anything. I liked the Coca Cola. It has more bubbles there. The potatoes are very big," he held his hands six inches apart, "and all the vegetables come in cans."

This astounded Kharkov. "In cans? Tomatoes? Carrots? In cans?"

Stéphane pondered a moment. "Well, maybe not carrots… But peaches and pears, and peas and beans, and they make *purée* out of apples. The wine is undrinkable. Papa said so. He said it gave him a headache." He paused, thought a moment. "And I've never seen so much *meat*! Really *good* meat! The *bifsteak* were as big as my papa's shoes!"

"Meat…" The concierge's look turned wistful, sad, eager, wanting.

"Hot dogs," said Stéphane in English.

"*Hot DOGS?*" The concierge knew a few words of English and was openly incredulous. "They eat the *dogs?*" He'd heard of this, he told the boys, in Russia; entire cities and villages devoid of cats, dogs, even rats, all trapped and devoured by a starving population, but in America? Could this be true?

"*Des petites saucisses dans des petits pains*," Stéphane explained. "You eat them with your hands, with mustard and tomato sauce." He paused, added, "And this green sort of jam they call *relish*, sort of sweet but not bad."

Jeanot chimed in, "I've had them! Sometimes the Captain brings some back from the American store. With the *petits pains*!"

The Russian shook his head in amazement. "Ah, *l'Amérique… Les saucisses… Les tomates…*"

"Tomatoes as big as my head," Stéphane said with the pride of a farmer who'd grown some himself. "And also watermelons larger than Jeanot. We saw them at a fair in the countryside. And huge chickens; chickens as big as geese, chickens that make ours look like pigeons…"

Kharkov was almost in tears by the time the boys left.

Back on the third floor waiting for their mothers to come home from the cinema, Jeanot asked if all Stéphane had said was true. Fruit really that large, meat in every plate, a sheer abundance of everything lacking in Paris? Stéphane swore it was all so, every word. His father had eaten so much during the trip he'd complained of gaining weight. They had televisions in all the hotel rooms and if you left your shoes outside the door at night, you'd find them the next morning all clean and shined.

Later that evening, Sergei Kharkov played his collection of John Philip Sousa marches very loud in his apartment, so loud Jeanot and his family could hear it coming in through their living room windows. Papa said that Kharkov must have had too much vodka and sent Jeanot downstairs to ask the concierge to lower the volume. Jeanot knocked on Kharkov's door and the concierge appeared, dressed in his White Russian uniform. His son was dressed up in his aide-de-camp regalia.

Kharkov was drunk. There had been so many questions, he told Jeanot, that he'd wanted to ask Stéphane, the traveler boy. Why were such opportunities wasted on a child! Were there, really, amber waves of grain? Was it true that in some areas the land was so empty you could see the curvature of the Earth? Lakes as large as seas! Canyons so deep rivers flowing there were obscured by clouds! Explosions of steam from the earth and giant waterfalls that crashed in thunderous spray!

Jeanot returned home without asking the Russian to lower the volume. Kharkov, Jeanot knew, was dancing to America.

Chapter 14

When his great aunt Tatie came to visit Jeanot, she took the train from St. Germain to the Gare St. Lazare in Paris with Guénolé. Each time she came, she recounted the half-hour ride in a private compartment where a waiter served her tea and lemon drop cookies, and each time the tale was slightly different. Guénolé, who traveled with her own thermos of *café au lait,* looked down upon tea drinkers. She said they were all related to the detested Brits who resided across the channel and harassed her exalted Brittany.

Once arrived, the maid was sent off to fend for herself, which usually meant walking two miles to a Breton café where for a few Francs she could get drunk on cheap wine and Khir and eat crêpes. Tatie would take a taxi the three blocks to the apartment on Rue de la Terrasse. She would converse a bit with Kharkov, then take Jeanot to drop in on her cousin Clovis Répaud and Soldat. She seldom had anything to say to Clovis' former wife, Jacqueline. She didn't like the woman and said she thought her haughty and above her station. As she once told Jeanot, "Jacqueline farts higher than her ass." Jeanot had laughed. He didn't know what Tatie meant but any mention of farts and bottoms was funny.

Tatie always brought something when she came to visit; an odd gift for the house, like inexpensive silk flowers bought at a shop near the Gare. Once some years before, she arrived with an elephant's foot end table from her time in Africa many decades earlier. It was wrapped in plain brown paper and the cab driver trundled it up the stairs, held to his chest like a coal scuttle. Maman refused to have it in the house and it ended up in cellar where rats ate it and all that was left was the brass plate attached to the toenails.

Each Christmas Tatie gave Maman an uncut gem; once a sapphire, another time a ruby, and at Easter she brought chocolate eggs for Jeanot, bought the year before during the post-Easter sales. The eggs, once the gold foil wrapping was removed, were no longer a deep brown but tannish and dusty, and they tasted exactly like what they were: faded chocolate.

Tatie always dressed the same; there was a faint mauve aura to her which stretched from hair to stockings. In the winter she wore a fox stole. In the summer, rain or shine, it was a formless raincoat the color of sea sand.

Jeanot loved Tatie because she never talked down to him. She treated him like a diminutive adult, asked his opinions and often acceded to his wishes. They had conversations about the nature of the universe, the traffic, education, language, history. The latter was Tatie's favorite subject; she had lived through a lot of history, had traveled to Asia and Africa as a young bride and had seen how the world had changed in sixty years. She told him who the people were with streets and boulevards named after them: Haussman, Roosevelt, Malesherbes, Lefebvre, Jourdan. He didn't always understand her comments but considered this unimportant. He sensed that even if Tatie did not know something, she would come up with an enlightening explanation not far from the truth.

One day they were walking near l'Opera and Tatie stopped, pointed to a pockmarked wall. *"Regardes, Jeanot…* Here the Boches lined up twenty young men and shot them. Some weren't much older than you. See the marks on the wall?" She pointed, "those are bullet holes."

Jeanot knew about the war in an abstract sort of way. The Germans liked France so much they wanted it for themselves, and it was people like his Papa and Maman who stopped them. Jeanot had never seen a

German. He imagined they were very tall with large teeth; he thought they probably roared when they talked. Although they may have been big, strong, and fearsome, he knew they could be beaten. His parents had proved that.

Tatie and Jeanot went to restaurants together. Tatie used *gros mots* occasionally; swear words rarely uttered in public passed her lips at random. A taxi driver who swerved too close to them was a *couillion*, a *chocolatier* whose treats were too costly was a *salopard*. Jeanot was grateful Tatie trusted him enough to know he wouldn't repeat those words in front of his parents. He would keep them hidden, unused. He was gratified simply to know such treasured expletives. He discerned intuitively that Tatie, purple-prosed or not, was every inch a lady from an earlier time, a vestige from another century when respect for feminine charm transcended all things. His Papa had often spoken of such a time, and no one represented that ideal to Jeanot more than Tatie.

Once Jeanot thought he would impress her at the restaurant by ordering something without her assistance. Because it made perfect sense he got the entrée with the highest number next to it. Tatie had to call the waiter back before the man could deliver a matched pair of whole lobsters to their table. From then on, Tatie ordered the main course and Jeanot ordered dessert for both. He learned she always got the same thing; *Pêche Melba*.

Once, after lunch, they went to the afternoon show of the Cirque Médrano on Boulevard Rochechouart.

The circus was housed in a gaudy old building and was well-known for its clowns, though Jeanot wasn't sure whether he liked them. They were frightening, with their loud voices and bicycle horns, and the way they ran up and down the aisles and among the spectators, spraying them with giant bottles of soda water. Tatie liked the clowns. They made her laugh, but Jeanot noticed that none attempted to douse her, and he wondered whether this was through her force of will or if perhaps the circus had a house rule against spraying old ladies.

They didn't mind spraying kids though, and one of the clowns, the meanest looking of the lot with a half-blue head and spiky red hair, got Jeanot right in the face, soaking him, his bag of peanuts and the Eskimo Pie Tatie had bought him minutes earlier. Jeanot was outraged. He yelled, felt tears of righteous anger well up and just as they were about to erupt, the very same clown gave him *two* Eskimo pies and a huge bag of peanuts. Tatie wiped his face with a small lace handkerchief that smelled exactly like her. She hailed a vendor, bought even more candy and in seconds all was right with the world again.

They watched roustabouts erect the cage for the lion tamer, but Jeanot was not impressed. He wished there were rhinoceros tamers. Now that would be something to see, but the man with the snapping whip and pith helmet was tired and uninspiring, and what he was doing didn't look dangerous at all. The big cats were slow and unmenacing and Jeanot barely applauded. His mind wandered and he remembered reading about lemmings, little animals that lived in America and jumped off cliffs. He had never seen a lemming, and he had never seen a cliff and so he imagined they leaped off like the divers at the swimming pool where he went one Saturday with the Louveteaux troop. None of the kids were allowed to go off the high board, but one of the bigger boys did it anyway, jumping off and landing on his stomach and making a huge splash. Jeanot knew that must have hurt, but you had to admire the *grand garçon* who didn't cry at all.

If the lion tamer left Jeanot cold, he went wild for the balancing act featuring tiny Oriental women. Before it was through he was planning a show of his own in the living room after everyone was asleep. He would get a couple of chairs and the little kitchen step-ladder Mathilde used to reach high into the pantry; he would learn to balance precariously on top of everything, just like the performer and impress Babette the next time she came over.

By the time the horseback riders appeared he was exhausted and a little nauseous. He nearly dozed off and Tatie settled him so his head rested on her lap. She didn't want to leave yet, telling him the aerialists were next, and that she saw the same show last week to make sure it was appropriate for a child. He would be fascinated by the men and women working without a net fifteen meters above the ring.

She speculated aloud briefly about the acrobats' lives, compared them to her own while Jeanot dreamily half-listened. For the past forty years, Tatie had been a widow living in the same home in St. Germain. The maid, Guénolé had been with her thirty-seven of those years and Maman often speculated on how in heaven Tatie managed to survive in such close proximity to the wicked little Bretonne whose "every exhalation is misery," according to Papa. They almost never spoke; their relationship of mistress and servant was clearly established and had never altered, as far as Jeanot knew. Papa said Guénolé was a cheat and a thief who every week snitched a few extra Francs by skimping on the food budget, buying yesterday's fish and bread, making do with household goods purchased from the nest of Breton thieves who lived near the train station and robbed the local stores at night. Tatie knew all this and more. She told Jeanot about how Guénolé had stolen jewelry from her and pawned it, and about how Guénolé kept a bottle of Calvados in her closet—the maid mixed the Calvados with milk and replenished the alcohol every three days from a giant jug in the cellar. Tatie knew almost everything there was to know about the daily habits of this tiny malicious woman who could barely cook and kept the house so poorly. Tatie exclaimed repeatedly that she didn't know why she kept her around so long. Maman said Tatie and Guénolé's relationship, was built on distrust and dislike and was as solid as anything either woman had ever experienced. It would end only in the demise of one or the other.

Tatie has told Jeanot she hoped Guénolé will go first.

This wasn't such a difficult thing for Jeanot to understand. He thought of his relationship with the late Dédé; remembered all the things he hadn't liked about the onion-eating boy, and thought that sometimes people could care very much and dislike very much at the same time, and things were all right that way.

The man on the flying trapeze launched himself into the air and did a triple flip. The audience—Tatie included—went "Ahhh" as he grabbed the outstretched arms of another aerialist and alighted on the platform so high above. Jeanot stirred, sighed deeply as he thought about his aunt, Dédé, and the high-flying trapeze artist. Tatie smoothed the boy's cowlick down but let him lie undisturbed.

By the time they left the Cirque Medrano the day had turned cool and the air smelled like burnt diesel.

Jeanot was subdued and held Tatie's hand as they crossed the street towards a taxi stand. He twined his small naked fingers into her equally small gloved ones and—a surprise!—made it a point to open the car door for her. The small gentlemanly act made her laugh, which in turn made the boy smile. She hugged him and all the way home in the cab she squeezed his hand, smiling as if to say she was supremely happy to be with this beautiful child who was not hers. Basking in that perfect happiness, Jeanot fell asleep at her side.

Chapter 15

One Tuesday, neither Françoise nor Madeleine came to the apartment. They always came on Tuesdays, and had dinner and stayed to talk or listen to the big RCA radio. Sometimes one spent the night while the other went back to her own home, but they always came. Jeanot couldn't remember them ever not coming before.

A second Tuesday passed, then a third. Jeanot asked his Maman where the girls were and she gave him a bleak look before turning her back and wiping her eyes.

That night, Papa came into Jeanot's room to explain that his sisters had to stay at their own house while things were sorted out.

"Things?"

"*Oui,*" said Papa. "Complicated things. You know your Maman was married before?"

Jeanot did. Though Madeleine and Françoise were his sisters and the three of them had the same Maman, the girls were not Papa's children. It was confusing because thinking of his Maman with another man defied logic. She and Papa were his parents, a unit. They were *together.* He knew they had met during the war, but that was a different time and a different universe. The war may have been only years ago, but Jeanot understood, of course, his Papa and Maman had been together since the beginning of time.

"Well," Papa continued, "your sisters' father wants them all to himself. He doesn't like that they come here."

"Because of me?"

Both Françoise and Madeleine occasionally complained that Jeanot made too much noise, asked too many questions, and was constantly underfoot when Madeleine practiced the piano and Françoise read books in English. He'd never thought his presence was that annoying. Was it? Had they complained to their Papa about it, and would Jeanot get in trouble?

"*Non,* Jeanot. This has nothing to do with you." Papa took a deep breath and Jeanot could see his father was going to try to explain something complicated.

"*Non,*" he said again. "What it is, your Maman and her first husband, his name is Marcel, he's your sisters' father. Well, he and your Maman got into a very big fight years ago, and unfortunately, they're still fighting. *Tu comprends?*"

Jeanot nodded.

"*Bien.* So sometimes, what happens when people fight over something for a very long time, they get help from other people, from lawyers."

"Other people to do their fighting for them?"

Papa looked surprised.

"There was a story in *Tintin,*" Jeanot explained. "About lawyers. I didn't read the whole thing. It was in that center section they have every week about what people do for a living."

"Ah," Papa nodded. "Well, sometimes when the lawyers fight, they fight sort of... not very nicely."

"Like the *grand garçons* do?"

"Hm. Maybe, yes."

"Last year," Jeanot remembered, "two of the *grands garçons* fought in the courtyard at school and one kicked the other right in the," he looked around and lowered his voice, "right in the *couilles.*"

Papa opened his eyes wide. "That must have hurt!"

"Lawyers do that?"

Papa laughed once, more of a bark. "No. But that would be something to see, wouldn't it?" Now he did chuckle openly, then ran a hand through his hair. "I think what they do is a lot more harmful… But anyway, the lawyers fight, and they say really bad things about the people they're fighting against, hurtful things. And sometimes they tell lies, too, and what happened, a few days ago, is that the lawyer for Marcel said some bad things about your Maman."

"What bad things?"

Papa pondered this for a second, and then shrugged. "The lawyer said your Maman was not a good mother to Françoise and Madeleine."

That, thought Jeanot, was plainly ridiculous. His Maman would have been a good mother to anyone. Hadn't she written a book about the girls? Hadn't she gone shopping and bought them clothes? Didn't she spend hours talking with them and remembering stories about Algeria and riding camels and eating funny foods? Of course she did.

"That's just stupid," Jeanot said with conviction.

His Papa agreed. "Well yes, it is. But still, it makes her sad. So you have to be extra nice to her, all right Jeanot? It's important."

Jeanot nodded. Now he wondered if the lawyers were also responsible for his Maman taking a lot more pills lately.

For as far back as he could remember, there had been a breadbasket full of medicines right in the middle of the dining room table, in the same place where other families had a basket of fruit, or flowers. The basket was woven osier and contained a dozen clear bottles, and metal tubes, and brown liquids in little glass vials, all replenished weekly. His Maman took some medicine at lunch and at dinner, and lately, he'd noticed, sometimes she took some between meals too.

"Will it be over soon? The lawyers?"

"I hope so," Papa said. "I really, really hope so."

Two afternoons later when he was in his room rearranging the cowboys and Indians, Jeanot heard the apartment door slam shut. His Maman was shouting and crying at the same time.

"Why does Marcel have to be like that? So cruel! What does he want?"

Jeanot stayed in his room but pulled the door ajar a bit and pressed his ear to the opening. "*Calmes-toi, chérie,*" he heard his Papa say. "It doesn't help anything to get this upset."

Maman was in no mood to be calm. "Did you hear what he said? That I was unfit? That I behaved like a *putain?* While he's cohabitating with that horrible, despicable woman and doing God know what in front of the girls!"

"*Chérie! S'il te plait.* Jeanot will hear you."

"Jeanot should know how horrible these people are!"

"*Non.* He shouldn't. Leave him out of this. Don't make him dislike his sisters."

The argument raged another fifteen seconds. Jeanot held his breath. He heard his parents go to the dining room. Someone took a pill bottle and shook it. Jeanot recognized the sound. His mother did that each time before taking the pills. He heard his Papa murmur something, and after a short while, both his parents went into their bedroom.

The same thing happened a week later, but this time it was his Papa who was unhappy. "You should have told me, Marité. That completely blindsided me."

Jeanot wondered what it was Maman hadn't told Papa. He, personally, had a few secrets. For example, he'd lifted two Indians and one cowboy from the toy store a month earlier. It had been a terrifying, exhilarating experience, and walking home after the theft, he'd been sure every single pedestrian glancing in his direction knew of the crime. He had tempted fate by placing the stolen items right in the middle of his tabletop diorama, among the other little figurines. Then, in the middle of the night, he's removed them, persuaded that Mathilde, who never missed a thing, would spot them and tell his parents. In the morning he had placed them back on the table and worried about it throughout the school day. When nothing happened when he got home, he didn't know whether to be relieved or disappointed. It troubled him that a mortal sin was such an easy thing to commit, that what he'd believed would immediately and inexorably lead to dire consequences simply had not done so. It was troubling, this realization that he could do something really bad and not be found out. It implied that what he'd been told by anyone in authority—Maman, Papa, Mathilde, even Babette—simply wasn't true. Even harder to understand was the joy he'd felt following the theft. Why would taking something not his cause such delight?

Now Papa was saying, "You told me nothing happened between you and him. And now this…"

"It was nothing, *chéri. Crois moi.*" His Maman's voice was flat and sad. *"Tu sais que je n'aime que toi."*

Well of course, his Maman loved only his Papa! Jeanot heard his father walk away. The big American shoes from the PX made loud clopping sounds. He thought he heard his mother sniffle.

At dinner that night his parents were quiet. Papa pushed food around his plate and drank almost a full bottle of wine. His Maman twice took pills from a small brown bottle, and then excused herself before dessert, saying she was tired. Papa asked Jeanot about school but wasn't listening when Jeanot told a story of the teacher who tripped and almost fell on his own untied shoelace. Three boys had laughed out loud and earned a half-an-hour each in separate corners of the classroom.

Back in his bedroom Jeanot leafed through *Tintin, Spirou* and *Mickey* without interest. He thought about his Maman being married to another man but couldn't quite picture it. Nor could he understand why the thought of it made his father sad. After all, that had been a long, long time ago, hadn't it?

More secrets, he decided.

One person who knew a lot about divorce was Babette. She came to visit with her mother who was picking up a dress from the *atelier*, and when Jeanot mentioned what was happening with his Maman and Papa, she smiled confidently and said, "I already know all about it!"

Babettes's parents had been talking about this openly at the dinner table, it seemed. "Maman says," Babette informed him, "that your maman is fighting to keep her daughters, because her other husband wants to take them away. Maman says that your mother got pregnant with you even before she was divorced from her other husband, her first husband, and that, of course, is very wrong. That is what all the scandal is about."

It was strange to hear his Maman and Papa referred to like that, like the character in a story. It was stranger still to think they were involved in a *scandal*, a word he knew meant, "something embarrassing and very bad."

Babette had a remarkable memory for her parents' conversations. She told Jeanot his Maman had had an affair with a married man during the war.

"What's *an affair?*"

She looked annoyed. "*Mon Dieu!* You're so young!" She heaved a meaningful sigh and said. "An affair is when someone goes to bed with someone they shouldn't."

Jeanot said, "Ah," for lack of anything better to say. His mother and father always slept in the same bed, and neither of them had ever gone to sleep with anyone else. Of course, there had been times, on trips to visit other friends, when Maman had slept in the same room with other women, and Papa had stayed with other men. He'd understood that there was nothing scandalous at all about that.

Babette continued, "And her husband found out and—"

"My Papa?"

Babette shook her head. "No. Not him. Her first husband. Your sisters' father."

"Marcel?"

"Is that his name?"

Jeanot could see Babette was pleased with this bit of information. "I think so."

"So yes, Marcel. Marcel found out your Maman slept with a man—"

"My Papa?"

"No, no!" Babette was getting annoyed.

"I don't understand," mumbled Jeanot.

Babette was quiet for a moment gathering her thoughts. "Écoutes moi bien. Your Maman, when she was still married to Marcel, slept with another man. Not with your Papa, that came later. Some man. And Marcel found out and he got livid; that's the word my Maman uses, *livid*. So he threw her out of their house…"

"Threw her *out!*" This was appalling.

"Yes," Babette said smugly. "Out. Right into the street. And then your Papa came along and he slept with your Maman which my father says made her an unfit mother, because they were not divorced yet, she and Marcel."

"But she was with my Papa!"

"But she shouldn't have been!" Babette said this victoriously, as if it explained everything.

Jeanot shook his head. This divorce and sleeping thing was complex, and he didn't know if Babette really had facts or was making things up as she went along. She did that sometimes.

Babette asked, "*Tu comprends?*"

He nodded yes, even though he didn't.

She put an arm around him. "*La vie, c'est compliquée.*"

He had to agree. Life was complicated.

Babette and Jeanot were rearranging cowboys and Indians on the table in his bedroom. She insisted on pairing braves with cowboys, making them look as if they were dancing, which annoyed him to no end. He knew she was doing it on purpose. Every few minutes she glanced at him, moved a figurine, and hummed to herself. He, with dogged perseverance, pulled the dancers apart.

When she tired of the game, she sat on the floor next to the table and said, "Did you know you're a Jew?"

"No, I'm not," said Jeanot. "I'm a Catholic. We've all been to church together, remember? Last Easter?"

She stood and stretched, hoisted herself on to the top bunk bed and lay down. "You're a Jew," she repeated. "My parents were talking about it yesterday at the dinner table. They said your Maman married a Jew the first time, and so automatically, you're one too." She smoothed her skirt, kicked off her shoes so they fell to the ground with a clunk, and added, "My Papa says, once a Jew, always a Jew." With that, she fell asleep.

Jeanot knew what Jews were. A number of his parents' friends were Jews, and they had tattoos on their forearms that he was not supposed to ask questions about. There were a couple of Jewish kids at school too, and they wore little round hats and people sometimes made fun of them, and he knew, of course, that Marcel, the man who had married his Maman before his own Papa did, was Jewish. Still, how that made him, personally, Jewish, remained unclear.

Babette, he'd learned from experience, was an inventive friend who made up answers if she didn't have them at the ready. She had once told him, when he was very little, that rhinoceros were elephants who had lost one tusk and that leopards were female lions that African people had spotted with black paint. He'd believed her until Papa had cleared up the confusion. There was, therefore, a strong likelihood that the Jewish story was one of Babette's blatant falsehoods.

He shook her awake. "So what is it exactly, being Jewish?"

She blinked her eyes and sat up. "Is it time for *gouté*?" *Gouté* was served at four every day in both their homes, usually hot chocolate and cookies to tide them over until dinner

Jeanot would not be redirected. "How would I know if I were Jewish? What's the difference between that and being Catholic?"

Babette frowned. "It may be a bit complicated for you to understand." She jumped down from the top bunk. "I am really ready for *gouté.*"

"Jewish."

She sighed theatrically. "Well," she said. "You have to learn a secret Jewish language, one only Jews speak. And there are special foods. You can't eat ham."

"No ham?" Ham was one of Jeanot's staple foods. He ate it four or five times a week in sandwiches, and his mother served it for dinner whenever she could get big American ham steaks from the PX.

"No sausages, either."

That would be okay. Once or twice a month, Mathilde fixed *boudin*, which Jeanot had been told was made with the blood of slaughtered animals mixed with other doubtful ingredients. *Boudin* was always served with mashed potatoes, and Jeanot had learned to mix everything in his plate to make it edible.

"Will I have to get a tattoo?"

The question silenced Babette. After a while she said, "No. No, I don't think so. I'm pretty sure those are only for grown-ups; for Jewish people who were in the war."

They sat in silence for a while and Jeanot wondered at the intricacies of things never considered before. Did it matter that his Maman was—or might be—Jewish? What about his sisters? Were they Jewish too?

He was still exploring the possibilities when Mathilde came into his room with a tray for their *gouté*.

Chapter 16

Jeanot was surprised and delighted when his Maman invited all who wanted to come to a five-day week-end in Benodet. Everyone was welcome, she insisted, including friends and workers from *Creations St. Paul*. She had rented a small house near the beach, a bungalow with three tiny bedrooms, an outhouse and a primitive kitchen. She wanted to—*had to*—get away from Paris, she announced. It would do people good to be by the sea, eat *moules à la Bretonne,* and bet on the horses at the local track.

Jeanot wondered if perhaps the air and the prickle in the back of her throat had finally become too much. Maman coughed often and said it was the atmosphere.

Jeanot was given a new bathing suit, a mask and fins, and his very own Tarzan towel showing the jungle-man swinging through the vines as evil white grave robbers tried to shoot him. Maman bought a daring bikini that Papa objected to. He said he thought it showed far too much skin, but when Maman asked if she now looked like what she was, the mother of three, Papa had to admit she did not. Other men gazed at her when the family strolled out onto the beach together, and Papa always looked pleased, although Maman was clearly uninterested in their attentions. Jeanot, too, was proud of his beautiful mother. He agreed with Papa that his Maman looked like no other maman that he had ever seen; the other children would no doubt be jealous.

Of the workers employed at Maman's *atelier*, only Cécile and Jean-Sylvain came for the full five days. Babette was invited to provide company for Jeanot. They set out from Paris Friday before dawn in two cars, Papa's DeSoto and Jean-Sylvain's even older Citroën. There were sandwiches, cheese and bottles of wine, and Orangina for the children. Cécile rode with Papa and Maman, Babette and Jeanot with Jean-Sylvain, who worried throughout the drive about the sleeping accommodations. "I refuse to sleep anywhere near that *pute* Cécile," he said. "Had I known she was coming, I might not have come myself…"

At the word *pute,* Babette, bored with counting cows, perked up. "Why is she a *pute,* Jean-Sylvain? Does she sleep with all the men? That's what my mother says *putes* do. She says my Papa has slept with all the *putes* in Paris. Has he slept with Cécile, do you think?"

Jean-Sylvain sniffed. "I have to dress her. Undressing her would be far worse." Jeanot had no idea what this meant, and for once, Babette offered no explanation.

Somewhere between Lavalle and Reines, everything went wrong. Jeanot said he had to pee so Jean-Sylvain stopped the car and both children leaped out. Babette squatted behind a bush as Jeanot sprayed a nearby tree. Jean-Sylvain looked for a map in the glove box, then got out of the car, looked up and down the road. *"Merde merde merde merde!"* Jean-Sylvain swore loudly, *"Merde!"*

Babette laughed, turned to Jeanot, "Jean-Sylvain said *merde!*" Then she started chanting the word, and in no time Jeanot chimed in and soon both of them were singing, "Merde merde, merdemerde-merde!" to the tune of *Alouette.*

Jean-Sylvain shouted, "Don't you understand? We're lost! Lost!" His voice rose an octave and his shrillness interrupted the children's song.

Babette said, "How can we be lost? The road is right here!"

Jean-Sylvain took a deep breath and said, more calmly, "I don't know where we're going."

Jeanot thought that was silly. "We're all going to the beach. Maman is taking us there!"

The exasperated man ran his hand through his hair. "Do you see your maman anywhere, Jeanot? Do you? Because I don't!"

Jeanot didn't either. A bolt of fear shot through his stomach.

"Òu est Maman? Òu *est Papa?* Òu *sont-ils?*" He turned to Babette. "Where are they? Where'd they go?" Then he burst into tears. Jean-Sylvain threw his hands up in the air and turned to Babette. "Tell him to stop crying! I can't think with the little bastard squalling in my ear!" Being referred to in the third person *and* with a bad word made Jeanot feel utterly lost and the intensity of his yowls increased.

Babette hugged him, patted his head, rubbed his back. Deep inside Jeanot knew that something terrible must have happened to his parents if Babette was being so sweet, so his sobs became hiccups and suddenly he threw up, narrowly missing Babette who leaped back with a "*Merde!*" of her own. He tasted bile and Orangina and the ham sandwich from an hour earlier, threw up some more. Babette handed him an old army canteen full of water and he drank, spat, and drank again. Babette kept her distance. "*Ça va mieux?*"

Jeanot was about to answer when Jean-Sylvain broke into an odd little dance, jumping lightly into the air and waving his arms over his head like an asylum escapee. He shouted "*Içi! Nous sommes içi!*" He took out his white handkerchief and waved it until the DeSoto pulled up and Maman and Papa both alighted from the car.

Jeanot stopped hiccupping; it was a miracle, both his Maman and Papa appearing as if by magic just when all was lost. He hugged his Maman's knees and she picked him up, made a face. "Jeanot? What happened here? You smell like—"

"*Il a vomi,*" Babette explained.

Maman took Jean-Sylvain's handkerchief, spit in it and wiped Jeanot's mouth, then balled it up and threw it over her shoulder into the roadside ditch. Jean-Sylvain looked shocked. Jeanot made a face. He found his Maman's spit clean-up repulsive but Maman did it anyway and far too often.

They returned to their cars and drove on, Jean-Sylvain staying no more than two car lengths behind the DeSoto and saying over and over again, "What a man! *Quel homme, ce Roland! Un héro! Un homme magnifique!*"

Jeanot fell asleep as Babette returned to counting cows.

When they arrived in Benodet, Jeanot thought the cottage looked like one of the little shacks that speckled the property around the chateau where Dédé had died. He'd been told by his father how each little house there had a particular use. There was one for drying and curing meat, another for storing root vegetables, a third for keeping pregnant sows away from the rest of the pigs. There had been one his father had not pointed to, but Jeanot had instinctively known that one had something to do with slaughtering, butchering, skinning. He and Dédé had peeked through a streaked window and seen a chopping block, many knives, and stains on the wooden floor. Dédé had said it smelled bad, like something gone rotten, and Jeanot had known the smell was death.

The little rental house was not far from the sea and Jeanot heard the pounding of waves on sand. He gathered his pail, shovel, new American sailor hat bought for the occasion, flippers, mask and Tarzan towel and was about to set out for the beach by himself when Papa stopped him.

"*Une minute*, Jeanot. We have to get set up first, decide who sleeps where. Find Maman and help her, then we'll all go together."

That took close to an hour. Cécile objected to sleeping in the same room as Jean-Sylvain, who felt the same. The latter suggested all the men sleep in one room, and the women in another but Maman insisted on sleeping with Papa, so it was decided that Jeanot and Babette would sleep in the smallest room which was hardly larger than a closet. Babette whispered to Jeanot, "You'd better not fart!"

Jean-Sylvain and Cécile got the second largest room. Jeanot helped carry in some of Cécile's baggage, and saw the two *atelier* employees setting their beds as far from each other as possible.

Cécile began to unpack some party clothes that Jeanot thought ridiculous for a trip to the beach. She had brought a red satiny dress and a pair of high-heeled shoes that looked painful to wear. She asked

Jeanot if he thought that his father would like the dress, and Jeanot, uncertain, tried to be helpful by saying that Papa always liked his mother's red clothes. For some reason, that answer didn't seem to please Cécile, although it amused Jean-Sylvain. Eager to get back to the beach, Jeanot excused himself as soon as he could.

The sea was freezing. Jeanot ran into it, holding his mask and fins and it wasn't until the water hit his midsection that he screamed, tried to turn back, but was bowled over by a medium-sized wave. Babette, in only up to her ankles, seized him by the arm and pulled him out. He was breathless, hiccupping with cold, wide-eyed. The wave had pulled his suit down to reveal the crack of his butt and he struggled to pull it back up, feeling sand in there and lower. Papa ran up, grabbed him under the arms and held him close. "*Doucement petit, prends ton temps,* take your time and you'll get used to the water." When Jeanot's trembling subsided, Papa put him down, walked to their towel and came back with some change. "Go buy something, get a *gaufrette* and a *diabolo menthe* and stay out of the water until you get warm. When you want to go in again, I'll go with you."

So Jeanot sat on the sand and began building a castle using his bucket and shovel; Jean-Sylvain helped by shaping the walls with a twig. Babette added shells to the ramparts, and everyone agreed that it was a shame there was no sandcastle contest today because surely Jeanot's creation would have won.

When the sand got too hot to walk on, Jeanot ran into the water again with his parents trailing behind. His Maman made shuddering sounds the deeper she got in and yelled when the water splashed over the lower part of her bikini. Papa laughed, picked her up bodily and threw her into the water. She came up sputtering, furious and cursing. "*Salop!*"

Papa dove at her, grabbed her by the waist and pulled her under. When their faces emerged seconds later, both were smiling. They walked back to the beach hand in hand and Jeanot noticed his Papa was hiding something in the front of his bathing suit. Cécile, sitting on a towel in a bikini even smaller than Maman's, must have noticed it too. She frowned.

Chapter 17

They ate lunch sitting in the front yard around a home-built plank table with benches. Jeanot ran his hands along the pale grey wood, warped and chipped, and Maman warned the children about splinters. A giant elm tree full of chattering birds dwarfed the yard. Maman and Cécile set the table with the house's mismatched plates and varied knives and forks gathered from the kitchen. Jeanot and Babette helped put out the *saucisson*, ham, three kinds of cheeses that got soft and runny in the heat, butter from a nearby dairy, *rilletes de porc*, rough country bread, radishes, celery stalks, a bean salad, figs, apricots, and three oranges from Tunisia.

Jeanot watched his father eating radishes. Papa split a red orb with a knife, shaved a small ribbon of butter, then added salt and pepper. It took him mere seconds to prepare a radish, and he ate a half-dozen without pausing. Jeanot disliked radishes because they made his nose itch, but he aped his Papa, adding too much pepper. He popped the radish in his mouth, then hurriedly took a drink. Cécile spread *rilletes* on a chunk of bread and smacked her lips. Jeanot thought *rilletes* were peasant food that stunk of pig fat. That was what his Maman called them. When Papa brought some back from the *charcuterie*, she made a face and called him a pig farmer. Cécile smacked her lips again. Jean-Sylvain obviously shared Maman's thoughts on *rilletes*. Jeanot watched him nibble at a slice of ham, trimming all the white fat with precision and pushing it to one side of his plate, then cutting the pink meat into minute square pieces. He peeled a fresh fig, offered it with a small smile to Papa, who nodded his thanks, mouth still full of radish, and reached for the bread.

The adults were drinking wine and both Babette and Jeanot were given small glasses of *abondance* to drink, one part wine, four parts water. This, they'd been told, would keep them from becoming alcoholics when they grew up. The wine tinged the water pink and gave it a sweetly metallic flavor. Jeanot, who had never been crazy about the taste, kept most of his *abondance* until the end of the meal and then drank the entire glass in one gulp. Babette sipped hers thoughtfully, imitating Cécile, and she agreed when Cécile stated that this was indeed an excellent rosé. Why was it, asked Cécile, that the good local wines never got to Paris? It was, she assured them, because the peasants were all drunks. Jeanot was sure that Maman had once called Cécile "the daughter of a peasant," and so he assumed that she spoke with authority. Papa recounted the story of the peasant who killed his entire family after drinking too much absinthe, which explained why absinthe was now illegal. The adults nodded. Jeanot, too, had heard the story before of Jean Lafray, the murderer, and debates still raged frequently at his own dinner table over the hold absinthe could have on a man.

They reminisced about the war. Cécile told of farmers she knew, neighbors who kept to themselves and sold produce to the Germans, even as they sheltered a family of seven Jews in a root cellar below their barn. At war's end, the family was accused of being collaborators but the testimony of the Jews made them heroes instead. The family said they had lived in the cellar for two-and-a-half years and had never missed a meal. They were fed richly, given wine, eggs and fresh vegetables. They also claimed to have heard the farmer's voice only three times in all those years. When the village mayor sought to decorate him, the farmer refused to be either honored or thanked. He did not change his silent ways and quietly returned to growing artichokes and spinach.

Jeanot, sleepy from the sun and food, found a tattered blanket and spread it beneath the elm tree. He lay on it and stared at the sky and soon Babette joined him there.

Jean-Sylvain peeled another fig meticulously, quartering the fruit's skin and arranging it like a rosette on his paper plate. "I used to live there. My mother and I had an apartment on Rue Nélaton." He waited for a reaction. There was none.

"Overlooking the Vélodrome d'Hivers. The Vel d'Hiv."

Now Jeanot saw his Maman look up. "We shouldn't be talking about this, Jean-Sylvain," she said. Papa buttered another radish.

Cécile said, "The Vel *quoi?*"

"Where they took the Jews," said Jean-Sylvain. "I saw it. I saw the women and the children all wearing yellow stars, they were crying and screaming and *flics* pushed them inside the Vélodrome, and later that night I saw a mother holding a baby. She'd somehow managed to climb to the top of the place and she jumped…"

Maman glanced towards Jeanot who hastily pretended to be inspecting a leaf. "Really, Jean-Sylvain. We're on vacation and—"

Papa shushed her. "Let him speak." Jeanot paid more attention. It was rare for his Papa to interrupt Maman.

"All during the night they were taking bodies out," Jean-Sylvain continued. "They wrapped them in blankets at first, and then in cardboard. I guess the blankets ran out. They kept the Jews there two days and on the third day dozens of buses came and took them away. Mostly mothers and little children. They piled them in the buses, squeezed them in and drove them away. There were thousands of them. Thousands."

Cécile was clearly trying and failing not to look aghast. "You mean the Germans, *non?* The Germans sent them off?"

Jean-Sylvain shook his head. "No. We did. I mean, the French, us. They were French policemen, not Germans. I didn't see any Germans at all. The *flics* were guarding the doors. I saw them turn away our *boulangère* who went there with a basket of bread. I stayed with my mother in our apartment. I didn't do anything…"

He bit into the fig. "In three days they were all gone and a bunch of cleaners came in, took out truckloads of garbage. Old clothes. Shoes. Old valises and stuffed toys. It stank. They brought in the fire brigade to hose the place down but it didn't help. It still stank."

Maman gave Papa a strange look, then nodded towards Jeanot, who busied himself with the leaf and pretended not to notice. Papa said, "He's old enough to know."

Jeanot wondered, *Know what?*

Jean-Sylvain didn't notice the exchange of looks. He wiped his lips with a napkin. "I looked in the paper the next day and the day after that and there wasn't anything written. As if it hadn't happened, and after a while I started to believe it hadn't, but then a couple of weeks later they found these three bodies in the basement of our building. Two boys and a girl, brothers and a sister, I guess. They had escaped somehow, and they'd starved. I guess they were afraid to come out. The police came for the bodies. They collected them like garbage. I've never forgotten that."

Jeanot yawned, and Babette did too. Maman stood. "Hush now! Let's not talk about this anymore. We're on vacation and it was a long time ago."

Jean-Sylvain shrugged. "Not long enough…"

That first night the children slept with a fan that made a reassuring noise. A young woman was hired to sit with them and she mostly listened to the radio and ate peaches, skin and all, popping the pit into her mouth and sucking until every strand of peach-meat was gone. The adults dressed in their best clothes and went to the casino.

Jeanot dreamed of warm waters and sand castles as big as homes. He woke once, peed, heard Babette stir, then returned to his cot and fell back asleep.

Not much later, Jeanot woke to the sound of his Maman's screams. Something hit a wall and shattered. Both Jeanot and Babette sat up, wide-eyed in the dark.

Jeanot ran out of his room to see his Maman with her hands on Cécile's throat. She released the younger woman and slapped her twice, hard, and Cécile fell to the ground in a heap. Jean-Sylvain took Maman by the shoulders and pulled her back, but not before Maman launched a kick that caught Cécile squarely in the stomach. Cécile coughed, retched and threw up. The acrid odor of vomit filled the room.

Babette stood behind Jeanot, hands blanketing her mouth. *"Qu'est ce qu'il se passe?"*

Jeanot could feel his heart beating like a Bastille Day parade drum in his chest. He looked at his Maman, now restrained by Jean-Sylvain, and heard her rain a string of words, only some of which he understood and knew to be the worst kind of insults, the kind that would guarantee a serious spanking and several hours in the coat closet.

Both women were breathing hard and Cécile was covering her face. Then Maman broke away from Jean-Sylvain and threw herself at the other woman. She spat at Cécile and the gob of saliva slid off Cécile's hair.

"Salope! Espèce de pute!!" She kicked Cécile hard in the ribs and was launching another blow when Jean-Sylvain pulled her away again.

"Marité! Arrètes! Calmes toi!"

Cécile got to her knees, to her feet, wiped her face. *"Mais elle est folle!* She's gone crazy!"

Papa stood in the bedroom's doorway. *"Chérie! Arrètes! Je t'en prie! Contrôles toi!"*

Maman shrugged away from Jean-Sylvain, turned to face Papa. Jeanot had never, ever seen her face so contorted and full of rage. She was crying, breathing in hard, short gasps. Her make-up streaked her eyes and cheeks, and Jeanot saw she was trembling, as if from the cold, though it was summer warm in the little house.

Maman glared at Papa. *"Contrôles toi?* You want me to control myself? You fucked that slut and you want *me* to *control* myself!!"* She started sobbing loudly now, making a keening sound as her chest heaved.

Papa was shirtless and his pajama bottoms hung low. There was a long red scratch that rose from his navel and ended just below his left nipple. Jean-Sylvain's eyes were glued to Papa's chest.

Papa took both of Maman's hands and led her out of the room, out of the house and into the front yard. Jeanot and Babette both rushed to the window. Babette clutched at him, but Jeanot squirmed away and ran to where his Maman was sitting outside. He rounded his arms about her waist and could feel her trembling. Papa returned to the house.

After a while, he came back with a glass of water and said, "*Jeanot, vas te coucher.* Go back to bed. Everything will be okay."

He gently separated the boy from his mother and pointed him toward the door. "*Va. Va.*"

Inside, Jeanot found Babette staring at Cécile. Jean-Sylvain was in the room, standing over the woman. "*Fais ta valise.* Pack your bag. I'll be back in a few minutes to drive you to a hotel. Do it *now.*" Cécile stayed mute, nodded her head.

Jean-Sylvain told the boy to go in the kitchen and make chocolate milk for him and Babette, who was now standing in the doorway wearing an inquiring look, her head cocked to the right. Jeanot stood his ground. Something terrible had occurred and could get even worse if he left.

Maman re-entered the room and fell into a chair. Jean-Sylvain took her right hand in both of his and squatted next to her. "*Calmes toi, ma petite.*" He stroked her hair, rubbed her shoulders. When a few minutes had passed, he said, "Nothing happened. That slut was all over him, but I never let him out of my sight. *Crois moi,* Marité. He wasn't alone with her for a moment."

Maman's shoulders slumped. "*Vraiment?*"

Jean-Sylvain nodded. "Yes, really. I wouldn't lie to you Marité, you know that. The bitch was trying to get to him but nothing happened. Nothing."

"She can't stay."

"She's leaving tonight."

Babette whispered to Jeanot, "I told you Cécile was a *pute*!" She snickered dirtily and Jeanot ignored her.

Papa stood off to the side, his head lowered.

"It's true, *chérie*. Nothing happened. Nothing at all."

Jeanot thought for the very first time ever that his Papa was lying.

After a while, Maman swallowed a handful of pills with a gulp of wine. Papa tried to embrace her but she pushed him off without a word, went into the bedroom they shared and slammed the door. Papa ordered Jeanot and Babette back to bed, then wrapped himself in a blanket and lay down on the too-small couch. Uncertain what else he could do, Jeanot returned to their room with Babette.

Shortly after that, Jeanot looked out the bedroom window and watched as Jean-Sylvain and Cécile left the house, she holding a small blue suitcase. He heard the ancient Citroën wheeze to life and drive away. When Jean-Sylvain returned in less than an hour, Jeanot was still awake. Babette was whispering the word *pute* over and over again, "I told you so, remember? I said she was a *pute.*"

The next day was warm and wet, a steady Breton drizzle that was more mist than rain. Jean-Sylvain and Maman went to town to shop and Papa took Jeanot and Babette to the almost deserted beach where he watched them splash in the surf but didn't go into the water himself. Jeanot thought his Papa looked sad, but didn't know how to broach the preceding night's events.

Then Papa stood up. He ran to the water's edge, picked up Jeanot and dove into the surf. Jeanot yelled, choked on a mouthful of brine, laughed and clung to his Papa as waves broke over them.

For the rest of the weekend Papa did not share a room with Maman. Jean-Sylvain suggested he take over Cécile's now vacant bed but Papa shook his head, no, and stayed on the couch.

They all went to the track and to the beach; they had *moules marinières* and so many *gaufrettes* both Jeanot and Babette began turning them down. Babette explained to Jeanot that his Papa probably had done something he shouldn't have with Cécile, who was a *pute,* which was why Cécile had left in the middle of the night. She added,

"All you men are the same." She didn't expound, and Jeanot took it that his gender, small or large, were all built in the same way. When he said this to Babette, she scoffed, "*Tu es vraiment un bébé!*"

Once back in Paris, Maman spent hours reading books and articles on *les États Unis*. She found a map of Washington and told Jeanot that city had been designed by Pierre l'Enfant, a Frenchman. The photos of the American capital showed a green place with plenty of land and parks, and not much else.

She went to the pharmacy with Jeanot and ordered twelve bottles of Seconal. The woman behind the counter eyed her strangely and told her to return later that afternoon; they didn't have that many tablets on hand and would have to call another pharmacy. Then at the flea market, she bought a dozen back issues of *Life* magazine and a small pair of used pointy boots for Jeanot, which he found difficult to walk in, though he insisted on wearing them home.

Later, mysteriously, as she put Jeanot to bed, she said, "I hear they have cowboys in Washington."

Chapter 18

They were going to America. Jeannot was terrified, elated, disbelieving, and dubious. He ceaselessly questioned Maman and Papa about *where, how*, and *when*. The *why* of it didn't matter. After reading a *Tintin* that explained why cowboys took their guns apart to clean them, he disassembled his best cap pistol and bathed it in olive oil. He wiped each part down with a rag, but when he put it back together there were three small pieces left over and the thing wouldn't fire anymore. Even Papa couldn't fix it, but it was clean and shiny, and he got into trouble because it left a stain in the right-hand pocket of his Louveteau shorts.

When Jeanot mentioned to other kids at school that he was leaving for *les États Unis*, he could tell they thought he was lying. Everyone wanted to go to America but very few ever did, though everyone knew someone who knew someone. Everyone had a distant cousin, or a neighbor, or a far-flung in-law met once over dinner who had gone and written back of miracles, or sent postcards that read simply, *"C'est magnifique, ici!"*

The only person who thought Jeanot was telling the truth was the concierge, Kharkov, who sighed wistfully. He and Jeanot exchanged tidbits about the English language, how *colour* and *vapour* and *savour* had a '*u*' in Great Britain but not in America.

His Maman moved quickly, allowing no time for the arguments of friends and family to change her mind.

She and Papa announced their plans to Grand-père Léopold over lunch with the family in the apartment, and Jeanot thought the old man put forth only the barest of opposition. Grand-père had visited the United States, he told them darkly, mere days after Maman married the Jew and begat the two grand-daughters he barely knew. He worried that Jeanot might forget his roots and become an American, but Maman promised Jeanot would come and visit him every summer. Jeanot nodded. He would visit, though why was unclear. Grand-père had never manifested the least interest in cowboys, Mohawks, Walt Disney films, crêpes made by Mathilde, or the Louveteaux, though the old man had brushed his hand through Jeanot's hair and mumbled something sorrowful after Dédé's funeral.

A worker from the shipping company came to the apartment to measure things for crates, and when Jeanot asked what he was doing, the man smiled and said, "Helping you move to America!" That made it more real than any parental promise.

Jeanot had a hundred questions, a thousand. Were they going to Texas? No, Washington. Papa opened the atlas and pointed to the capital of the United States. Jeanot measured the distance with his thumb and forefinger. It didn't look that far away from Texas, so maybe they could go there on weekends.

Were Françoise and Madeleine coming too? No, but they would visit during the holidays.

Could Babette come? No, but she could visit if her parents allowed it.

Could he wear cowboy boots to school, and would he be taught to shoot a rifle? Would they live on a ranch with buffalos? Would they have a television and could he have one in his own room? He *was* getting his own room, wasn't he? Could Tatie live with them? And Oncle Répaud and Tante Jacqueline? Could the family get a dog? *Two* dogs, a small one to play with and a big one to protect the house from coyotes, mountain lions and rattlesnakes. Could they get a horse, or at least a pony, maybe a few ponies so he could ride with his friends?

Papa took the questions seriously, smiled and nodded and told Jeanot there were a lot of children his age in America but he would have to learn American English to speak to them. American English? English without the *U*s in it? Jeanot wanted the lessons to start immediately so Papa taught him, "Where is the bathroom, please." It came out heavily accented but understandable. They moved on to other essential phrases and in a few days, Jeanot could recite many sentences, as well as his full name, a telephone number of random digits, an American sounding address, his age and date of birth, "God Bless You" in case someone sneezed, and "Am I in the right place?" in case he wasn't. Papa told Jeanot he might have an aptitude for languages and Jeanot nodded. He liked the word *aptitude.*

Maman had no aptitude. She insisted on pronouncing each syllable as if it were part of a misspelled French word. Try as she might, she could not hear the difference between "paper" and "pepper," "better" and "batter," and the various pronunciations of "cheep," "chip," "cheap," and "chick" or "cheek." Worse, she had what Papa called a shockingly guttural Germanic accent when she tried to enunciate. Jeanot chose not to comment.

At school, Jeanot found a young teacher who spoke English fluently, and at recess they discussed the differences between British and American English. The young man had spent six months in the United States and between puffs of Gitanes cigarettes, explained how Brits said *lorry* and *lift* while the Americans preferred *truck* and *elevator.* If Jeanot didn't understand the details, it didn't really matter. He was amassing knowledge that would come in handy when talking to the natives, he was sure.

At home he pored over the back issues of *Tintin* and *Spirou.* Both magazines' centerfolds were often devoted to photos and drawings of historical events in foreign nations. He read about the Great Chicago fire that had been caused by a cow, about influenza, about slavery (an idea he didn't quite understand), about alligators, buffalos (he already knew a lot on buffalos), rattlesnakes (ditto), prairie dogs (who were not dogs) and bears (black, brown, Kodiak, grizzly, polar). One day Papa came home with a massive book entitled *Les Mystères de l'Amérique* which raised more questions than it answered. Why were Indians on reservations? Was cotton gin a liquor, like Armagnac or Poire?

Then Papa was gone for more than three weeks, traveling by ocean liner and train to Washington for a series of work interviews. Thanks to a wartime friend's help, he was hired by the Voice of America as head of the French language desk. In a letter to Maman which she read aloud to Jeanot, Papa explained he would be responsible for airing three-hours of programs six days a week to the francophone world.

Jeanot knew from school that some 200 million people spoke French. They were in Europe, Canada, Africa, Asia, and a few islands whose names he always forgot. His Papa would be talking to all of them.

Papa also wrote in a second letter that he'd been looking at homes in the city and suburbs and taking copious notes. He'd spent a morning peering at used cars. He told them he liked almost everything he saw.

When he returned, Maman and Jeanot met him at Le Havre where the monstrously large transatlantic ships docked, dwarfing the buildings and dockworkers. Jeanot wondered how in the world anything that large could float. When Maman told him the family would cross the ocean aboard such a ship, he began practicing his breast-stroke while lying in bed at night on his stomach. You never knew. Ships sank sometimes. He knew all about the Titanic and the Lusitania.

Maman had decided to tell Françoise and Madeleine about the move while they were all at the Parc Monceau. They always liked walking there and the ice cream vendor was an aged Italian with the best cones in the city. Jeanot ordered a *cornet praline,* and the girls had strawberry and chocolate. Marcel had agreed to let his daughters come by themselves, so it was just Jeanot, Maman and her girls.

Françoise and Madeleine had different reactions to the news of their Maman's move to America. Françoise, the younger, burst into tears. Madeleine shrugged, examined a broken fingernail. "But you don't speak English, Maman." Madeleine had spent a month in London and considered herself a linguist.

Maman led them to a bench, sat them down, one daughter on each side with Jeanot looking on, trying to catch the praline drips before they rolled to the ground.

"I'm sure I can learn," she told Madeleine. "Roland has already taught me a few phrases. The important thing I want both of you to know is that I'm not going to be that far away, and you will come and spend the summer. There are airplanes now that make the trip in less than twenty hours. You leave from Le Bourget and you land in Iceland where you can buy sweaters, and then you fly to the United States."

Madeleine frowned. "We'll have a house," added Maman, "and each of you can have your own room. And we can go to California and see the movie stars!" Françoise was a passionate reader of movie magazines. Madeleine, once an avid fan, had since moved on.

"We're going to go to Texas," Jeanot said. "To see cowboys. And you can come. Papa said he was looking at cars, and American cars are big, bigger even than the DeSoto. We can all go!"

The girls didn't react.

"To Texas," he added limply.

Later that afternoon the girls went home and Maman looked sad. At dinner, she took more pills than usual and went to bed without eating dessert. Jeanot and his father were left to share a slice of Mathilde's beet pie.

Papa told Jeanot he liked America. Papa spoke English fluently, having been raised largely in London. In the United States they spoke his language, sort of. He said his British accent always garnered respect and interest. He had been to America once before when he was much younger, when he traveled as a British Lord's secretary.

Jeanot knew the situation was more complex for his mother. Papa explained that it was a chance to start over. Maman announced she was throwing a going-away party for herself.

Ten days later, friends and employees came bearing bottles of wine, announcing they'd been told the wines in America were syrupy, undrinkable, and caused migraines. Others brought cheese, and a few offered baguettes to bring with them to America, which made Jeanot wonder how smart some of his Maman's friends were.

It wasn't much fun. Madeleine and Françoise were allowed to attend; Jeanot saw Madeleine sneak a dollop of scotch whiskey into her Orangina. Shortly after drinking it down, she became sad and tearful. Françoise rushed to the door every time a new guest appeared, then retreated glumly to the platter of prosciutto canapés. She wasn't allowed to eat ham at her father's home, she explained, as she crammed a half-dozen hors d'oeuvres into her mouth.

Jeanot, for reasons unclear even to himself, insisted on donning his toreador's suit of light, though Papa would not let him wear the sword. In spite of this, the evening was muted. The last time there'd been such a grown-up party, Dédé and he had wreaked havoc with their potato guns. Now Dédé was gone for good. It made Jeanot wonder and miss their fun.

Babette was there with her family and said she thought of Dédé too. She still carried the little square of the dead boy's pillowcase, and when she hugged Jeanot she whispered tragically, "He'll always be in our hearts…" Jeanot wondered whether she'd read that someplace, or heard it on the radio.

Dédé's father made a brief appearance but his mother didn't. She was still too distraught, Monsieur Bourillot explained, to participate in any revelry. The amateur cinematographer with the dirty film came as well, also without his wife, whom Babette said had left him after the naked nazi debacle. He seemed none the worse for it and brought an immense wedge of smelly Roblochon cheese.

Grand-père Léopold stayed long enough to shake a few hands, but Yves remained much longer. Jean-Sylvain came in a canary yellow suit and elegant tan shoes. He hugged Papa several times and kissed him on both cheeks upon arrival and departure, and left dabbing at the tears in his eyes with a mauve handkerchief.

The evening was a parade of everyone Jeanot knew or had met. Oncle Répaud and Tante Jacqueline, Tatie, Stéphane and his divorced mother, the painter with the bad breath, the concierge and his son.

Later in the evening, a very young man showed up and Jeanot saw Françoise run to him and kiss him on the cheek. She introduced him as Vincent. He was pale, tall and slight with aquiline features, the beginnings of a mustache shadowing his upper lip. He nodded and shook Jeanot's hand gravely. After a moment Françoise hurried him away and took him to Maman. Even from a distance, Jeanot could see Françoise was blushing furiously. Later, when there were fewer guests and Vincent was smoking a cigarette by himself, Françoise found Jeanot and whispered, "I'm going to marry him someday..."

Vincent would be a fixture around the apartment in the weeks before the departure. Françoise said her own papa did not approve of him, so at every opportunity, Françoise would sneak away from her father's home and come to the apartment where Vincent would meet her. Vincent told Jeanot that in America there were contests to see who could have the longest cigarette ash, and he, Vincent, a master of the art, would win hands down, since he could maintain a cylinder of ash almost as long as the cigarette itself. Jeanot decided he would start smoking once in the United States.

Vincent had other bits of lore: In America, there were white rats as big as rabbits and carnivorous too. He warned Jeanot against being outside at night. Sometimes wild horses stampeded in the suburbs, trampling children and adults alike. Some cannibalistic Indians had blowguns and liked to shrink children's heads to the size of walnuts.

Jeanot nodded and smiled. Vincent, he knew, was telling ridiculous stories.

There was more. Americans rarely wore socks or underwear. They only bathed once a week. They brushed their teeth with twigs. There were no baguettes, croissants, *pains au chocolat, saucissons*. There was plenty of chewing gum but Jeanot shouldn't use the black one because it would turn him permanently into a Negro. It had happened to one of Vincent's friends, who had been forced to change his name from Emile Laure to Sydney Bechet. Jeanot considered that and the relationship between Negros and banjos. If you turned into a black man, did you automatically know how to play the banjo? Jeanot was intrigued by the idea of turning into a Negro; wondered for a moment if that might not be useful, once in America. After some consideration, he decided that he preferred being himself. America, however, was getting more baffling by the day.

The last two weeks in Paris were a jumble of frenzied activity, tears, frustrations, unwanted visits and miraculous achievements. Maman sold the contents of *Créations St. Paul* at a price that had her humming to herself. She bought Jeanot a new pair of dress shoes that he didn't like, and agreed that a new cap pistol might be a wise idea. Jeanot wrapped the old one that smelled like olive oil and gave it to Karkhov's son.

Items Jeanot had grown up with suddenly vanished. A spectacularly ugly broken floor lamp that Jeanot was vaguely afraid of was picked up by the concierge who claimed he would fix it. The faded cherry red sofa under which Jeanot hid and fell asleep when he was a tiny child (he did it so often Mathilde kept a blanket and pillow there for a year) was carried away by two huge men. A set of lacquered end tables with drawers where Maman kept her extra packs of Pall Malls disappeared while Jeanot was in school, as did a liquor cart and three dark paintings of ships battered by storms at sea. Jeanot had stared at the middle one for hours wondering what it must be like to be a pirate without a raincoat.

Both family friends and complete strangers came by to look at the furnishings. There were tears and loud words when Papa realized Maman had sold his Royal portable typewriter without telling him. Jeanot had spotted it in the back of the hallway closet but neither he nor Maman knew Papa had carried the machine throughout the war, had written dispatches on it that were aired through the clandestine radio station he had run for four years. Papa was furious! She had sold the machine cheaply, too, to someone whose name she didn't know, an old man with a beard and a shabby overcoat. Over dinner, Papa seethed and told her that she'd stolen a part of his past, and for what, a few francs? His blood and sweat were on that machine! Maman apologized and yet sounded unrepentant. If the typewriter was so important, why had it been gathering dust in the back of the closet? She'd get him another typewriter, a brand new one. The offer made Papa even angrier, so he stomped out of the room, slamming the door on his way out.

Jeanot and Maman ate dinner alone, and when he asked, "*Où est Papa?*" she told him he was at work and would be back soon, which Jeanot knew was a fib. His Papa always wore a white shirt and a tie to go to work, and he'd left wearing the threadbare sweater he always put on when assembling the frames for Maman's paintings. Only once before had Jeanot seen his Papa angry, and that was years ago when Maman had spent all the money they'd been saving to repair the DeSoto on a set of brushes which had supposedly belonged to someone called Picasso.

When it was his bedtime and Papa still had not returned, Jeanot began to panic. What started as a dim apprehension in minutes turned to full-fledged terror, and soon he was breathing in shallow gasps, unable to get enough air to fill his lungs. He screamed once and thought he might faint. Mathilde, who was swabbing the corridor as the last chore of the day, sprinkled his face with mop water.

A few minutes later, Papa came home smelling of brandy. Jeanot heard Mathilde whispering and then Papa was in Jeanot's room, standing next to the bed. Jeanot and he talked late into the night, far past Jeanot's bedtime. Papa said he would never leave the family.

"*Jamais. Promis juré*, Jeanot," which Jeanot knew was the highest form of promising that the family had. Papa told Jeanot they both had to be strong for Maman's sake, because going to America would be great fun but hard work, too. Jeanot thought it might be a good time to negotiate a visit to the toy store where they sold tin Indians and cowboys and perhaps purchase three braves and two chiefs, as well as a pair of cap pistols with a leather belt and holsters. Jeanot told his Papa that going to America unprepared would not be wise, and Papa agreed.

Chapter 19

By the second day aboard the *Ile de France*, Jeanot knew everything he needed to know about the liner. It was the largest transoceanic ship in the French Line, he told his Maman, and weighed 44,000 tons! It was 241 meters long and sailed at 23 knots, he explained to Papa, and asked what a knot was. Did they know the ship carried 1800 passengers and were they first class? No? Second, then? Not that either, Papa explained. They were in third class, which was perfectly acceptable.

Jeanot made a deal with Maman allowing him to roam at will as long as he agreed to be in the cabin by six every night. She pinned a note with his name and cabin number to the lapel of his coat and set him free. Jeanot met the ship's captain, the chaplain, two of the nurses and one of the radiomen. He admired one sailor's tattoos so much that the young man used ballpoint pens with green, red and blue ink to create a heart-and-flower motif with "Maman" in the middle of Jeanot's left arm.

"There aren't many children to play with," he told his parents one night over dinner, "but that's fine. This is an amazing ship!" He declaimed more numbers—fuel used, kilometers traveled in a day. "They use 3,000 carrots for the salads! And 800 kilos of flour every single day!"

He wandered the decks alone in full cowboy uniform, the cap-pistol holster riding low across his butt, swaggering a bit as he walked.

He found a secret passageway that allowed him to wander into the first- and second-class decks. An American man fed him a nip of bourbon whiskey and he swallowed it without a tremor which, Jeanot could tell, impressed the man. An American lady gave him a dollar bill. Jeanot kept it hidden in his shoe. Maman and Papa would tell him to return it if they found it.

A bored American teenager returning home from visiting a divorced parent in France taught him some new words, and Papa told him to never, *ever*, say them out loud. In fact, Papa whispered, don't even think them. There were very strict laws in America about small boys using bad language, and in some cases children were sent back to France without their parents for uttering such dread expressions.

A man from Maine gave Jeanot a pack of Blackjack gum, but Jeanot didn't dare chew it, remembering the admonition about becoming a Negro man. He traded it for a pack of commonplace Wrigley's at the ship's store and did not turn into anything. After that, he was seldom seen without a wad of gum working his jaw. Someone else offered a French sailor's hat with a red pom-pom in its center and Jeanot wore it with pride, abandoning the cowboy hat.

He ate with Maman and Papa in the morning. He learned to say, "more bacon, please" which was always rewarded with more food. He developed a taste for pancakes and cornbread, but said to Papa the runny scrambled eggs were *dégoutant*. His Maman agreed. He'd stuff a roll or two in his pockets for a midmorning snack. For lunch he ate roast beef sandwiches and ice cream, often by himself in a deck chair. He decided he might become a sailor if he couldn't be a cowboy, but changed his mind when the ship was hit by a storm and he became violently ill.

He discovered a movie theatre on board that showed Westerns and offered a strange snack called popcorn in big paper bags. This was salty, buttery, free and guaranteed to ruin your appetite, but there was no one there to say "no." In the ship's library he found a cache of old *Look* magazines. He pored through them with increasing concern—there were no cowboys or Indians anywhere in the pages. This oversight worried him. How could it be that in the land of Lucky Luke, Gene Autry, and Roy Rogers, his heroes were not even mentioned?

Papa explained that there weren't that many cowboys in America anymore, and then changed his story. "They're too busy riding the range to stop and pose for photographers. Cowboying is a lot of work, what with the steers, the buffalos, the Indians, the rattlesnakes and the gunfights."

That made sense, coupled with the fact that most horsemen were on the other side of the country. Jeanot recited the names of the cowboy states he'd memorized; Texas and Oklahoma and New Mexico and the Dakotas, North and South. Papa added in a whisper, "It might have something to do with the beans the cowboys eat at every meal. They probably didn't want to be around each other after the beans." Papa made a farting sound and Jeanot laughed. All of it made sense. It was extraordinary the things his Papa knew, how he could throw light on mysteries, laugh and reassure, all at the same time.

The lights of New York appeared on the ninth day; a faint glow in the predawn night. Papa woke up Maman and Jeanot and trundled them up to the tourist deck where they joined hundreds of passengers getting their first glimpse of America. Papa hoisted Jeanot, still in his pajamas, onto his shoulders. Jeanot held onto Papa's head and Maman admonished them both for standing too close to the guardrail. Jeanot made it a point to lean over the edge as far as he could to see deep water sharp as cut glass.

There wasn't much on the horizon yet though soon the running lights of other great ships became visible. Papa found out from a passing steward that the *Ile de France* would not dock until mid-afternoon as several other liners were scheduled before her.

As the ship edged closer to the port, Papa began pointing out sights. "That's the Statue of Liberty, Jeanot. The French people gave it to the Americans. There's a smaller one in Paris."

Jeanot looked. It was a big statue with a spiky funny hat. "Why?"

"Why what?"

"Why didn't we keep the big one? It's a nice statue."

Papa didn't know, shrugged and skipped to a skyscraper. "That's the Empire State Building. It's the tallest building in the world."

"Taller than the Eiffel Tower?"

Papa wasn't sure. Jeanot answered his own question. "Probably not. The Eiffel Tower is really tall, but that," he admitted, "looks more useful. Do people live in there?"

"No. It's all offices."

Jeanot watched as most of the *Ile de France's* passengers opted to have lunch on deck, many standing as they looked at the skyline. They were nearing the best of all worlds. France may have had its charms, but America was the future. Even Jeanot knew that.

Two tugs brought the *Ile de France* in, and Jeanot watched the process with fascination. He could see into the wheelhouses where stocky bearded men shouted orders and threw levers into position as they controlled the rudder with one hand turning the spoked wheel. It was slow work, but in time they had the ship pointed in the right direction and the giant hawsers, thicker than a strong man's arm, grew tight as bow strings. The *Ile de France* moved with exquisite slowness, getting closer and closer to the American shore. Jeanot clambered up on his father's shoulders again, one hand holding his French sailor hat in place. The wind, an *American* wind, picked up and fluttered the scarves of the women and the pant legs of the men. Jeanot leaned forward. There wouldn't be any cowboys here, but that was OK; it was still *L'Amérique*, a land of possibilities and endless horseback dreams. He pointed. *"Papa! Maman! Regardez! Regardez! Des Américains!"*

Chapter 20

In a few hours, they'd been told, they would begin to disembark from the Ile de France. Jeanot was holding his Papa's right hand with his left one, as his own right hand rested lightly on the butt of his cap pistol. You never knew.

"Do you think so? Really?" Maman asked.

Papa nodded. "Absolutely. It's an amazing place. You're both going to love it! It's so big, not crowded and grey like Paris. We'll have a house, not a cramped apartment. And it's so clean in America; in Washington, the buildings are white and there are trees everywhere, not just in the parks. You'll get there, you'll never want to leave."

Jeanot could see Maman was unconvinced.

"Easy for you, maybe. You speak English. You're a *man*. It's always easier for men."

Papa squeezed her hand. "How are you feeling, *chérie*?" He pronounced the words in English slowly, as if to a backward child. For weeks now, he had made it a point to speak English to Jeanot and Maman, asking simple, everyday questions in the new language.

Maman hated learning another tongue, Jeanot could tell, but she did her best to respond.

"I am well, thank you. This is a very nice boat. Ship? Boat?" She pronounced well "ouelle" and Papa looked as though he was trying not to smile.

"Either is correct," he said. "Or, you can say, both are correct."

Maman nodded. Jeanot too thought it was complicated. Both, either. Ship, boat. Why was English such a silly language? Why couldn't there be one simple way of saying things that needed to be said? And then he remembered that in French there was *bateau* and *navire*, and *chaque* and *tous*…

"I am glad you are feeling better," Papa enunciated.

Maman nodded, though it was obvious she *wasn't* feeling better, not in the least. Jeanot had been with her to the pharmacist shortly before leaving Paris and she'd bought a lot of pills. She'd tried to get even more but the pharmacist had refused. "*Vraiment, Madame,* this is enough for a year!"

"Hardly," Maman said, and then turned to Jeanot and added, "Who knows if they have these in America?"

He'd noticed that lately she swallowed two doses of each drug every morning, which was twice the amount she routinely took in Paris. Jeanot wondered if Papa had noticed.

They had been standing on the deck for half-an-hour. "I am a little…" Maman struggled for the word, said it in French, "*étourdie.*"

"Dizzy," Papa said.

"Deezzee," Maman repeated.

"Dizzy," said Jeanot with a somewhat better accent, then said, in English, "I will be back." He disappeared behind a lifeboat and returned seconds later wearing a bright orange life vest. "One of the stewards gave it to me. He said I could keep it!"

Maman shook her head. "Really…"

Jeanot thought it important to make a point. "The steward said there were deep and dangerous waters in America, and I should wear it at all times. Those were his words, 'at all times.'"

Jeanot adjusted the vest, squared his shoulders and fixed his French sailor hat. "Do you want me to see if I can find you one?" When neither parent responded, he ran off between the deck chairs, climbed a vertical ladder to an upper deck and vanished again. Six minutes later he was back, trundling two more life vests. "You should put these on."

Neither Maman nor Papa did so, so he asked, *"Vous êtes sure?"* When Papa nodded, Jeanot returned the vests to where he'd found them.

A minute later, Papa squatted down so he could look into Jeanot's eyes.

"You know, there won't be any cowboys when we get off the boat. You're not going to be disappointed, will you?"

Jeanot thought he wouldn't be.

Papa continued, "They're farther away, on the other side of the country. That's where the buffaloes and the Indians and the geysers are, too."

Jeanot knew that. *Everybody* knew that. He'd seen pictures of New York, with the giant buildings and the teeming streets and there hadn't been a stallion in sight. "Cowboys are in Texas, and in Wyoming," he said.

"Also in Nevada, the Dakotas and Maryland," Papa added.

"Not Maryland." Jeanot was no fool. He knew a *lot* more about the proud men on horseback than Papa did. "Definitely *not* Maryland."

Chapter 21

Jeanot concentrated on the ball. It was small and very hard, harder than any French ball he'd ever handled, with red stitches that reminded him of a cut he'd once gotten on his arm when he fell off a swing at the Parc Monceau.

Ten yards away, the American boy, Tommy King, scratched at the ground with the toe of his rubber-soled Keds, spit, looked to the left and right, and launched into a complicated dance involving a raised leg and a vertical arm. Then quick as lightning, he flung the ball with amazing speed towards Jeanot, who raised the big round glove to his chest and braced for the catch. The ball was thrown high and struck Jeanot square in the forehead. He uttered a small sigh and dropped like a beast at the slaughterhouse.

He heard Tommy King say, "Shit," and saw him run off into the woods behind the family's backyard. Then he closed his eyes and concentrated on the little starbursts exploding in his head.   Footsteps rushed to where he was lying in the grass and Maman moaned, *"Mon Dieu!"* Madame King, the American lady in whose house they were staying said, "It will be all right," which he understood to mean he was not dead or seriously injured. Still, he could feel a massive headache forming behind his eyes and he wondered if perhaps his head had cracked open and was oozing brains. There was a trickle of something thick and wet on his forehead.

He opened his eyes. Tommy King had returned and was standing above him with an expression of serious worry that, in any language, was also a plea. "Don't tell!"

Soon they were all in the kitchen, Jeanot in a chair, eyes open but dazed. There was a large lump on his forehead to which Maman was holding a dishtowel full of crushed ice cubes. He saw Madame King grab her boy by a shoulder and drag him to his room. She was not happy and Tommy was frightened.

In the summer of 1959, Jeanot thought America was not living up to some of his expectations. Tommy King was a mean kid just like the *grands garçons*, the bullies at Jeanot's school in Paris. Tommy's sister, Betsy, had a round moon face dusted with acne. She avoided both her brother and Jeanot. Tommy often spied on her as she was dressing— Jeanot had followed him once and seen her in her bra and underwear, which was completely uninteresting since in Paris, in his Maman's *atelier*, he'd gotten used to half-naked models.

Then there was the poison ivy. Who had ever heard of such a thing, plants that attacked people? In the south of France, Jeanot had trod through patches of fiery nettles, but their sting vanished as soon as his Maman rubbed a solution of vinegar, chopped fresh parsley and water on his legs. There was no such cure for the treacherous shiny leaves and now Jeanot's face and arms were dappled with pinkish calamine lotion.

On the positive side, the ice cream was better, thicker and more flavorful, and the amount of food Madame King served was beyond belief. Breakfast was eggs, thick *crêpes*, bacon, sausage and orange juice, *orange juice,* a treat served perhaps once a year in France! Lunch was a meaty sandwich on cake-like white bread. Dinner was often steak or chicken cooked outdoors on a grill called a barbecue by Monsieur King, who had a perpetual booming laugh and was so big and large he scared Jeanot a little.

Papa explained to all that the term came from the French *barbe au cul,* which meant from beard to butt. No one believed him; Monsieur King said it was once again the French taking credit for a good invention like the telephone and the airplane. Jeanot thought he might argue if he had more English words, since he had read in both *Tintin* and *Spirou* that the French had indeed invented both the telephone and the airplane.

Monsieur King loved cooking on the barbecue. He used a spatula almost as big as a shovel to turn whatever he was making and a little brush to put on his special sauce, a sort of reddish, slightly sweet and spicy concoction Jeanot wasn't sure he liked.

Still, for all the large meals and treats, Jeanot found America odd and forbidding. The woods behind the King's home were dark and endless. Regardless of Madame King's assurance that it was just a 100-yard-wide strip of forest between two housing developments, Jeanot refused to enter them. There might be animals in there he wouldn't know how to handle despite his familiarity with buffaloes and coyotes, garnered from his collection of *Lucky Luke* comics. Also, the houses all looked the same, with small green front yards and painted mailboxes.

Just the day before Jeanot was walking up and down the sidewalk concentrating on manhole covers and smaller, square metal plates set into the street when an urge to pee took him to the wrong front door and into the bathroom of a neighboring house. The woman there, short, stocky and very blonde, had given him milk and cookies, smiled, and led him by the hand back to the correct home. She and Madame King had had a good laugh at his expense while Tommy made a face that implied Jeanot was both an unwanted foreigner and very stupid.

It had been four weeks since their departure from Le Havre in France aboard the Ile de France, and almost three weeks since their arrival in New York. Dorothy and Gene King, wartime American friends of Papa, had welcomed the family into their home in the Maryland suburbs of the American capital.

From New York, Jeanot and Maman took the train to Washington, a five-hour journey through several states, Jeanot was told, though he saw little difference between one state and another. Papa and Monsieur King drove Monsieur King's car, laden with luggage, and arrived at about the same time.

Jeanot, familiar with trains, noted that the American wagons smelled better than the French ones, or perhaps they simply smelled different, less of tobacco, onions and garlic. He recognized the familiar stink of body odor. That hadn't changed from France to America.

The train had rolled through a uniform countryside. Maman told Jeanot she thought the vast flat buildings they passed were where things were made, though she had no idea what those things might be. Tires? Gasoline? Cars perhaps? She brightened when she recognized a large sign that read *Johnson & Johnson* and Jeanot knew this pleased her. Maman bought Johnson & Johnson products when she could at the American PX in Paris. He used that company's little sticks with balls of cotton on the ends to clean his ears.

There were small and medium-sized towns too, with acres of shingle roofs, vast green spaces Jeanot thought might be parks, and many churches. He wondered about that as well. There were churches in Paris, but not on every street corner like here, and the ones in Paris were tired and uniformly grey. These were bright white, clean, with colorful stained glass and sharply defined steeples.

Maman said, *"C'est évident! Les Américains sont trés religieux."*

Jeanot was not sure if it was that obvious, but certainly it would seem people went to church all the time here, not just on Sundays like most French people.

Maman smiled, "Maybe we could join a church! Meet new people, make friends!"

Jeanot considered the idea. He could see the family in its Sunday best standing on the steps of a house of worship and knew he'd have to wear the leather shoes that hurt his feet. He didn't welcome the idea but nodded. Maman needed to be cheered up, not argued with. Maybe here, where things were different, it might be good for his Maman to go to church. She almost never did in Paris, and Babette had said that people who went were always happier because they knew they'd be going to heaven. Maybe, Jeanot thought, Maman isn't sure if she's going there or not, and attending church might make her feel better, safer.

Chapter 22

Maman was having a difficult time of it. She had taken to watching *I Love Lucy*, *What's My Line* and *Search for Tomorrow* and Jeanot knew from the look on her face that she didn't always understand what was playing on the small screen.

She had already told both Jeanot and Papa that when they got their own house, she would draw the line at eating and watching television at the same time. She had once read in *Paris-Match* that Americans commonly did this, which explained their difficulties with good literature, and the country's lack of appreciation for the finer arts. Plus, she'd added, the French health authorities interviewed for the article believed viewing while eating was bad for digestion and risky to overall wellbeing.

Jeanot, personally, found something fascinating about those little meals designed to be eaten in front of the TV; the neat shiny aluminum trays divided into three sections, each containing an immaculate portion of perfectly colored food. Madame King had served such TV dinners to the children the night before, when there'd been no time to cook. The kids had loved them. Jeanot, ever a fussy eater, thought the food was pretty tasteless and in need of salt, but he had been captivated by the trays. After eating, he had rinsed his and used it to separate some of the marbles in his collection; cat's eyes from agates from clay. Tommy and Betsy had pointedly thrown theirs away in the kitchen trash cans, whispered and giggled. Jeanot was sure he was the subject of their laughter.

Without really knowing how he knew, Jeanot sensed that though Maman would not admit it, America overwhelmed her. The truth was, it overwhelmed him too, sometimes. The people were so large, they took up so much space; they had big, forceful walks and their shoulders rolled even when they were standing still. They had huge hands and skulls and foreheads and large mouths crowded with white teeth. It came to him that five Parisians grown-ups could stand in the space one American occupied and there would still be room for a kid or two. Even when they talked, it was as if they filled the air with word balloons, like in his *Mickey* magazine. Maman tried to explain to him that if she were forced to name everything she saw-in French and in English—then she would drown. That's how she felt, as if American waters were circling her neck and rising fast, coming at her both from above and below.

Drowned. The word terrified Jeanot. Drowned, like Dédé had drowned? That was a horrifying thought that left his stomach angry.

Jeanot, too, found the newness of everything disconcerting. In the King household, every piece of furniture, every rug, painting, dish and glass, every knife and fork and coffee mug, all of it was new. Even the floors looked like they had been installed days before and had never been walked on.

In the apartment in Paris, everything had been *old*. The table linens came from his grandfather, as did the cracked and weathered furniture. Hundreds of people had sat on the couches and chairs, and eaten off the dining room table. His Papa had explained that there was value in old things, and Jeanot had sort of understood, though actually, it hadn't mattered. He hadn't thought about the origins or ages of what was around him until he'd arrived in America. Here, it appeared, nothing passed from one generation to another. There were no scratched furniture or family photographs of stern grandparents and cowed children to remind the family that others had come before them. Not a single thing, in Madame King's house, had ever belonged to someone else. This would be unheard of in France, and it made Jeanot wonder if Americans even had grandparents! Was it possible that they didn't?

He had mentioned it in passing to Papa, who had nodded. "It's a brand new country, Jeanot. They don't want things that have been handled by others. They're odd that way. That's why they wash their hands all the time, so they don't leave marks on all their new things. If something gets dirty, then they can't claim it's new anymore."

Jeanot had overheard Madame King boast that her home was only six years old and loaded with all the latest amenities. A monstrously large white metal box, Jeanot discovered, was a refrigerator that hummed in the kitchen. A smaller spare icebox in the basement was for beer and children's drinks. There was an electric oven, a machine that made coffee, fans over the stove and in the bathrooms to get rid of smells. The other houses on the street were similar, with identical bay windows, screen doors, driveways and yards. Here might be a tree whose flowers were ever-so-slightly different from the tree next door, or a sidewalk that wound to the left instead of to the right, but the sameness was such that Jeanot had accidentally walked into a stranger's home, leading to the wrong bathroom incident.

Jeanot had never realized France was an *old* country. When the family went on vacation near the Mediterranean, the tiny house they rented in Cannes dated from the 1300's and no one found it odd that the floors were still dirt, packed so tight by centuries and generations that no dust escaped. America, on the other hand, was almost virgin land. What was there before, Jeanot wondered; teepees and the naked red Indians he so admired?

He had also noticed there were no smells in American kitchens or stores; the aroma of daily life had been scrubbed away or had never existed. He missed the overpowering presence of the *boulangerie* fifty meters from the apartment's doors, and the peppery world of Monsieur Lippman, the dour épicier.

Their third day in the new country, Jeanot and Maman had gone with Madame King to an enormous food store where people pushed huge metal carts—*carts with wheels*—down endless aisles of canned tomatoes and peas and tuna fish. There too, the air had been scrubbed clean. In the store's bakery, the goods were all packaged in clear plastic bags or wrapped in colored paper so you couldn't tell if the bread was really fresh or not, and the only cheese was a yellow block of something that Maman said looked like the wax Mathilde had used on the floor of the Paris apartment.

Madame King had noticed their discomfort. "It takes some getting used to, all the newness, and how big it all is in America. Every time I come back here from visiting France, I have a week or so where I miss it, even the bad things like the entire country stinking of old tobacco."

Jeanot watched Maman's eyebrows arch. Madame King laughed, "It's true, Marité. Maybe you don't notice it because you smoke, but Paris is like a giant ashtray, a *mégot géant!* Also," she added, "I really don't like that dogs poop everywhere in Paris..."

Jeanot was willing to concede that point. Walking through Paris was an exercise in avoiding the *crottes de chien,* a truth that worked very much against Jeanot being allowed a four-legged companion. Whenever he pleaded for the family to get a dog, Maman said, "*Ils sont sales.* Dirty, filthy animals and their owners are no better." She might, she told him, entertain the idea of getting a cat once they had a home of their own, but cats didn't interest Jeanot. You couldn't train a cat, he said, or take it for a walk, or teach it to fetch things. Dogs might be dirty, Jeanot told his mother, but cats were just plain dumb.

Papa focused on the recently purchased car and tried to teach Jeanot automotive basics. The car was an odd maroon color with a lot of chrome, and it ran so smoothly that when waiting for a green light, you had to strain to hear the engine.

Days before leaving Paris, Papa had sold the old DeSoto to an Algerian entrepreneur who had tousled Jeanot's hair and told them he would paint the car glossy white, chrome and all, and rent it out for weddings. Papa pocketed a thick wad of bills, and later Jeanot suspected him of not being entirely forthcoming with Maman. He listened to Papa explaining the details of the sale, telling her he'd had to bargain hard with the Algerian. Everyone knew, said Papa, Algerians were hagglers, almost thieves, really. They wore you down until you just wanted them to take whatever it was and leave. He had been lucky, he said, to get what he did for the car. Papa gave Maman a couple of bills and Jeanot kept quiet. Something important had just happened between Maman and Papa that required his silence.

The new car was a 1948 Buick Roadmaster with an automatic transmission; a *Dynaflow* transmission, Papa said. Monsieur King said Buicks were excellent cars. Jeanot thought this one was slick and shiny and so rounded and curvy it looked like it was speeding along while standing still. There was one small tear on the passenger side seat, and Papa sewed it up with heavy matching thread so the repair was almost invisible. The interior had a push-button radio, two-speed windshield wipers, and a roof antenna manipulated by an inside knob. Jeanot became quite the expert at pulling in radio signals by twisting the knob this way and that. At both the front and rear were tank-like chromed bumpers featuring pointed cones that Maman said looked like large armored breasts. The car started when Papa inserted and turned the key and then floored the accelerator; none of that business like with the decrepit DeSoto, of having to cover the engine with a blanket during the winter and light a newspaper fire around the car-buretor to make it turn over.

Jeanot and Maman both liked the Roadmaster. Jeanot thought the Roadmaster's back seat was even more comfortable than his bed, and when the family went for a drive, he often fell asleep in the back, lulled by the car's gentle vibrations and the uniformity of the unfold-ing vista.

After two weeks in America, Jeanot and his parents drove to Gettysburg, Pennsylvania, a two-hour trip, and Jeanot learned a lot of people had died there about one hundred years ago. Papa bought him a Union soldier's cap and a couple of bullets fired by an unknown rifleman at an unknown enemy.

Maman said she felt this was in bad taste; Jeanot's head shouldn't be filled with visions of violence. To him, though, there was something mystical about the spent ammunition, about the horrible and fascinating fact that someone, somewhere had actually used these things with intent to kill.

The owner of the tourist shop spoke halting French. He told them he'd been in D-Day with the 5th Field Artillery Battalion, 1st Infantry, and when the war was over he'd stayed in France and traveled around the country for eighteen months. He assured Maman that the bullets had been dug out of embankments. There were thousands, no, tens of thousands buried in the soil of the fields and woods surrounding the village, so these two were bloodless, had neither killed nor wounded.

Maman was not persuaded and dragged "her two men" to the milliner next door, a plump woman who just happened to be the wife of the artifact seller. The woman, too, spoke basic French and Maman was delighted. She bought two church hats with discreet feathers and veils, and a jaunty green cap that set off her eyes. Papa said it looked like a beret, which throughout her years in France Maman had criticized as provincial and worn only by bumpkins, so she disagreed. They didn't make berets in America, and therefore the green cap could not be one.

Within a month Jeanot, Papa and Maman moved into a yellow three-bedroom clapboard house on High Street, a half-mile from the District line on the Maryland side.

Maman wasn't sure the purchase was a wise one. She told Papa within Jeanot's hearing that a few years before, an aged woman had lived in the house and collapsed dead in the backyard; it seemed like an ill omen, and, she said, "Don't you think this might be a bad thing for Jeanot? To play in a yard where someone died?"

When Jeanot heard about the old woman's demise, he found it creepy but intriguing. One afternoon he lay on his back in the yard on the very spot where he thought the dead lady had fallen and tried to communicate with her, but she didn't respond. Obviously, she didn't speak French.

There was a single large black walnut tree in the half-acre back-yard, and Maman had plans for a vegetable garden which was never dug out, though Papa would become expert at growing peppery white radish and Big Boy tomatoes from Burpee seeds. At Maman's request, Papa planted a flower bed in front of the house and Jeanot insisted on burying a sardine next to each plant, since he had learned from an article in *Tintin* that when Indians grew corn, they used dead fish as fertilizer.

Within days the bed was ravaged by feasting raccoons, one of which hissed menacingly at Maman in broad daylight when she tried to chase it away with a broom.

Maman demanded a car of her own. Jeanot and his Papa went in search of one, and Jeanot thought a 1947 Ford two-door coupe would fit Maman well. The car belched clouds of white smoke when started, then settled down to a purring idle. It was dark cherry red and had rust spots but Maman didn't seem to mind. It had been almost cheap—183 dollars—and she told Jeanot she felt like the Queen of England when she drove it, though at first she had problems with the car's size. It was too large and hard to park. The power steering led her to misgauge where the curb was, and she blew out two rear tires in a week.

The Ford's last owner, a doctor, had installed seat belts and explained their use to Papa, but neither Papa nor Maman ever buck-led up. Soon Maman complained the seatbelts mussed her dresses, so Papa and Jeanot took them out.

Jeanot thought the back seat was adequate, but not as spacey as that of the Roadmaster.

They were the first two-car family on High Street and the pur-chase of the Ford invited sidelong glances from their neighbors. Papa took Jeanot along and they visited the people in the front, at the back, and around the sides of their house. Jeanot could tell that everyone was impressed with Papa's British accent.

A few weeks later, Papa invited the neighbors to a backyard pic-nic. He bought beer, French wine and soft drinks and Maman made a pâté no one except Jeanot and Papa ate. Jeanot only ate it because he felt he had to. Nor did the neighbors appreciate the spotted *mortadelle* Maman had paid a fortune for at the French butcher, or the baguettes bought at the European bakery in Bethesda.

"*Ce sont des cons,*" she told Jeanot, who did not really agree. He hadn't thought much of the pâté either and much preferred Wonderbread to the crusty baguettes that were hard to chew.

"You are becoming a little *Amerloque,*" she told him, smiling only slightly. "You like hamburgers and those mashed potatoes that come in a box more than my *pâté de campagne* and *purée.*"

"I like hamburgers too," Papa said, and then stopped talking when he saw the look on his wife's face.

"You and your son, you're both *nigauds,*" she said.

"Dummies," Papa translated the word for her benefit. "Or chumps, but that is old-fashioned," he added.

The furniture shipment from France arrived four weeks after they moved in, on a very large truck driven by a tanned, muscled man and his assistant. Jeanot watched them unload everything with remarkable efficiency, and they followed Maman's directions on what should go where and how. Jeanot was waiting for one particular medium-sized box.

He had wrapped each individual lead cowboy, buffalo, coyote, papoose-bearing squaw, Union soldier, brave, chief, and foldable tee-pee with matchstick poles, horse, longhorn steer, and other livestock in pages of *France-Soir* and *Le Figaro*. He had swaddled them carefully on a bed of discarded fabric from Maman's *atelier*. His Méchano erector set—212 separate pieces, three electric motors, 12 wheels with real rubber tires, and an assortment of nuts, bolts, washers and springs— was positioned on top of the Wild West collection as added padding. His Maman had covered the box with brown paper, had sealed it with tape moistened with a wet sponge, and had written his name on each side with heavy grease-pencil strokes. Most of his other playthings were either discarded on the promise of new and better American toys or thrown haphazardly into a faded brown suitcase. Bobo, a rocking horse too rickety and large to transport, had been donated to the Colonial Fund for African Children in Need of Toys. It pleased Jeanot to think that somewhere in a village of thatched huts and bare-breasted women, a dark child his age was astride a wondrous horse that, faraway, had been the source of many cowboy dreams.

One of the movers carried the box in, placed it in front of Jeanot, smiled and said, "I bet that's yours," in a voice so deep Jeanot could only stare at him.

The box was slightly scuffed and pushed in at one corner. Jeanot took it to his room and laid it on the bed. He slit the tape with the pocket knife from his Oncle Répaud, removed and unwrapped the collection item by item. He asked Maman for a folding card table and began arranging the soldiers, cowboys, Indians and animals just as he had in Paris.

Then it struck him that he did not need to build a diorama of the American West. He was *in* America, and even if Texas and Oklahoma and Wyoming were far from his house in Maryland, why recreate a model of where you already lived?

It was kind of silly; it made him feel childish. There were plenty of other activities available to him in the new land, so he aligned the small figures on his window ledges. In time some fell and broke, others' colors faded, while others still vanished as old toys do. Some he gave away, and five he traded for a Daisy bb gun that didn't shoot. When Jeanot wasn't looking, a neighboring boy, Jeff Thomas took two—an Indian chief and a sleeping cowboy—and stuffed them in his pocket. At least, that was what Jeanot suspected. The thief never confessed, but when the toys disappeared, Jeanot just *knew.*

Chapter 23

It was Jeff Thomas who taught Jeanot how to say "Fuck."

Jeff was a small kid who lived the next street over, and they both wore glasses though neither ever mentioned it. Jeff's specs were always dirty and he never tried to wipe them clean, whereas Jeanot had been taught from the very start that *his* glasses were important, expensive, and irreplaceable. He was never without the small blue cleaning cloth given to him by the optometrist in Paris and he used it several times a day.

Jeff told Jeanot his mother was divorced. The two lived in a ramshackle house with a weedy garden, and when it rained, Jeff said, water poured from the ceiling onto the floor of his room. Jeff also said there were uncles who came and stayed at their house for days or weeks but rarely longer. One had bought him a bike; a racy model with thin wheels and curved handlebars. Jeff had only ridden it once before falling, seriously scraping a knee and wrecking the little pyramid of cogs on the rear wheel. He showed it to Jeanot, who couldn't understand why the bike was in Jeff's backyard with a poison ivy vine growing between its spokes. The black tape on the handlebars was melting from the summer heat and the skinny tires were flat.

Jeanot learned that sometimes Jeff was not allowed to enter his own home. If his mom put a red scarf on the handle of the house's screen door, Jeff would wander the streets until four o'clock in the afternoon or later. Jeanot was not too clear on the why of this, and thought it sort of unfair that he, Jeanot, had to check in with his family every couple of hour or so. That Jeff was allowed such freedom was hard to fathom; the boys were roughly the same age, and Jeff did not seem to appreciate his incredible good fortune. Instead, he kicked at rocks and was irascible, short-tempèred and unfriendly, saying things like, "Fuck Uncle Joe!" or "Fuck Uncle Harry," or "Fuck Mom!"

Jeanot also thought Jeff was lucky to have a lot of uncles. Jeanot had been told he had two on his Papa's side but they were in England, and he hadn't met them. His Oncle Répaud had given him a pocket knife, but the rest of them, including his Maman's brother, Yves, had never given him much of anything, much less a bicycle.

Jeff taught Jeanot the word "fuck" because both liked the way it sounded. Jeanot spent the better part of a morning first learning the correct pronunciation—not *fock,* but *fuck,* like truck—then repeating it to himself a thousand times. He didn't know of a word like that in French. "*Merde*" was soft and squishy and lacked character, while "fuck" had impact, soft at first like a musical note, do re mi *fa,* and then POW, the k like a stone hitting glass. A useful expression, it might, he thought, become a practical part of his vocabulary. He came home humming, "fuck fuck fuck fuck, fuck fuck fuck fuck," to the tune of *Frère Jacques* but then Papa grabbed him by the shoulder, dragged him to the back of the yard, and said there would be serious consequences if Jeanot ever uttered the word again. The look in Papa's eyes was such that Jeanot decided this was indeed an even more powerful term than he'd first considered. He filed the knowledge away.

Jeff Thomas said his real father was Superman, which didn't impress Jeanot much until Jeff showed him a DC Comic with the Man of Steel on the cover. Jeanot was willing to admit that Superman was indeed inspiring, but it seemed the likelihood of a superhero fathering Jeff was slim. Jeff was a sissy who cried over a rosebush scratch, and in any case, if Superman had X-ray vision, then why did Jeff have to wear glasses as thick as Jeanot's? Jeanot was always being told that he was the image of his own father, while Jeff, red-headed, freckled, frail and occasionally smelling not very fresh, looked nothing like either the caped hero or Clark Kent.

Still, Jeanot only smiled politely when Jeff talked of Superman. There was no reason to get into an argument with his only American friend, and anyway, he lacked the right words. In French, he might have been able to make his points succinctly, but in English he could only shrug his shoulders. Let Jeff have Superman as a father; who knew what might or might not be real in this new country? Parents were strange beings too; powerful, magical at times. Jeanot's Papa had recounted a story of swallowing a needle as a child. Twenty years later, he felt a sensation in his middle finger and, with his teeth, pulled the needle out of his fingertip! The tale had horrified Jeanot who for days afterwards refused to eat anything more solid than boiled carrots.

Jeanot could tell instantly that neither Maman nor Papa liked Jeff Thomas. Maman believed physiognomy revealed the inner self, and she thought Jeff looked like a ferret. *"Il a un petit nez pointu,"* she told Jeanot, and the boy had to agree. Jeff's nose *was* unusually pointy and occasionally twitched, like a sniffing rabbit. Papa noted that Jeff seemed to take everything in the first time he came to the house, paying particular attention to the new RCA television set that dominated the living room. Jeff looked at the silverware when the boys were served lunch; he asked if Maman's pearls were real. Papa said this was an unusual, if not a disturbing question coming from a child.

For both Jeanot and his Maman, English came hard at first, but it became easier after a few months. Maman went to the Americanization school where, she related over dinner, she was taught how to shop, pay bills, and avoid making hand gestures that Americans might consider rude. She learned there was no bargaining at the Giant Food store, and that she should never ever go into a bar alone, which, though she missed the cafés and their outdoor seating, she hadn't considered doing.

She gardened, enlisting Jeanot's aid to dig, weed and mow. Despite their best efforts, Maman had a brown thumb and so she gave up on real stalks and petals and filled the house with silk flowers from E.

J. Korvette's, a store she considered heaven-sent. She often dragged Jeanot there and he got lost once, somehow separated from her in the ladies' undergarment section.

It caused a stir, Maman in tears and babbling in a frightful mix of French and English no one understood. Announcements echoed over the store's loudspeakers as security guards scoured the restrooms and supply closets. A kindly large woman shopping for a girdle in the plus-size aisle found him fast asleep sucking his thumb, and for the first time dreaming in English.

Jeff Thomas stole $10 from Papa's wallet when he found it unattended on the kitchen counter next to the family car's ignition and trunk keys. Jeanot watched him steal the money and couldn't figure out what to say or do; it was such a strange, outlandish thing that he was left speechless. He went to the bathroom to pee and while he was there Jeff stole the rest of the bills in the wallet, then ran away.

The theft was quickly discovered. Both Maman and Papa questioned Jeanot, who denied any knowledge of the crime. For years after the thievery, Jeanot would wonder at the depth of his resistance. It made no sense, defending and protecting Jeff Thomas, a thief who'd betrayed him and put him in an impossible situation. Yet he'd done just that, lying to his parents for no good reason other than the fear of harming the sole friend he had in America. Even that wasn't right, because Jeff was not a friend at all, just a foul-tempered whiny kid with a bunch of uncles and a make-believe Superman father; a kid who never cleaned his glasses, who stole and lied and let a perfectly good bicycle go to rust.

Papa called the police. He told Maman to leave the speaking to him. They must not, he said, confuse issues; police officers were the same the world over, simple men who wanted simple explanations. He insisted Jeanot be present and told him to be quiet unless directly spoken to.

Two detectives came in a plain car, an old tan Chrysler with soiled whitewall tires. They wore rumpled suits and rumpled expressions; they each accepted a glass of ice water and pulled out ruled steno notebooks and ballpoint pens. Neither of them looked at Jeanot, which terrified him. They could read his mind, he knew; they saw on him the guilt of aiding and abetting a thief, not to mention lying to his Maman and Papa and not a small fib, either, but a huge monster of an untruth. This was big trouble, the kind of thing that lead to a life of crime.

He decided to tell, took a breath, opened his mouth... and was struck mute. No words emerged. He felt like the aquarium fish at the pet store he'd visited a week earlier, tiny monsters with bulging eyes and stupid round mouths that pulsed without a sound. He was a prisoner of his own body; he believed he might burst from the sheer pressure of the lie. Why couldn't he just say, "Jeff Thomas took the money"?

He couldn't. It was as if Jeff was in the room and had him in a stranglehold, something Jeff did often to prove a point or demonstrate the innate superiority of American boys over smaller foreign ones. Jeanot gasped. Everyone in the room looked at him, so he pretended to cough and excused himself to get a drink of water.

When the policemen had established that close to a hundred dollars had indeed been taken, they began asking more pointed questions. A hundred dollars was a lot of money, and the transgression went from petty crime to felony.

Did the family lock its doors? Had they noticed any strangers in the neighborhood, any Negroes or vagrants? Was anything else missing?

The detectives looked at Jeanot and spoke of prison sentences, juvenile detention facilities with large and unkind boys who were closer to men than to adolescents. One of the detectives shuddered and, addressing Papa, said, "Lemme tell you, I wouldn't want to be a little boy in a place like that!"

After a while, Papa turned to Jeanot, and spoke in French so the policemen would not understand. *"Tu as quelque chose à dire, Jeanot?"* Was there something Jeanot wanted to tell them? Jeanot shook his head. There wasn't. He sipped at his glass of water with concentration, found he couldn't swallow.

"*Tu es sure?*"

Jeanot wasn't sure of anything anymore. Night could have fallen at noon, he wouldn't have noticed. He allowed the water in his mouth to dribble back into the glass. The two detectives looked at each other. Papa stood and took Jeanot's hand. "Gentlemen, would you mind being patient for a moment?" To Maman he said, "*Tu leurs fais un café, chérie?*

"My wife will make coffee for you. I'll be back in a moment." He led Jeanot to the front door and they both stepped out into the yard.

They walked around the house to the garage, to the dug-out plot where the tomatoes and radishes were growing, to the back fence that abutted a few acres of unattended wooded land. Papa opened the yard's rear gate and walked them through, down the little path that led to a creek. It was Jeanot's favorite place; there was a rock in the middle of the streamlet where he could sit and count minnows, spidery boat-men on spindly legs skimming the water's surface, and tadpoles. Once he'd seen a huge turtle there, and he knew of a thick black snake that lived between two rocks a few yards away.

There was a small beach of rough brown sand and Papa sat down, heedless of the moisture. Jeanot sat too.

"*Alors?*" Papa picked up a pebble and threw it into the water.

Jeanot shrugged, swallowed. "It wasn't me."

Papa said, "I know that. You're not a thief, Jeanot." He threw another pebble in.

There was more silence.

Jeanot's resolve was ebbing away. Papa saw it, added, "*Tu as été bien élevé.* We raised you right. You wouldn't do something like this, steal from your Papa and Maman." He paused, tossed a bigger stone that splashed and made small waves. "So who did? I think I know, but I'd like your opinion."

Jeanot wished he were anywhere else, in Paris, in Africa with the leopards, in the frozen North. He tried to remember if his Papa had ever asked for his opinion before. An immense weight bowed his shoulders, the pit in his stomach roiled and tears pooled in his eyes. Finally, he muttered, "Jeff. *Jeff est un voleur...*"

"A thief," Papa said in English.

"Tief" Jeanot hated *th* words. They always came out as *t* or Z. "Tief," he repeated.

When they returned to the house the policemen were gone though they'd left a number to call. Maman said both men made faces when tasting her coffee, a liquid Papa claimed was as dark and bitter as the portals of hell. In fact, neither man had taken more than a sip, which Maman thought rude and typical of some of the people in this country. Maman called American coffee *jus de chaussette,* sock juice, so pale it was almost transparent. She claimed the Maxwell House served by American friends tasted brown. She prided herself on brewing a serious cup, a soldier's cup, to which she would add scalded milk and brown sugar when asked. Neither of the policemen had, so she'd served it black.

Papa called the police but the detectives weren't back yet so he left a message. When they called back he sent Jeanot to his room before speaking.

The next day, Jeff Thomas tracked Jeanot to the rock in the middle of the creek. The police had been to his house and talked to his mother, he said, and she'd started crying. Jeff had denied stealing anything. Had Jeanot seen him taking the money? No, Jeff said, Jeanot hadn't seen anything, and invented the crime, and was a stupid foreign kid that nobody liked and who should have stayed in France where they wore no underpants.

Jeff hit Jeanot hard in the stomach, then stuck his head under water until Jeanot was sure he was drowning. Jeanot swallowed a mouthful of creek water, choked, and tried to scream. An image of Dédé face-down in the water floated past his eyes. Jeff cursed at him, using the fuck word several times, and kicked him in the shins. He promised horrible and painful things if Jeanot said *anything* to *anyone* about *anything.* Then he started sobbing and ran away.

Two weeks later Jeanot learned Jeff had been sent by his mother to live with his estranged father in Minnesota, so he went to Jeff's house and in halting English asked if he might have the weed-covered bicycle. Jeff's mother smiled, a sad smile, Jeanot thought, kissed him on the cheek and told him, yes, he could. She also handed him an envelope and told him to give it to his father and mother.

He carefully disentangled the two-wheeler from the poison ivy vine and half-rolled, half-carried the thing back to his house. The rear wheel wouldn't turn and the chain dragged on the ground, but he would fix everything, paint the bike bright red and replace the tape on the handlebar. He gave the envelope to his father who opened it and found a check for $100, which he tore in half and threw away.

Jeanot never got around to fixing the bike and a year or so later, Maman put the thing out on the curb with the trash. It was gone the next morning.

Chapter 24

Jeanot was not a good student. He blamed this on his lack of English but he hadn't been a good student in France either. Schoolwork bored him; he found trying to pay attention to the drone of teachers a skill he could not master. He fidgeted, made faces, doodled, and sighed loudly enough that everyone heard him.

He had hoped that in America there might be a different curriculum, one based perhaps on Wild West lore, or survival in the woods, or even bow and arrow construction taught by an Indian. No, this was the same old dried and tired stuff; math, geography, spelling and handwriting, this time in a language that made no sense at all.

The kids in the class weren't very friendly. They peered at the meals his Maman packed him—*mortadelle* or *saucisson* sandwiches, a small jar of herring in cream sauce, a handful of hot radishes—and jeered. One boy made retching sounds, staggered around and held his stomach as if ready to vomit, and everyone found this absolutely hilarious. Even the teacher, Mrs. Calhoun, wrote a note for Jeanot to take home, suggesting to Maman that preferable meals might include Wonder Bread, baloney, yellow mustard and orange slices, instead of the smelly and odd-looking foods packed in Jeanot's lunchbox.

There was another problem as well. Maman took the bright red lunchbox she bought him at People's Drug Store and painted it an amazing array of colors, with a spotted cow on the front panel and a large dog of indeterminate breed on the back. This was beyond the comprehension of the other kids who started making mooing sounds whenever Jeanot sat down to eat. He bore it all with varying degrees of patience. Once, he got into a fight with a kid who took his *saucisson* sandwich and flung it across the lunchroom. Jeanot got a bloody nose and the other kid got sent to the principal's office and then home, which made it worth it.

During dodgeball, Jeanot got smacked in the face right away. The big kid who threw the ball yelled, "I got the dirty furner!" Jeanot stepped out of the circle of classmates and didn't respond. Big kids were the same everywhere. He muttered "fuck" under his breath and looked around to make sure no one had heard him, but the kids were yelling and screaming and focused on the game.

Then, there was the underpants song:
There's a place in France
Where they wear no underpants…

He heard it every day from different voices, almost always boys, but once in awhile a girl's reedy soprano joined in. It may have been funny the first twenty-five times, but American kids, Jeanot decided, had little imagination. The song was sung in the halls, in the boys' room, at recess. The teachers tried to stop it but the more they admonished, the less they succeeded. After a while, Jeanot ceased paying attention, and as soon as this happened the singing diminished though it never quite stopped. One morning, to his horror, he awakened with the tune stuck in his head. It stayed there all day; la la la *lala* lalala la la la *la.*

Jeanot was simply no good at math. In Paris at the école maternelle, his lack of mathematical skills bewildered his teacher. Nor could he draw even a crude map of France, or name the major cities, or recite lines from Lafontaine, Molière, or Victor Hugo. He knew the teacher thought he might be a little slow; he'd heard her whisper to another teacher about those unfortunate post-war city kids whose malnutrition left a permanent mark. The teacher, Jeanot knew, had a son his own age; both had been raised on pale bluish mare's milk and bread soup; there'd been little else available in Paris immediately after war's end. Now her boy was spindly, prone to every cold and childhood illness. He had poor teeth. Like Jeanot, he wore glasses and was incapable of reciting a single stanza of memorized poetry.

In the French school, the only ability Jeanot manifested in class was a beautiful cursive hand, so that when he took dictation, he at least handsomely formed the many misspelled words. Maman had told Papa, "He can learn to spell any time. You can teach him that. That beautiful writing? He got that from me."

In America, handwriting didn't seem to matter much. At Westwood Elementary School, One girl wrote cursive like Jeanot, but he didn't trust her; she was German. Everyone else, he noticed, relied on big, blocky malformed letters, sloppily assembled and lacking any elegance. A lot of the kids had trouble reading too, and Jeanot found that incomprehensible. He couldn't remember not reading; illustrated books and magazines—*Tintin, Bécassine, Les Pieds Nickelés, Spirou, Paris-Match*—were among his first visual memories. He remembered copying the dialog of a Tarzan book on to random pieces of onionskin writing paper.

There was even one time when he copied a poem and claimed it as his own. Maman had gotten tremendously excited, had thought she perhaps had a *génie* as a child, like the little girl, Minou Drouet, whose poetry at age seven had electrified France and stunned the critics.

Minou was so famous she had met the President of the Republic, and even the stuffy *Le Monde* newspaper had called her writing "the voice of post-war optimism." Her photo was everywhere, posed with proud parents as she toured France and read her works out loud to huge audiences.

Maman, thrilled and full of hope, had shown Jeanot's poem to Papa, whose reaction was quieter. Papa had spoken with his son, and Jeanot, not quite understanding, had sensed there would be deep trouble if he maintained the lie and continued to claim authorship. He had shown his Papa where the poem had originally come from, a volume with a red cover and gold lettering that read *Collections des*

Oeuvres Modernes Inconnues. Papa recognized it as a wedding gift neither he nor Maman had ever looked at.

For Jeanot reading and writing were as basic as breathing. Without reading to help him escape, the world became paler on the brightest day and most things stopped making sense. In America, where logic was hard to find, reading was a necessity.

Chapter 25

KC Post was a small, golden-haired girl who lived next door, with a horde of brothers in a scruffy house with an overgrown yard. She was fond of cheap jewelry. There were clips and bands in her hair, plastic bracelets around her wrists, and beads she had strung herself in multiple strands around her neck. She was always barefoot and her feet were dirty; her exhausted mother had long ago stopped telling her to wear shoes. Her full name, KC told Jeanot, was Katherine Catherine, in honor of two aunts who hardly spoke to each other.

KC had green eyes, almost invisible freckles, and a crescent scar on the left side of her chin. Jeanot often found her sitting on the curb in front of her house reading books; not comic books, but real books from the lending library, with hard covers and no pictures. She had told him the world would soon end in a storm of fiery rain that would suck the air out of people's lungs, scorch the trees, and in particular, destroy her home and all who lived within, except her.

Jeanot was in love. Sometimes when they talked she held his hand and he no longer thought of Babette in Paris.

Maman liked KC as well and let her rummage through discarded costume jewelry. She fixed the little girl sandwiches made with ham and Camembert from the French butcher's shop, and KC devoured them, asking for extra cheese. KC also enjoyed Maman's undrinkable black coffee into which she would pour six teaspoons of brown sugar.

On a bright summer day, Jeanot and KC sat on Jeanot's front porch in a swinging chair Papa had built three weeks after he and Maman had bought the house on High Street. KC and Jeanot talked about the coming end of the world and sipped from plastic glasses of red Kool Aid, which Maman told Jeanot was one of America's greatest resources.

"First, all the animals will run away," KC said, "because animals are smarter than we are, you see, and they know when bad things are about to happen. So everybody's pets will be in the streets, all the dogs and cats and parakeets."

Jeanot knew KC's family owned several dogs, three cats and two parakeets in constant warfare with one another.

"And the buffaloes?" Jeanot still had a fondness for buffaloes, though he'd been in America for a while and had yet to see one.

KC considered the question seriously, which he appreciated. "Yes, them too. And wolves and gophers and groundhogs and hedgehogs. All the animals, even the slugs and butterflies and things that live under rocks…"

"Everyting," Jeanot said.

"Every *thing*," KC corrected him.

"*Thing,*" he repeated, very much wanting to please her. "Every *thing.*"

This would be quite a show, a Noah's Ark in reverse, and he hoped if it happened that the animals would parade down High Street.

KC never made fun of his accent. She helped him find the right word when he stumbled and did not know the underpants song. Her brothers feared her.

There were six Post brothers and KC was the only girl. She learned quickly to deal with the boys on their own terms, with punches and kicks and arm twisting and kneeling on backs until the fallen cried "uncle," a form of submission she could demonstrate but not explain to Jeanot. Sometimes, she told him, she helped with their homework, which left them in her debt. Every morning, she dressed the youngest one. Jeanot had noticed that the youngest Post now, too, often went shoeless. The brothers left her alone and no longer picked on Jeanot either, though they did snicker, and hummed the underpants song within hearing. Jeanot didn't care.

He was never as happy as when he sat on the curb and talked with KC about the end of the world. He had wings, he soared, and a smile split his face almost painfully. He routinely gave her his ice cream and Kool Aid and she accepted both with minimal thanks, as if this was the way things should be; Jeanot was meant to give her stuff. He tried to force his *Tintin dans le Congo* on her but she was smart enough to refuse it because, he realized, she sensed even this early in life what his Papa had once told him - there are things a woman should never ask of a man.

"You should keep those," she suggested. "You'll want to hand them down to your children after the Apocalypse."

"A-poc-a-lypse?" Jeanot had never heard the word.

"When everything will be destroyed, mostly my brothers," she explained.

Though the Post brothers all went to the local public schools, KC did not. She attended the St. Margaret of Antioch's School for Girls, on a scholarship granted by the diocese to Disadvantaged Catholic Students. She had won the award by being the only child in her Sunday school class able to recite from memory the names of all the books of the Bible in the correct order, from Genesis (1440 BC) to Apocalypse (68 AD).

It took her less than five minutes to memorize them, she told Jeanot, because she had "phonographic memory." To demonstrate her talent, she read a random page of his latest Superman comic and recalled, in order of appearance, all the speech balloons involving Lois Lane, Jimmy, and Clark Kent, as well as the explanatory text beneath the panels.

On yet another summer day she invited Jeanot into her house. It was dark there, shuttered and blinded, yet surprisingly orderly and not at all like the overrun front and back yards with the towering milk-weeds and rampant ivy. Jeanot noticed there were pointy-ended can openers on strings hanging from doorknobs in every room. KC told him this was because her father liked to open his cans of Pabst Blue Ribbon beer anywhere in the house. She further explained her father had his first Pabst at six in the morning and always carried two spares in the side pockets of his workpants. He drank a can every half-hour and drove daily to Paul's Spirits Emporium to replenish his supply.

KC's father did not officially work. He was wounded by a Japanese soldier during the war and had full disability, KC told Jeanot. "That means he gets money for doing nothing."

Still, Papa hired KC's father to replace some shingles on the roof, and the man proved to be surprisingly nimble in spite of his disability.

KC led Jeanot by the hand.

"We've been in this house forever," she told him. "Grandpa died right here on the couch last year. He was watching Perry Como and closed his eyes and never opened them again. Momma thought he was asleep and left him there and Dad found him the next morning. Dad complained he didn't even have time to open his first beer."

"Really?" asked Jeanot. When he was not totally sure of what had been said, he had taken to answering, "Really?"

KC nodded. "I used to like Perry Como, but now I don't. Not even *Catch a Falling Star.*" She hummed a few bars but Jeanot didn't know the song.

KC's house smelled strongly of dog, cat piss, old tobacco, beer vapors, and undershirts worn one day past their prime. It was otherwise clean, with thin area rugs, pictures of Jesus, Mary and assorted saints pinned carefully to the walls. A large framed black and white photograph of all the Posts hung in the hallway. KC was in the middle of the photo, and there were so many Posts that the boys on either end had to lean in to stay in the frame, bodiless heads grinning like hobgoblins.

The biggest television set Jeanot had ever seen, at least two feet across, dominated the living room. There were two copies of TV Guide, one at each end of the couch where Mr. and Mrs. Post battled for channel primacy.

KC's bedroom was painted canary yellow. She was the only Post child with a room of her own. There was a blue and white parakeet in a cage near the window. She led Jeanot to her bed. They lay together in the empty-of-Posts house listening to the squeaks and groans of timbers settling in the eaves. KC's breath tickled his left ear. She held him tight, sighed deeply and pretended to fall asleep, but he knew she wasn't sleeping because she was giggling, making small snuffling sounds. After a while, her entire body started shaking with laughter.

Then they heard the front door slam. The excited voices of boys just let out of school carommed up the stairs, voices full of possibilities and freedom in the afternoon sunshine.

The Post brothers were home. Jeanot and KC leaped out of the bed and were sitting on the floor playing with Lincoln Logs when the oldest brother peeked in and started humming the underpants song.

Maman approved of Jeanot and KC's friendship. Papa did too, but he never seemed to have time for her when she came to visit. Papa was preoccupied, thought Jeanot, worried about Maman's state.

One day, Papa asked, "Jeanot, *les pillules*; is your Maman taking more of them when I'm at work?"

Jeanot hesitated. This was a difficult question. In a dim and dangerous way, Jeanot knew any answer was a betrayal. He shrugged, but Papa insisted. "*Pense, Jeanot. C'est important!*"

Jeanot looked up, bothered, and Papa added, "It's okay. You can tell me. Sometimes Maman forgets and takes too many. And that could be dangerous. Remember, that time just before we left?"

Jeanot did remember, of course. When everything was being packed up in the apartment on Rue de la Terrasse, after the *maison de couture* closed, Maman took too many pills and slept eighteen hours straight. That scared everyone, even Mathilde, but Maman eventually woke up and things went back to normal.

"Sometimes she takes pills in the afternoon," Jeanot told Papa. "Yesterday morning, I think, she took some, and then again at noon." He hoped this was an answer that would satisfy. Jeanot saw his father's face sadden. "Keep an eye out, Jeanot, and tell me if you think Maman isn't acting normally."

"Normally?" Jeanot thought about it. "She sleeps a lot during the day."

"Really," said Papa. "How much?"

"She's always asleep when I come home," Jeanot explained. "Well, almost always. Sometimes she doesn't wake up until you get back."

Papa was quiet for a moment, then nodded and said, "Well, your Maman tires easily."

Jeanot didn't know if that was true. His Maman, for as long as he could remember, had always been full of energy.

Papa changed the subject.

Maman plied KC with rhinestone pins and earrings, multicolored ribbons, and music from the 40s which KC seemed to love. She taught KC to sew and to draw, and even Jeanot could tell KC was unusually adept. She was quick to understand shades, brushstrokes, and stitches, and he was proud of her. She was as creative, he thought, as Maman herself.

Jeanot knew Maman missed his two sisters who remained in Paris. There was little contact with them save bimonthly, long-distance telephone calls broken by operators, sizzling undersea cable noises, hisses and crackles. He had not spoken to either Françoise or Madeleine since leaving France; the calls were too costly to exchange more than the most basic information, and he wouldn't have known what to say even had he talked to them.

KC, Jeanot sensed, was helping his Maman deal with Françoise and Madeleine's absence. He was mostly fine with that, but not entirely; KC was at the house every day, but too much of her time was spent with his Maman and not with him. He experienced a strange jealousy that he didn't know how to display. He wished his Maman would simply go away for a while and not encroach, not demand, not usurp. The truth was, Jeanot was terrified of losing KC to anything or anyone, to circumstances, people, family, geography. He wanted to witness the end of the world with her; to partake in the delicious

Apocalypse that might reduce them both to cinders. He imagined this process would burn a bit, as when he was too long in the sun the last time the family went to the Côte d'Azure. This and more he was eager to undergo with her, and yet there were other people who demanded KC's time; her parents, her brothers, even his own Maman. It was almost unbearable.

One rainy morning, KC asked him, "That boy Jeff Thomas, he was your friend?"

Jeanot said yes, though he thought lying might be better. "But not my best friend," he added.

KC nodded. She was silent for a while then said, "I didn't like him. He tried to touch me *there*," and she pointed to her middle.

"Why?"

She shrugged. "I think it's because he's a sex fiend."

"Sex fiend?"

"Yes. Someone who *has to* touch girls. My mom says my dad is a sex fiend. Anyway, I wouldn't let him."

Jeanot was pleased by this. He didn't want anyone touching KC anywhere.

Chapter 26

After a while, even Papa seemed grateful to have KC around the house. When Jeanot told her this, she shrugged and replied, "Well of course! I am smart and patient and I'm your friend. And let's face it, Jeanot," she pronounces it *Djeeno*, "You don't make friends easily. Me, I like everyone. You…" She let the sentence trail off.

It was true, Jeanot realized. Now that Jeff was gone, KC was the only friend he had left.

"The thing is," KC continued, "that you're sorta small, and the glasses don't help. You're one of those kids who's gonna get bullied." Then she smiled and took his hand. "But don't worry, I'll protect you!"

Later that same day she asked, "Did your mom and dad just decide one day that you were coming here, to America, or did they ask you about it first?"

Jeanot had to think about that for a moment. "No, they didn't. We talked a little. Then, one day the men came and…"

"The movers?"

Jeanot nodded. "Yes, big men, they came and took the furniture and all the boxes."

KC pondered that for a moment. "Boy, I don't know what I would do if the same thing happened to me. If people just said, 'You're moving!' That'd be hard."

Jeanot thought, and decided that it had been sort of hard. His Maman, he knew, was still reeling from the shock, though she hid it well. Maybe not that well, though. Maman was definitely taking more pills.

KC said, "You're lucky I'm here. I'm a godsend. Where would you be without me? Your mom, though, she seems to be having a hard time."

Jeanot knew this was true. He couldn't help but notice that every day brought a new complaint, a new protest regarding the unavailability of celery root or worthwhile vegetables. Maman railed against iceberg lettuce, the very existence of which she could not seem to understand. There were objections to how things were done here; the new country had not revealed itself completely and each day brought small and mildly unpleasant surprises.

Why, for example, if the price of an item was openly outrageous, beyond comprehension, why couldn't said price be discussed with the seller and adjusted to make for a more pleasant purchase? Why could she not smoke her Pall Mall cigarettes in the movie theater? Why was there not a single store in Washington D.C., the capital of the United States of America, selling decent art supplies? Such local shortcomings were offset by the discovery of Hostess Twinkies, on which she soon became dependent, and Lady Clairol Champagne tint that gave her hair a strange gold and occasionally pink hue.

One day, Maman discovered the dentist who treated the local French population was the son of Camille Chautemps. Chautemps, three times Prime Minister of France, had granted married women financial and legal independence, the right to enroll in university, and to open bank accounts. Monsieur Chautemps, now old, was living in Washington with his wife. They had both been exiled shortly after the war for his role in the hated Vichy government. Jeanot wasn't particularly interested in the lives of elderly politicians from days long past, but was happy enough to see that the connection pleased Maman.

She decided to invite the entire Chautemps family for dinner, but Papa reminded her it was Chautemps who turned France over to the Nazis. Jeanot heard this and immediately decided he would hide if these people came to his house. Papa said, "That's why we went to war! Doesn't it matter to you that the man was a traitor?"

"A long time ago," Maman replied. "Times have changed."

"I really don't like the idea."

"But if Chautemps hadn't been such a traitor," Maman insisted, "I would never have met you!"

The argument was so ridiculous that Papa laughed. Jeanot could tell Papa would humor Maman, as he usually did. The Chautemps family would be invited.

When the Chautemps arrived for lunch on a Saturday, Jeanot noticed the dentist had strikingly yellow teeth and very bad breath. His sister, Genevieve, a tall brunette with a ponderous hairdo, dealt in real estate and sported bounteous breasts and an extravagant cleavage. Madame Chautemps, the dentist's mother and wife of the politician was now shrunken and gnomish, a victim of scoliosis and too much makeup so that she looked almost clownish. Maman insisted that the woman had once been a stunning beauty, but Jeanot had doubts. The dentist's father, the former premier, wore a tired and hunted look for most of the evening. He recounted stories that seemed somehow inappropriate, which jarred with the picture that Maman had painted of his triumphant role in history.

"Do you know," he asked the company in French, "What has one forward speed and five reverses?"

Even Jeanot had heard this one. It was possibly the very oldest World War Two joke.

He piped up, "An Italian tank!"

The former premier shot him an unhappy look.

Jeanot saw that Maman, nervous at having celebrities—even faded ones—for dinner, had taken two Miltowns before the company arrived. She became a calm and impeccable hostess who served eggs in aspic, a *poulet au persil,* and as a private joke, sauerkraut. Neither Papa nor Maman related that they were in the Free French during the war and that they'd fled France when Monsieur Chautemps ceded the country to the *Boches*. It would have been impolite to do so, Jeanot was sure. Chautemps never asked what Maman and Papa did during the war, and so peace was maintained. Jeanot noted that Papa glanced at Genevieve Chautemps chest several times, which made sense, as he couldn't help looking himself. There was just so much of it. He saw, however, that Maman noticed it too, and she did not look pleased.

In time Maman discovered more people of interest. Jeanot couldn't help but notice that none were American save the husband of Ôdile, a petite French woman who ran a store in Georgetown.

Ôdile's husband did not speak French and, when Maman invited the couple to a largish dinner party at the house, none of the guests made any effort to include him in the conversation. The American did not seem offended; he wandered the front and back yards inspecting the paltry plantings. He gazed at the art on the walls and the books on the shelves. He examined the fake Persian rug with great care. He picked up a Mediterranean seashell mounted on a block of wood, hefted it appreciatively, held it to his hear and then replaced it.

Eventually, Papa came to speak with him; Jeanot heard them talk about the weather, tomatoes, and the new Caravelle airplane produced in France. "Five-hundred miles an hour," said the American admiringly, and congratulated Papa as if Papa had built the thing himself in the basement.

Later Jeanot, bored by the adults, found the American on the back porch. The American seemed to be in good spirits. He asked Jeanot how he was doing. Had he been following the baseball season and the Senators? Jeanot shook his head, no. He clearly remembered getting hit on the forehead with a hardball that second day in America. Jeanot asked the American if he'd been to Texas, and indeed the man had. He told Jeanot stories of Choctaw Indians, Davy Crockett, the Alamo, and floods along the Rio Grande. Jeanot understood every third word and said "really" a lot.

Maman came upon them there some time later, and ushered the American, whose name was Hubert, into the dining room and to the table. Dinner was a buffet, and Maman had worked all day and had outdone herself with the preparations and the meal. Jeanot helped to open cans of chickpeas, and tore the stems from mushrooms. Having done his part to prepare the dinner, Jeanot tasted every delicacy, including French and Italian hard sausage, artichoke hearts, couscous, chicken breasts steeped in Marsala and paper thin slices of marinated veal cooked in a batter of egg yolks and flour.

As the evening wore on, Jeanot became warier of this Hubert. He noticed the American's smile was disconcerting in its steadiness and unvarying intensity. He watched the man fill his plate with this food and that, and saw Maman pour him a glass of Beaujolais. The American said, "*Merci,*" and that one word led Jeanot to suspect this man could speak French if he wanted to, but had chosen not to do so for reasons of his own.

Later, Jeanot overheard Maman tell Papa, "I think it's a matter of pride. They're very confident, these Americans."

Papa agreed. "When you win every war you fight, you get that way."

Weeks later, Maman told Jeanot and Papa that she'd learned from a friend that Hubert actually spoke French quite fluently, as well as Italian, Portuguese and Russian. He worked at the Central Intelligence Agency and monitored meetings of foreign nationals.

Papa thought this was very funny, and Jeanot laughed to be included in the joke, but he didn't truly understand it.

Papa said, "Imagine that! We've been singled out for surveillance after such a short time in the country."

Maman was not amused, and was so offended, in fact, that she never invited Hubert and Ôdile to her home again.

"Who'd think of such a thing," she told Jeanot and Papa over breakfast. "*Spying* on us, *tu imagines?* I knew it right from the start. You can't trust them." Then, lowering her voice, she whispered to Papa, "I told you so."

Chapter 27

The hurricane made Maman once again doubt the wisdom of coming to America.

There had been grainy images on television of Southern states where palm trees were almost bent to the ground. Roofs were torn from seaside bungalows as impossibly large waves battered the beaches. Jeanot had been watching this with interest. Weather like this had never happened in France, though he had read in *Tintin* about monsoons in India and Borneo. This hurricane was in Florida, a thousand miles from Washington and almost in a foreign land. Neither Maman nor Papa seemed overly worried, at first.

At school, Jeanot was told that if the hurricane struck Westwood Elementary School, he should get under his desk and make himself very small. The children practiced this until Mrs. Calhoun was satisfied there would be no casualties among her students. The girls complained about getting their dresses dirty, and the boys smirked as they tried to catch glimpses of panties.

From the television, Jeanot learned the hurricane was Beatrice, the second of the season, born in the Atlantic and rotating counter-clockwise as it gathered strength and speed. The hurricane slammed into the coast of Central Florida, paused there, and began a leisurely travel up the East Coast. It caused thunderstorms, heavy winds, waterspouts and a tornado or two that took out a Virginia Beach trailer park without causing injury to its residents. The tail end of the winds hit Washington, D.C. at 11 p.m. as Papa and Maman were returning from a bridge party in Foggy Bottom.

They were zipping along in the Roadmaster on Rock Creek Parkway when the canopy of a large Dutch elm caught the wind like a sail and uprooted the tree. Papa told Jeanot how the tree came crashing down on the car, caving in the roof not eight inches behind where they were sitting. The impact stopped the car dead and blew all four tires out. Miraculously, neither driver nor passenger was seriously injured. Maman got a bloody nose and fat lips when her face hit the dashboard and Papa bruised four ribs on the steering wheel. They were stuck in the Roadmaster until the rescue squad arrived, pried the car's right door open with crowbars and brute strength, and extricated them.

A photographer from the *Evening Star* was two cars behind and got a shot of the half-crushed Roadmaster and of a dazed Maman being wheeled away on a stretcher into the ambulance. A second photo showed a shocked Papa clutching Maman's purse. Both pictures made the next day's paper.

Jeanot was dozing through the storm at KC's house. Maman had paid Mrs. Post three dollars to babysit Jeanot, and Mrs. Post had confessed she was mildly taken aback that the French couple stayed out so late on a weeknight.

It was two a.m. before Maman and Papa could pick Jeanot up. He woke for a moment, looked wide-eyed at his Maman's swollen face, then fell back asleep. He woke again as she tucked him into bed and he heard her tell Papa she wasn't sure she wanted to stay in a country where the trees tried to kill you.

"*C'est complètement fou,*" she said through swollen lips. "That would never happen in France! Never!"

Papa was willing to admit hurricanes were rare in Europe, but he pointed out there were other threats. "Separatists," he countered. "Basques and Britons and Flemish. They've been known to attack people, and believe me, if they get you, they'll give you more than just a bloody nose!"

Maman wasn't listening. "First, a child robs us. Then they send a spy to our house. Now this!" She wanted Papa and Jeanot to chop down the black walnut in their backyard; she'd never liked the tree and claimed its shadow was killing the grass. "Just watch! There will be another hurricane! *Tu vas voire*, that tree will try to kill us in the middle of the night!"

Papa tried to reason. "*Allez, chérie*. Now you're being silly…"

She ignored him. "I have no idea what could happen in this country. *Aucune idée…*"

Jeanot was hero-for-a-day at school and Mrs. Calhoun pinned the photos of the destroyed Roadmaster and its distraught passengers on the cork bulletin board in her classroom next to the color portrait of Mamie Eisenhower. She used the hurricane incident to explain how great America was, welcoming immigrants who were spared a crushing death only by the goodness of a God who spoke English. She further drilled her wards in squatting beneath their desks and, while there, reciting the Pledge of Allegiance to the Flag.

The hurricane was the first of a series of events Maman, always slightly superstitious, saw as dire omens.

A week or so later, Maman and Jeanot were raking grass clippings from the lawn when she disturbed a nest of mud daubers and was stung five times in quick succession. She took it stoically, sponging the wounds with white vinegar, but there was no doubt in her mind something was up with America. The country was not as welcoming as it had promised to be.

Then for no reason at all she turned her ankle at the Giant food store and knocked over a stacked display of Chicken of the Sea tuna fish. The manager rushed to her aid and was so solicitous and afraid of a lawsuit that he gave her, free of charge, all the groceries in her cart. Maman told Jeanot how once again bad luck had struck. Not only did she hurt her ankle, but there were merely five inexpensive items in the cart at the time. Had she stumbled a few minutes later after buying a week's supply of meat as planned, she would have collected a much better assortment of provisions.

Six days later, the oil in which she was deep frying eggplant *beignets* caught on fire. Papa, who was preparing radishes, reacted quickly and threw a pitcher of iced tea into the fryer. The flames leaped to ceiling heights with a frightening whooshing sound. The curtains near the range caught on fire and Papa, using the sink sprayer, was successful in putting them out, but his efforts pulled loose the sprayer hose, shooting a stream of water straight up into the air.

The stove was ruined, as were the *beignets*. In time, they discovered the heat of the fire had melted the soldering in the plumbing above, so that water dripped from the ceiling lights every time someone flushed the toilet in the second floor bathroom.

Jeanot found the entire episode highly educational, and when his parents were out, flushed the upstairs toilet several times to watch it rain from the kitchen ceiling.

Plumbers, plasterers, drywall men and painters paraded through the house for a week and Maman swore the water pressure was never the same.

Shortly after the kitchen's near destruction, Papa complained of a headache over dinner and the next day was bedridden by a bout of malaria, a disease he'd caught at the very beginning of the war. The whites of his eyes turned a ghastly yellow and he could only eat boiled rice and broth.

Jeanot was scared. Papa had never been this ill, and the sight of him shivering under blankets was terrifying.

"Is he going to die?" It was such an unthinkable possibility that he could only whisper it.

Maman reassured him, though he could see she was scared too. "*Non.* Don't worry. He'll be up in a week or so."

"*Tu es sure?*"

Maman held her son's shoulders, then hugged him hard. "*Oui.* He'll be fine."

Jeanot, despite his mother's assertion, remained uncertain. He checked on his Papa several times a day and even brought KC in to take a look and offer a second opinion. She observed the bedridden man gravely for a moment. He smiled at her with his yellow eyes and she pronounced him on the verge of recovery. Jeanot was relieved. It wasn't that he lacked trust in his mother's words, but he thought it wise to get an American assessment.

To keep his Papa alert, Jeanot said, "Tell me again how you got to England!"

Papa sat up in his bed. "You've heard the story a hundred times."

"But KC hasn't! She's really interested!

KC played her part. "I really am!"

Papa looked at them both, sighed and said, "Go get the atlas, Jeanot."

When Jeanot returned with the large book, Papa opened it to the page that showed southern Europe.

He began. "I was in America…"

Chapter 28

"On September 3, 1939," began Papa, "Britain, France, Australia and New Zealand declared war on Germany. The news reached me in San Francisco shortly before I boarded *Queen of the Pacific,* a small liner that was to take me and my employer, Sir Julian Willingham, across the Panama Canal and back to England. Most shipping lines didn't want to go to Europe. By paying a lot of money, Sir Julian booked passage for us both to Lisbon, though he disliked the Portuguese even more than he did the French."

"Sir Julian was fat?" War stories were Jeanot's favorites. Papa seldom spoke of those days, and when he did, Jeanot had questions.

"Very fat! *Comme ca,*" Papa spread his arms out in front of him and puffed out his cheeks.

"You left America?"

"Yes, and after ten days on the boat…"

"Did you see any cowboys?

"No, because I never—"

"I would have stayed in America until I'd seen cowboys," Jeanot said, and added, "Buffaloes, too."

"But this isn't your story, is it?"

This was true. Jeanot nodded.

KC looked at Jeanot. "Will you let him talk?"

Jeanot pointed to the map. "You got to Portugal!" He knew where Portugal was, inside of Spain, which was far to the south of Paris.

Papa nodded.

"In Lisbon," he continued, "I paid a waiter in a bar 75 Escudos for a ride to the Spanish border. The man left with my money to get a car but never returned."

"Portuguese!" Jeanot scoffed.

"The next day, I woke up thirsty and feverish."

"Like when I ate that bad soup," said Jeanot, making a face.

"It wasn't the soup, Jeanot, it was all that cake you ate," insisted Papa. "Yes, like that, except worse. I tried to get out of bed, and I threw up and coughed so hard I thought I'd explode."

"Malaria," said Jeanot. His Papa had had a recurrence two years earlier, but not as bad as the present one.

"That's what it was," agreed Papa. "A Portuguese doctor gave me Atabrine, a pill to take for two weeks, and I lost seventeen pounds. While I recuperated in a cheap hotel, my passport was stolen.

"For a little money, the hotel's desk clerk arranged transportation for me from Lisbon to Navarre aboard his cousin's fishing boat. I even bought a large American gun from the boat's first mate."

Jeanot's eyes went wide, but KC shushed him before he could interrupt.

"I slept that first night in France under a bridge and wrapped in a blanket," said Papa. "I found a newspaper the next morning and realized for the first time how hard it would be to get to England through occupied territory.

"I didn't have a passport or a national identity card," he told Jeanot and KC. "And I wasn't fully recovered from the malaria, and the Germans had already set up the *Service du Travail Obligatoire* which sent men and women to work in Germany." To KC he added, "That means you didn't have a choice. If they wanted you to, you went."

On the map, Papa traced for them the route from Lisbon to Le Touquet. Jeanot wanted to hear the part about his papa fighting off the robbers.

"The trip took two months. Here," Papa said, "three men tried to rob me but I fought them off-"

"With your fists?"

"Of course with my fists! I was a boxer in England, remember? So I hit one of them on the nose, POW! And he fell down! And the second one had a stick and he hit me on the head with it but not hard enough so I kicked him…"

"In the balls!"

Papa embarrassed, looked at KC who shrugged.

"I know what balls are," she said.

"Yes, *dans les couilles*, and he fell down yelling, and the third one ran away."

At that moment, Maman walked into the room. Papa and Jeanot snickered, but Maman paid them no mind. KC sighed.

"*Là*," Papa pointed at the map again, a little farther north, "a very nice man gave me a bag of apples. Most of them were bad and I had to spit out the worms—"

Jeanot squinched his eyes shut and held his hands over his ears. When he lowered them, Papa smacked his lips, "Though they didn't taste bad. A bit squishy. A little bit like salted beets. I think your mother is making some for dinner tonight."

"She's not!" Jeanot wasn't fooled. KC rolled her eyes.

Papa continued. "In this place, a family took me in and served me the best meal I've ever had in my entire life. There were fresh radishes with salt and butter, a chicken done just so, potatoes and carrots and bread and jam and cheese and an apricot pie. After the meal they gave me pear liquor they made themselves, and that night I slept in their barn for 15 hours! *Imagines ça,* Jeanot! I slept with the cows and the horses. And the next day that farmer put me in touch with the Maquis, the—"

"The secret fighters!"

"They gave me clothes, maps, but at first they didn't trust me so they asked me many, many questions and I had to be very careful answering because if I answered wrong, *zoop!*" Papa ran his index finger along his throat. "Because everywhere there were collaborators, men and women who would betray you without a moment's thought."

"*Les collabos...*" Jeanot explained the term to KC, "They were the people who helped the Germans. And there were the BOF, too. That means *Beurre Oeufs Fromage.* Butter, eggs and cheese. People who didn't share their food or sold it to the Boches."

"Boches?" KC didn't know what that was.

"The enemy."

"There were some close encounters," said Papa. "I was offered shelter by a family that looked too well-fed, and I only escaped minutes before a squad of Germans poured into the outbuilding where I had been sleeping.

"Just outside Bordeaux, when I hadn't eaten in two days, I stole a chicken."

"You *stole*," Jeanot liked to emphasize the word. "*Stole!!*"

KC, annoyed, hissed, "Would you *please* be quiet?"

Papa smiled. "The bird made such a racket that a farmer appeared in the courtyard with his shotgun and fired the weapon into the dark. I got hit in the leg and I was forced to crawl from the site, birdless and bleeding...which is what I deserved for stealing. You should *never* steal."

"Even if you're starving to death?"

"That's not going to happen to you Jeanot. As long as you eat all the food on your plate. Remember, there—"

"—are children starving in China."

"That's right," said KC, who had heard the same thing from her mother. "Millions and millions of them!"

"Exactly," agreed Papa. "In any case, the first time I encountered the enemy, two Germans stopped me in La Rochelle and demanded to see my papers. They were barely sixteen and full of themselves. I gave them a few banknotes but they shoved me and demanded more. I kept my eyes downcast, gave them all I had in my pockets, and they left to find a café. They both spat on my feet as they left. I was shaking from fear and malaria most of that night."

Jeanot wasn't at all sure that Papa was telling the truth about that part. Papa had, as far as Jeanot knew, almost never been afraid of anything. Papa was probably just trying to make it a better story for KC, and that was fine.

"Often," said Papa, "I walked thirty kilometers a day, avoiding the main roads. When I reached a village or small town, I could tell within minutes what kind of people lived there. Vichy communities looked at strangers with suspicion. I always knew who they were…"

"Because they were fat, like the Englishman?"

"That," agreed Papa, "and because they walked with their eyes down. They wouldn't look at me in the face.

"Other places were different. In those I found that telling a bistro owner *'Je vais en Angleterre,'* would get me a free *casse-croute,* a sandwich, fried eggs and strong coffee, a baguette of that morning's bread and a shot or two of local brandy.

"Once I twisted my right knee so badly I thought my leg was broken."

"But the widow helped you!" Jeanot liked it when others realized his father's value.

KC asked, "Was she pretty?"

Papa thought for a moment. "No. She was very sad. She'd lost her husband."

"Lost?"

"He died."

"Oh."

"Yes, Jeanot. The woman took me in, a stern figure in black who massaged my leg until I screamed, and then bound it tightly in bandages made from her wedding dress. I stayed at her house eight days and she never spoke more than ten words at a time. But she fed me, mended my shirt, cut my hair, took my shoes to the local cobbler and had them resoled. One night she crawled into my bed and held me until dawn. I could feel her tears on my shoulder. She kissed me hard on both cheeks and then turned her back the morning I left."

"Sad," murmured KC.

Papa nodded. "Very sad.

"In some places," he told Jeanot and KC, "I stayed a few days; others I avoided entirely. Whenever I could, I collected maps of the region, and on these I scribbled observations. The information might be important, I thought, once I reached England.

"Over the course of another four weeks I traveled north, circling around the larger cities."

"And you walked every day?" Jeanot could walk all day, if necessary. He was reasonably sure he could have survived the war too, and he wanted to impress KC with his father's strength.

"Wherever I went," Papa told them, "I could count on a growing community of petty criminals and deserters. They often lived near the railroad tracks and I banded with them when necessary, sometimes riding boxcars through the countryside. It was slow but safe, and I found most railroad workers agreed with the underground's cause. Food and bottles of cheap red wine were left near empty freight wagons; the armed guards who patrolled the train yards looked the other way when they spotted us hiding in empty grain wagons. I learned to carry ground pepper to confuse the German shepherd dogs roaming some rural depots.

"In St. Nazaire near the Loire River, I ran into members of the Sao Breiz, the Breton resistance."

"Like Mathilde?" The family's part-time maid in France had been a Bretonne.

"Yes. Mathilde was in the Resistance too. Didn't she tell you?"

"No, she didn't," said Jeanot. "Mathilde only talked to me about gossip and people she didn't like. Mathilde," he told KC, "was our maid."

KC peered at Jeanot and his father. "You had a *maid?*"

Neither answered her question but Papa kept talking.

"Members of Sao Breiz cells rescued downed Allied airmen. When I told them I had relatives waiting for me in Le Touquet, one family fed me, another gave me fresh clothes so I looked like a Breton worker, and a *patissier* with a secret printing press gave me fake German papers. A shipper of artichokes took me all the way to Beauvais in Picardy.

"When I arrived in Le Touquet, I was carrying a small suitcase with a change of clothes, a fake French passport, the counterfeit identity papers, and the .45 caliber revolver I bought on the fishing boat."

"A Smith and Wesson!" Papa nodded. Jeanot knew his guns.

"I bet you felt strong, having a gun like that," murmured Jeanot. "American guns are powerful!"

Papa gave him a serious look.

"The gun scared me," he said. "I had gone pigeon hunting once when I was your age, and I didn't like it. A farmer friend of my own Papa had taken me to a wooded area and shown me how to fire.

"In le Touquet, I looked up the address of a cousin I had only met twice."

"*Le cousin Raymond*," Jeanot remembered, "The one with the dog."

"The man was a gardener," explained Papa, "employed by the city's parks; tall, unmarried, with rough hands. He knew nothing of the war, had no opinion on politics, and believed that 'every country gets invaded, that's how history works.' He worried about keeping his job. 'What if the Germans bring in their own gardeners? What will I do then? It really has been difficult for us. Médor probably suffers more than anyone,' he insisted, pointing to a brown dog sleeping by the door. 'The butcher doesn't give me scraps anymore. He sells them for stew. It's all very distressing.'

"The room smelled of damp and old newspapers, chicken broth and boiled potatoes," Papa said. "Raymond had no news from England, since he hadn't talked with his family in many years. At first, I wondered if my cousin might be a collaborator, but I decided he was too stupid to be of any use to the enemy. I bedded down on the floor and slept fitfully through the night.

"Raymond fixed coffee, carefully measuring out teaspoons of ground acorns into a blue enamel pot. He looked outside and shrugged. 'No work for me today. Too wet. Thank god for the unions. Do you have unions in England?' Eventually I said, 'Raymond, I need to get a boat. Do you have one, or do you know where one is available?'

"He said, 'a boat? Whatever do you want with a boat? In this weather?'"

Jeanot interjected, "Why didn't you just tell him you were going to England to join General de Gaulle?" Jeanot had learned almost at birth who *Le Grand Général* was.

Papa's yellowed malarial eyes looked stern. "Are you going to interrupt me every five minutes?"

Jeanot fell silent.

"I told Raymond," Papa went on, "that I needed to get to England.

Raymond shook his head. 'England? You mean across-the-Channel England? Are you crazy? I had to get special permission to go to eight kilometers to Arlène for manure. You don't even have proper papers, do you?' He got angrier and angrier as he talked. 'And it's raining, so who would want to go to England when it's raining!'"

I said, "I have family there."

"Raymond began shouting. 'They're not nice people, the family! They treated me very poorly. That's why I came here…'

"'A boat, cousin. I need a boat with a small engine, and I need gasoline. Can you help me?'

"Now Raymond was really afraid. 'No, no! I'm sorry I can't! I really can't. I have to work here you know, and take care of Médor and keep the parks clean. No. This just won't do. You should leave. Please leave.'"

"This is the best part," Jeanot told KC. "This part is when he steals the the boat!" Jeanot liked the idea of his father doing something bad, so he said it again. "He *stole* the boat! Just like he stole the chicken!"

"In this case, I borrowed it," Papa corrected Jeanot, but looked at KC.

She asked, "Did you ever give it back!"

"I borrowed it for a while," repeated Papa.

"And there was a storm!" This was Jeanot's favorite moment of the tale; his father battling the elements, battered by rain and wind, single-handedly manning the tiny vessel through black waters.

"And there were sharks!"

Papa laughed, reached out to tousle Jeanot's hair. "No sharks; I've told you that before. Not in the Channel; the waters there are too cold."

"But there could have been sharks! Or whales!"

Papa gave the notion some thought, shook his head. "No. No whales. No sharks. No octopus, either. But there were some really big mackerels! *Grand comme ça!*" He held his hands two feet apart.

That satisfied Jeanot. Sharks, whales, octopus, mackerels, they all lived in the mysterious and dangerous seas. He'd read about them in the *Tintin* books. He wished he had a shark submarine like Tintin did, and said so.

"Will you please stop interrupting?" KC glared at Jeanot. "I want to hear the rest, so be quiet!"

Jeanot rode the imaginary shark submarine to shore.

"So I borrowed a little boat; actually, I bought it," Papa lied. Jeanot knew it was a lie, because he'd memorized this part of the story from so many times before. "I just never met who I bought it from. I left money and a note in an envelope tacked to the piling near the boat. I got in and it was *very* small, *tout petit*, and I tried to start the engine and at first it wouldn't. I was afraid someone would come or call the police, but then just when I was about to give up, *vroom*, the engine started and I headed for the sea.

"The waves were not high, and the mist had cleared. The British coast was due west and I set a compass point; I thought I had to travel about thirty miles. I headed north towards Calais and the Strait of Dover. There were two full 20-liter gasoline tanks and I thought I could reach England in six hours.

"I was unshaven and dressed in the clothes the Sao Breiz had given me. Next to the gas tanks I'd found a wadded up slicker with a hood, and I wore that as well, trying to protect myself from the spray. I was getting seriously seasick when a five-man German patrol boat found me."

Jeanot looked at KC and whispered, "Les Boches!"

She said, "Shhh!"

Papa gave Jeanot a warning glance. "I stopped the engine. They threw me a rope. I had no choice. I tied my little boat to theirs and this giant soldier jumped and almost landed on me and started yelling in German, and I'll tell you, I was so scared."

"You almost peed in your pants!" Jeanot giggled. That was still such an impossible thought, his Papa being that scared. It defied everything he knew. But then the idea of Papa peeing his pants, now that was outrageously funny!

"Don't laugh, Jeanot! That's not nice." Papa looked stern, then softened. "I was sure he would shoot me and dump me in the water and suddenly—"

"You threw up on him!"

KC sighed in exasperation.

Papa laughed. "I did. All over his leg and his shoes. And I *knew* I was dead!" He paused for effect. "But all the other *Boches* thought that was the funniest thing they'd ever seen, and the big soldier—he wasn't really that big, actually, and he was very young, just a boy—he cursed at me and was taking his pistol out when an older German gave an order, and the young German got back into his boat and they left. I could still hear them laughing, and there I was—"

"You'd peed in your pants in the middle of the ocean!"

KC raised her voice. "Would. You. Please. Shut. Up!"

"In the middle of the Channel, Jeanot. It's not an ocean. But yes, all by myself again. So I took a deep breath and started the engine up and six hours later I was on the beach and there was Dover and I was soaked and very cold, I was trembling and I had no food and I didn't care." He took a sip of water. Jeanot noted his Papa was sweating heavily. He'd been told this was caused by malaria, but he remembered that he, himself, sweated when he was nervous.

Papa said, "I think that was probably the very best moment of my life.

"The Dover police picked me up on the beach; the force patrolled the area since there were rumors of a possible German invasion. They took me, shivering and numb, to the station; they gave me hot tea and hard biscuits, and carefully examined my fake papers. Then they made me write down everything that had happened to me. I spoke to several people and mentioned Sir Julian. I was fed warm soup and bread, and spent the night in a cozy cell wrapped in a wool blanket.

"The next morning, an elegant man in his forties introduced himself as Monsieur Durant, the Free French representative in the area.

"Monsieur Durant asked if I was interested in joining and I told him I was. Bilingual speakers were always in need, Monsieur Durant said. Do you know what bilingual is?"

KC said, "It means you have two tongues. Like a lizard."

Jeanot exhaled loudly. "It means you speak French and English, like me."

KC sniffed. "Not that well."

Papa coughed. "Two weeks later, I became an aide-de-camp to Charles de Gaulle, the commander of the Free French forces."

"Did you get a medal?" Jeanot thought his Papa deserved at least one.

"*Non.* But soon I was sent back to France with some men. They gave us a radio station that broadcast from a truck, and we told everybody about how the Germans were losing."

That pleased Jeanot. He could tell KC was impressed.

"Having been at war for weeks," Papa went on, "I now finally wore a uniform."

Papa looked tired. Maman came in, ushered the children out, and that was the end of the war stories for that day.

Chapter 29

Over the course of the latest bout with malaria, Papa lost twenty-five pounds. Doctor Rouget prescribed massive doses of chloroquine and quinacrine.

Jeanot liked Doctor Rouget. She gave shots that didn't hurt.

To calm down Maman, she suggested a new and promising drug, Valium, which, she explained, "is not an opiate, so there's no risk of becoming dependent!"

The Valium soothed Maman's nerves, which she explained were frayed from encounters with storm-battered trees, insects, malaria, slippery floors and kitchen fires. It did not, however, allay her suspicions that perhaps America was not a land one could live in safely.

Maman told them of her concerns. "I don't believe in good luck or bad luck," she said, though both Papa and Jeanot knew she did, "But you have to admit something is going on! First, there were all these injuries, the car getting wrecked, wasp stings and fires and now, look at you, Roland, you look like a Chinaman! Maybe we should move to Canada. They speak French there, or at least a version of French…" Maman had met a woman from Quebec who worked at the nearby pharmacy while food shopping with Jeanot. She'd been amazed by the woman's accent.

Papa reasoned with her from his sickbed. "The fire was a freak accident. So was the hurricane. Here, they call that an Act of God. It could have happened to anyone, anywhere!"

"Not in Paris," Maman replied. "There has never been a hurricane in Paris. And a French God will not try to kill you with a tree."

One day Papa received a get-well card written in a feminine hand.

Maman opened it, of course, and though the thoughts stated in the card were nothing short of banal, the sender's identity bothered her. "Why is that Chautemps woman with the breasts you like so much sending you a card? How does she even know you're sick?"

He looked at the card. "You probably told someone who told them. It's a very small society here, as you know. *Toute petite,*" he added to further his point.

Maman took back the card and deposited it in the bedside waste-basket. "I don't like that woman," she said.

"Neither do I," Papa said earnestly.

Maman often spoke with Doctor Rouget on the phone. She had also found Docteur Anatole Bianci (he insisted on being called *Docteur*), born of Italian parents but raised and educated in France, who was both an internist and a specialist in allergies. Doctor Agosto Csapláros, a displaced Hungarian from a wealthy Magyar family that had moved to Paris shortly after the Great Revolution, was married to a French woman and was a favorite of the embassy staff.

Maman visited them all, often with Jeanot in tow, and spoke of her difficulties in adjusting to the new country, her frustrations, fears and anxieties. The doctors understood. They too had faced the aggravation of America, the paperwork, and the interviews with sour-faced bureaucrats. The doctors nodded and dispensed. Maman left their offices with a handful of prescriptions for a variety of medications.

Jeanot hated the treks to the doctors. "*Encore?* Why do we have to go there so often? Their offices smell funny!"

"But they give you candy!"

"Lollipops," Jeanot said.

"*Quoi?*" This was a new word.

"Lo. Li. Pop," Jeanot pronounced it carefully. He'd heard KC say it a week earlier. "It means *sucette.*"

More and more often, Jeanot would translate for Maman. It was a thankless task. His Maman was not that interested in learning and oftentimes was affronted by the senselessness of English.

"Lo. Li. Pop. What a stupid word! Who can remember a word like that?"

Jeanot could, but found no reason to boast.

After the doctor they went to the local People's Drug Store where the French Canadian pharmacist overfilled the doctors' orders with a smile and a wink. Maman made a great show of gratitude, but once they left the store she told Jeanot, "I don't know what language that woman thinks she's speaking, but it certainly isn't French."

The recently bought drugs went into the wicker breadbasket in the middle of the dining room table. They joined the collection of small tin boxes, glass bottles, paper envelopes with loose pills, liquids in dark glass beakers, and tiny vials for dispensing drops in eyes, noses or ears.

Every meal began with a selection of tablets Maman popped into her mouth and swallowed with water. Papa, worried over Maman's medicinal intake, voiced some concerns while buttering a hunk of bread. Maman replied that the only person in her family who had developed a true reliance on the drugs was her brother Yves.

"Un vrai habitué," Maman said, recounting how Yves went away to an undisclosed clinic in Switzerland where he tromped through the Lower Alps and bathed in freezing lakes in the hope of curing his addiction.

"Opium," she told Jeanot and Papa. "Poor Yves. Now *there* is a man with a *grand problème.*"

Chapter 30

Papa and Maman once again had two cars—the Roadmaster had been replaced by a 1951 Plymouth Cranbrook with a windshield visor that Jeanot thought looked sinister. Their house was now a home and Jeanot's sisters, Françoise and Madeleine, had been invited to come and spend a few weeks in America. Both had refused. For a day or two Maman had spent costly hours on the phone trying to persuade the girls but without success. Madeleine had a new boyfriend in Paris and didn't want to leave him. She really liked this young man, the son of a photographer for *Paris-Match*, and she and Maman argued over several long distance calls with Maman ending up in tears.

Françoise could not come either; her exams at the Conservatoire were all-important. Even two weeks away from Paris might jeopardize her hard-earned standing in the class, which could be disastrous.

Jeanot had found the process of calling France highly mysterious and listened carefully as his Papa first talked to a lady who worked for the telephone company in the U.S. He gave her a lot of information, including the exact time of day in France and the numbers both in America and in Paris. Then, miraculously, minutes or hours later, the phone rang and there was Françoise, a scratchy and far-away voice, or his Tatie whom they'd called once and then spent ten minutes coaxing into breathing deeply after she'd burst, long distance, into inconsolable tears. Jeanot had not managed to talk his parents into calling Babette; they'd refused, citing costs and time constraints, so he'd tried to do it himself. He'd hung up as soon as he heard the telephone lady's voice.

The new kid arrived two weeks into the school year. He was slightly Asian, spindly, wore wire-rimmed glasses just like Jeanot's, and carried a look of open surprise. The teacher introduced him as Robert Van der Van, a weird name Jeanot knew would be slandered before the end of the day. The teacher said Robert's family worked for the State Department and had just returned from Indonesia. None of the kids, save Jeanot, knew where that was. Robert lived on High Street, a block away from Jeanot's house, and though Jeanot was tempted to approach him after school, he decided it might be wise to wait. Robert Van der Van might be one of those unfortunate kids who are natural fodder for bullies.

For one thing, he had huge, monstrous Dumbo ears attached to the sides of his head, ears that in a high wind might propel him down the sidewalk, ears that would foster out-loud comments even among adults. Also, he wore a suit, a tidy, double-breasted thing with elegant lapels and gold buttons. His shoes shone; his brow was dewy with perspiration.

When introduced, Robert rose from his seat in the back row and smiled shyly, then bowed his head. He said, "'Ello." Two of the more popular girls tittered. Sally and Helen, both blue-eyed blondes with tiny hands and red nail polish, were inseparable and, Jeanot thought, insufferable as well. Neither had ever spoken to him directly, though he'd distinctly heard Sally, the prettier of the two, hum the underpants song, and not just to herself.

When school let out, Jeanot saw that Robert Van der Van was intercepted in the hallway by Timmy Burke, a large and obnoxious kid whose eyes were set too close together. Timmy Burke stood in front of Robert Van der Van and said, "Robert van de Crank? Is that your name? Van de Crank?" Timmy Burke cupped his crotch and added, "You want to see my crank, you homo?"

Robert smiled, faked a move to his right and then darted left, past the bigger boy. He sprinted to the street where an elegant Asian woman sat in a brand new jet black Lincoln. Jeanot, standing alone nearby, thought Robert's mother—if that indeed was who she was—looked like one of the evil women in *Tintin in China;* very out of place yet commanding attention. As Robert climbed into the front seat of the car, he looked back, caught Jeanot's eyes and smiled.

The next morning everyone was referring to him as Robert Japo. It had been Timmy Burke's idea, because, "That little homo is sneaky like a Jap." The name spread around the school like food poisoning did three months before, when the cafeteria served a batch of bad fish-sticks and two-thirds of the teachers and students became violently ill. Jeanot had no idea why Japo was insulting, but knew it had to be, or else the other kids wouldn't be chanting it.

If Robert Van der Van was in any way bothered, it didn't show. He sat at a desk in the middle of the class. He was left-handed and wrote in that weird way lefties forced to sit in righty desks did, arm and wrist making an uncomfortable-looking semi-circle around the page, pen held painfully upright as if stabbing the paper.

Jeanot, three desks away, noticed that in spite of the constricted writing stance, Robert's cursive letters were well-formed, rounded and elegant, just like the ones in the banner above the blackboard. In fact, they were even *better,* because somehow Robert shaded his letters just so and they appeared to be alive, cavorting and dancing on the yellow lined paper. Mrs. Calhoun didn't like it, though. She stood over Robert, took the page he had written upon, and shook her head.

"This is very fancy, Robert. I guess it's the way they teach you in foreign schools." She said 'foreign' as if it were a bad word. "But that's not how we do it here. This is writing, not art class. You shouldn't confuse the two." She dropped the paper back on Robert's desk and it slid to the floor. Someone, Jeanot was pretty sure it was Timmy Burke, muttered, "Japo homo writing," and snickered. Mrs. Calhoun pretended not to hear though she had.

Robert was unfazed. He inspected the paper, folded it in half, then in quarters, and placed it in his leather book bag. He used a wooden ruler to tear a fresh piece of paper from the pad on his desk, squared it and began writing again, the letters shaded and beautiful, skipping across the page like flat stones on still waters.

On the way to recess, Timmy Burke deliberately jostled Robert, then snatched the new sheet of paper from the boy's desk. He passed it around to other boys. "Homo writing," he told everyone. "Japo writes like some weird foreign homo girl."

It took Jeanot a full three days to approach Robert Van der Van, even as the class largely ignored the strange-looking boy though Timmy Burke never failed to make veiled threats of violence.

Actually, it was Robert who came up to Jeanot after school, struck out his hand and said, "You're the French kid. We should be friends." Then he said it in French, "*Tu es Français, n'est ce pas? Soyons amis!*"

Jeanot hadn't heard a child's voice speaking French in such a long time that for a moment he didn't recognize the language. It was at that exact moment that Timmy Burke attacked. The bigger boy shoved Robert hard once, then tripped him. Robert seemed to fold upon himself; his knees buckled and he rolled away in a backward somersault. Timmy launched a kick at the boy's side, and Robert caught the foot, twisted once hard and brought the bigger boy to the ground. Then he stood, dusted off his pants and shirt, and when Timmy charged, deftly stepped aside and launched a high kick that caught the bigger boy square in the chest. Timmy collapsed, the wind knocked out of him. Then Robert grabbed Timmy's shirt with one hand and punched him once hard in the nose with the other. It was over. The fight had lasted less than four seconds, not even long enough for other kids to gather.

As Timmy sat in the dirt, nose bleeding and trying to gather his breath, Robert beckoned to Jeanot, said, "*Allez, viens,*" and then in English, "Would your mother fix us hot chocolate if we go to your house?" They did, Jeanot slightly concerned that his new friend might turn on him and leave him bleeding on the sidewalk too. Robert didn't, however, and Maman fixed them both *chocolat au lait* and *tartines* with strawberry jam.

Since Robert lived just a few houses away, he walked home by himself after thanking Maman in excellent if accented French and bowing slightly at the waist. Maman asked if perhaps the boy had been raised in Indochina, and it turned out he had; his mother was from just outside Saigon and they spoke French at home. Maman was delighted. Another French speaker, not even a kilometer away! She told Robert she would call his mother soon and both families would have dinner together.

In the end, however, Maman and Mai Hanh Nguyen Van der Van had very little in common other than language, and they never became friends. Maman said Robert's mother smelled of garlic and was far too thin as well as snobby in an Oriental sort of way.

Jeanot disagreed. He found Robert's mother soft-spoken and very pleasant, if a little unapproachable. He noticed that Robert called her *Mère* very formally. It reminded him of his own grandfather back in Paris who insisted on being called *grand-père*.

Robert spoke French, English, Indonesian and Vietnamese with fluency and had a smattering of Italian and German. He had started learning Pencak Silat, a martial art, at the age of four and had practiced it every day for three years while in Jakarta. He explained to Jeanot that it had everything to do with letting big boys like Timmy Burke defeat themselves through their own clumsiness. He demonstrated by showing Jeanot how to step aside when someone rushed him, and taught him very basic techniques of self-defense which Jeanot performed alone in his room until he got bored.

KC and Robert got along well, almost too well, thought Jeanot. KC was fascinated by Robert's travels and confided that as soon as she turned fifteen, she was going to run away and go to, well, she wasn't sure. She had heard good things about Paris from Jeanot, but now Indonesia sounded even more tempting. She had saved almost fifty dollars over the last few years and thought that might suffice for a while, but Robert warned her that travel was expensive and that she would need a hundred dollars at least. Jeanot felt a pang of fear and jealousy at the thought of KC moving so far away, perhaps even with Robert, so he suggested that fifty dollars would go a long way in Paris and wove tales of inexpensive movies, circuses, street shows and pastries. He also threw in the services of his Tatie. KC said she'd think about it. She liked the idea of going to France, but having to be with an aged French lady who probably smelled like faded violets wasn't all that tempting.

Chapter 31

In August of that year, Maman's older brother Yves, while on holiday in the seaside town of Bénodet, was hit by a Velo Solex driven by a drunken Breton. The motorized bicycle struck Yves as he was stepping off the sidewalk into Rue Maubière. He fell, hit his head on the cobblestones and died three hours later at the municipal hospital. Maman told Jeanot and Papa about the death of her brother without shedding a tear, though she did sniffle once or twice.

She and Yves had never been close. Jeanot remembered his uncle as tall, elegant, and apparently well-known; a concert pianist who traveled internationally and played for large crowds. He hadn't been a warm man. Jeanot had never particularly liked his uncle, and he was certain that Oncle Yves hadn't been very fond of him, either.

Later that day Maman said, "Yves has records, a lot of them, but they're the works of others. He never composed anything of his own. My father always liked him best. He was the *enfant prodige*. He was to carry on the Février name." She snickered and added, "Of course, he didn't marry, or have children."

Papa threw Maman a warning glance she ignored. "I've always wondered if my father ever figured out Yve's... preferences," she went on. Papa looked nervous, but Jeanot was already well aware that Oncle Yves had been a homosexual. Mathilde had never tired of whispering gleefully about that behind Yves' back.

There was a photo in the living room of Yves with other famous men. Maman had written names on the back; Stravinsky, Cocteau, Ravel, Coco Chanel, and Poulenc.

Maman had also told Papa and Jeanot how unkind her *wünder* brother had been. Oncle Yves had once glanced at one of Maman's paintings of Montmartre and had dismissed it as "daubing on cardboard." Jeanot remembered Oncle Yves calling him *un crétin insoumis* when he once stumbled and caught himself on the side of Yves' Steinway, leaving small fingerprints on the ebony surface.

Papa persuaded Maman she must go back to France for the funeral with Jeanot.

"It will be good for him to go back for a little while. He needs to remember where he comes from. He should see his sisters, and maybe Tatie. She can help take care of him."

Jeanot was happy to go. Although he wouldn't have dared admit it aloud, America had turned out very slightly less magical than he'd hoped, and, every now and then, he missed his first home in France.

The next few days were a flurry of activity with Maman shopping for her daughters; she had decided she must bring them the best America had to offer. She selected dresses and costume jewelry from E. J. Korvette, coats for both from Woodward & Lothrop, blue jeans, movie magazines, a box of assorted Mars candy bars, a history of Washington, D.C., and a picture book of Monticello.

For her father she bought a green, blue and red regimental striped tie from Murphy, and for Tatie a mauve hat with a veil like the one Mamie Eisenhower wore in a recent *Look* magazine interview. Since Maman liked the hat, she also purchased one for herself in pale blue and without a veil. She explained to Jeanot that she found veils morbid and funereal.

They took the train from Washington to New York's Grand Central Station, then a taxi to LaGuardia airport. The plane, an Air France Caravelle, flew from New York to Reykjavik, refueled, and seven hours later landed at Le Bourget Airport outside of Paris.

During the flight, Jeanot read magazines, slept, ate and got a second helping of dessert from the smiling stewardess.

Maman complained of the time change. It had been four in the afternoon when the Caravelle left Reykjavik, and six in the evening when they arrived in Paris. She was exhausted, she said; her ears had not recovered from the landing and take-off in Iceland and now pained her. She was partially deaf, struggling with too much luggage. She told him she thought she'd lost her passport, then found it in the pocket of her jacket. The Mamie Eisenhower hat was askew on her head and Jeanot noticed no other woman had a hat even remotely similar.

She had told Jeanot someone might be at Bourget to greet them. Perhaps, she suggested, Françoise and Madeleine had come in a taxi, but as it turned out, there were no familiar faces in the waiting crowd at the gate.

Jeanot was struck by the French faces; the men jowly, unshaven, Gauloises and Gitanes hanging from thin lips. The women were slimmer than Americans, their hair long and wavy, cheekbones high and taut, aquiline noses and thin eyebrows. The air smelled of cigarette smoke and diesel with a faint overlay of body odor, *eau de toilette*, strong coffee and garlic.

They went through customs without having their bags opened and the *douanier* welcomed them back to France. Maman smiled, said, *"Merci Monsieur!"* and with those two words they both slid back effortlessly into being French in a country created by and for them. They took the metro, changed trains twice, alit at the Parc Monceau stop where a young man in his early twenties insisted on carrying two of their suitcases all the way to the entrance of 3, Rue de la Terrasse. Maman tried to give him a ten Franc note but he raised his hands in mock shock and shook his head. *"Mais voyons, Madame! Il n'en n'est question, ce fût mon plaisir!"*

They paused before ringing the bell, both wondering if the irascible Sergei Kharkov, the building's White Russian concierge, might still be on duty. They had only been gone a year, but it seemed decades, centuries.

Jeanot saw immediately that the street hadn't changed. The *boulangerie* was where it was supposed to be, as were the flower shop and the épicerie. There was a new coat of varnish on the giant *portes cochères* leading into his building's inner courtyard where, generations ago, large-wheeled coaches pulled by teams of horses had been hitched. The hitching rings were still mortared into the *pavés*.

The building wall at sidewalk level was stained from countless urinary visitations by Soldat, the three-legged dog owned by Oncle Répaud.

The past washed over Jeanot; a torrent of memories and emotions, feelings barely suppressed. He looked down, saw the faintest trace of letters scratched into the wall, MTHHF, Marie Thérèse Henriette Hughette Février. Those were his Maman's initials etched into the surface of the wall when she was barely seven years old. Years before, she had told him of scratching at the mortar over several days with a teaspoon filched from the silver drawer. This had been her response to her father's admonition that she be a good girl and stay silent in her room for hours on end as Yves practiced his endless piano scales.

The initials were almost gone, MTHHF worn away by wind and weather and diesel fumes and the eroding cacophony of invading armies.

The Germans, Jeanot knew, had never discovered Rue de la Terrasse; it was too small, too narrow, too grey, and so they had taken over better buildings overlooking the Parc Monceau. His grandparents and uncle had weathered the war in style and comfort while Maman and her first husband had fled the country for Algeria when the Germans arrived in Paris.

Maman opened the door that had been cut into the *portes cochères*. The concierge's window was closed and curtained, so she rapped on it. A light appeared, then the curtains were drawn back and the window thrown open. Sergei Kharkov, frowning, older and thinner than the last time they had seen him, said, *"C'est l'heure du déjeuner!"* He pointed to a sign hung on the doorknob that did indeed say the concierge was at lunch. He was about to shut the window when he looked at Marité. *"Mon Dieu! Madame St. Paul! C'est bien vous?"*

Chapter 32

Jeanot listened, sitting on a stiff chair that had horsehair cushions which scratched his bare legs. The concierge's *loge* was how he remembered it, and Kharkov's Russian accent was exactly the same—thick and heavy as curdling cream.

"God in all His malevolence has visited our building not once, but twice in less than a week," Kharkov said. First, He had taken Monsieur Yves, struck by a drunken lout in the middle of the day; such a talented young man, one could weep over the loss. Then, this very morning, God had taken Madame's father, Monsieur Léopold. The concierge described how the old man had crashed to the floor after a *petit déjeuner* of coffee with scalded milk and toasted *tartines au beurre,* followed by a dram of Armagnac to thin the blood and bolster circulation.

Louise, Monsieur Léopold's maid, he went on, had heard the dull sound of her long-time employer's collapse, and she was now in the same hospital as the late Monsieur Léopold, though of course she was alive in a shared room and Léopold was neither. How unfair was that, Kharkov asked, that the lowly maid should survive while the master succumbed?

By the time the doctors and the ambulance arrived, Kharkov lamented, it was too late. Monsieur Léopold had had his last *petit déjeuner*, and what, Kharkov asked Maman, would happen to them now? What? With Monsieur Yves and Monsieur Léopold so cruelly taken, would Madame St. Paul inherit the building, and would she keep Sergei Kharkov, the most loyal of employees, because certainly now was when a faithful concierge's assistance in matters great and small was not just necessary but absolutely required, didn't she agree?

Maman, stunned by the news, sat in the *loge* living room on a spindly chair with uneven legs. Kharkov had given her a strong cup of black tea with two cubes of brown sugar and a Russian cigarette which remained unlit in her right hand. She glanced at Jeanot without seeing him. He knew instinctively that his Maman was afraid to take the elevator (had it been repaired?) up to the fifth floor because if this was true, if Oncle Yves was dead and Grand-Père Léopold was dead and Emma, who had passed away some years ago, if Emma was *still* dead, then she, his Maman, new resident of the State of Maryland in America, owner, with Papa, of a sunny house in Chevy Chase with a yard and two cars, two American cars that both ran, and a closetful of nice dresses from Woodward & Lothrop and EJ Korvettes, she… It was too much, Jeanot knew.

Maman nodded at the concierge who had been hovering, lighter in hand. He lit her cigarette; she inhaled deeply and coughed. She took a sip of tea, then another and gathered herself.

She told Jeanot they would not spend the night at 3, Rue de la Terrasse. They would get a small room in a two-star hotel a block away. She would call Papa in America. She would call Françoise and Madeleine. She would call her father's attorney, what was his name, Maitre something-or-other, Maitre Malpassant. First, however, she and Jeanot had to go to the hospital—which hospital? She asked Kharkov the address. Hôpital Bretonneau on rue Joseph de Maistre, he informed her. Could he get her a taxi, and could she leave her suitcases here? Yes, assuredly; it would be his pleasure and duty to guard her luggage with his life, said the concierge, and Jeanot, looking at the Russian, knew he meant it.

The next day, Maman clipped the obituary notices that appeared in both *Le Monde* and *Le Figaro*, with Yves' death notice in the papers on the same page as that of his father. She read them aloud to Jeanot.

The writer for *Le Monde* said Yves was a genius and his father no less so for not being as celebrated. *Le Figaro* had more praise for Léopold, comparing him favorably to Maeterlinck, and pronouncing Yves "the darling of the ermine set." Both newspapers called father and son men of great musical appetites, and *Le Monde* noted that Yves had never married while Léopold had, twice. In all, there were more than 300 lines of print devoted to the Févriers, *père et fils*. Nowhere was it mentioned that Yves had a surviving sister and Léopold a daughter. Jeanot asked why that was, and Maman had no answer, save, "Maybe they forgot."

Soon, it was over. Both Grand-père and Oncle Yves were entombed in the family crypt at Père Lachaise cemetery, Grand-père above Oncle Yves. Before and after the memorial service, Jeanot had been hugged and patted on the head a hundred times or more. Maman had shaken countless hands and said her wrists pained her; there'd been so many embraces she claimed to smell like a miasma of perfumes, good and bad—but mostly bad. The last guest had left the reception held at the fifth floor apartment Grand-père had occupied and Oncle Yves had dominated. Louise the maid, back from the hospital herself and strangely cheerful, was gathering glasses, plates, teaspoons and cloth napkins in a large tin tub normally used to hand-wash Oncle Yves' socks and undergarment. Maman and Jeanot stood in the middle of the living room festooned with Oncle Yves' awards, framed scores of Grand-père's operas, dark paintings from insignificant artists, and vases that had never held flowers. They both stared at a large and ugly portrait of Grand-père with his second wife, Emma, standing stiffly side by side. Maman said, "I think in twenty-three years of marriage, no part of either of their bodies ever touched the other." Her eyes teared for the first time and Jeanot wrapped his arms around her waist.

She pointed to the statuettes and sconces and threadbare Oriental rugs. "There's not a single photo of me, not one picture of their three grandchildren. How can that be?"

She began to shake, cry, then laugh. She summoned Louise, with whom she had been closer as a child than either parent and held onto her. The elderly Bretonne woman, now frail and as pale as her always white apron, held Maman in her arms and whispered, *"Ca ira, ma petite. Ca ira…"* Then she beckoned Jeanot into the embrace as well.

Maman's last act of the day was to tell Sergei Kharkov that he would remain as concierge, that she planned to sell the building but would make sure his tenure was honored by the purchaser. Jeanot saw that Kharkov, proud White Russian that he was, allowed a single tear to moisten his creased left cheek.

Jeanot asked Maman where Tatie was, and she told him Tatie was recuperating from pneumonia in a hospital near the hotel where she summered in Montreux. Jeanot remembered Oncle Yves once announcing to a room full of friends and family that he wouldn't deign to even attend Tatie's funeral, and Jeanot thought it somehow fitting that Tatie couldn't attend his. He asked if they would see her before they left, and Maman said no, probably not.

Françoise and Madeleine had not come to the service, and Maman hissed, "That *salope!* That Mamé." Jeanot pretended not to hear the reference to Maman's first husband's new wife.

The girls met them in the lobby of the hotel near the Parc Monceau. Madeleine, eighteen and just returned from London where she had spent a month attending a prominent bilingual secretarial school, mocked Maman's French accent when, at Madeleine's insistence, the two conversed in English.

"You speak like an American and your *th* sounds are all wrong, *mater*," Madeleine declared in what Jeanot could barely identify as English. "It is inelegant and hard to understand your accent."

He noticed Madeleine had switched from *maman* to *mater*. Maman tried several times to hug her daughter, who resisted.

Françoise was somewhat friendlier, and within minutes announced she would marry Vincent, the young man she had introduced to the family a year earlier. Maman's lips went hard. She said nothing, then reconsidered. "You're fifteen," she smiled.

"In three years, then, when I'm eighteen and he'll be twenty-one." Françoise paused, added, "You were married at sixteen…" It was a mild accusation, a statement of fact.

"But then of course, you left him," Madeleine added, in English.

Before Maman had time to build a response in any language, Vincent entered the hotel lobby. He wore a deep blue suit with a red tie and was smoking an American cigarette. Françoise rushed to him and kissed him on the cheek, which the boy seemed to dislike. *"Maman, tu te souviens de Vincent!"*

Vincent stood stiffly at attention, blew out a cloud of blue smoke and bowed slightly at the waist. Maman offered him a blank look. The young man glanced at her, annoyed, and took a step back.

They went to lunch, the five of them, at a bistro on the Boulevard Malesherbes and Jeanot thought perhaps Vincent's presence made things easier even though he smoked throughout the meal, which was slightly annoying. Vincent spoke mostly of himself and his accomplishments, which impressed Françoise and bored Madeleine. He had recently performed a series of concerts in a tour of *villes de provinces* and great things were predicted, he told the four. Ten months earlier, he had placed second in the international Mozart competition held yearly in Spain for young pianists. He had astonished the judges with his rendition of the Sonata K545. "It is popularly considered easy," Vincent said, between puffs, "but knowledgeable people recognize it is an extremely difficult piece to perform." He raised his hands and widened his fingers to proudly show the distance he could span on a keyboard, then explained that he should have won first prize but the Spanish judge had voted for a demonstrably lesser candidate from Catalan.

They ate chicken with *pommes frites.* Jeanot noticed that Vincent's wine glass was never empty. He drank almost two carafes of *vin ordinaire* by himself and by dessert was lecturing them on why the late Oncle Yves' work deserved some but not much respect.

"He had a good grasp of some of Poulenc's work, but it was rather pedestrian, perhaps overly familiar. I would have told him so had we met…"

The following day Françoise came by herself and with Jeanot and Maman walked through the Jardin du Luxembourg, one of Jeanot's favorite places in his earlier Parisian life. Madeleine, Françoise told Maman, was not at a work interview as she had claimed, but out with a new boyfriend, a married man twice her age whom she had seen several times last week and who gave her inexpensive jewelry and a silk scarf from Hermès.

Françoise reported this with a certain amount of venom and Maman asked if Vincent ever gave her anything. Françoise was silent for a moment, then said, "No. But he's very poor. He can't afford to buy gifts."

Maman said, "He smokes expensive cigarettes."

Françoise shrugged, and during a twenty-minute walk through the park, interrupted by Jeanot feeding the carps, Maman drew from her daughter details of the relationship with Vincent, who lived with an aged father in a walk-up off Rue St. Dennis.

Vincent seldom offered to buy coffee or a pastry, Françoise confessed. Their rare outings were paid for by Françoise's meager allowance, and she often did his and his father's laundry and ironing at their home when she was not at the conservatory taking classes. She also cooked, cleaned their place once a week, and was a better pianist, she thought. She believed Vincent might be jealous. Still, she loved him madly. He was so handsome and smart that sometimes her head swam. She wanted children with him as soon as possible, and she would encourage his studies and piano practice.

She then told Maman and Jeanot a secret. Vincent was somewhat lazy. He often did not practice at all, whereas she spent an average of four hours daily on the hard piano bench. He claimed to have reached a plateau and this worried her. She had known very gifted young musicians who were at their best in their teens, and then did not have the wherewithal to graduate from child prodigy to working musician. She was concerned by the road Vincent seemed to be taking.

Maman listened quietly. Jeanot kicked at stones and sent them skittering down the park lane.

Maman reached into her purse, found ten twenty dollar bills and pressed them into Françoise's hands. Françoise looked at them, and Jeanot wondered for the first time about French currency versus dollar bills. The French money was large, colorful with sharply defined portraits of historical figures. Dollars were green, almost grey, and all the same size, which made no sense at all. He thought French money would be happily spent, all those colors changing hands and bringing smiles. Dollars looked like bills that had been hoarded by tightwads.

Maman said, *"Tiens, prends ca..."* and Françoise did take them, folding the money carefully into her small white purse. Then the three walked to a Crédit Lyonnais bank and exchanged the money for a pile of French currency that widened Françoise's eyes.

They passed the afternoon together and later Maman called her ex-husband, Marcel, to ask if Françoise might spend the night with them at the hotel. It was a brief conversation. Marcel refused.

Later that evening Jeanot and Babette met. *"Alors,"* she said, "You've become an American? You *look* like an American."

Jeanot stared at his best friend of not that long ago. Babette had changed. Her hair was shorter, her lips a red he didn't remember, and there were now slight curves to her chest and hips. She was wearing a well-fitting skirt and a white blouse with a beige sweater thrown casually across her shoulders. She was taller, too, taller than he was, and she wore an expression of vague but unmistakable authority.

"So what is it like, being *un Americain?*"

Jeanot shrugged. "I don't know. It's not that different. We eat more meat. Papa doesn't like the wine and Maman says the cheese tastes like wax."

"I have a boyfriend," Babette said. *"Un petit ami.* His name is Lionel. He's sixteen and goes to the Lycée St. Louis. Maman does not like him."

Jeanot would not be outdone. "I have a *petite amie* too. She's American and blonde. Maman likes her a lot."

Babette made a face. "It doesn't count if your Maman likes her. The whole point of a *petit ami* is to annoy your parents."

That made no sense. "Why?"

Babette wore an exasperated look. "*Mon Dieu! Tu n'as pas changé!*" She peered at him closely. "Have you gotten taller? I can't tell."

He had, he knew. Papa had measured him monthly and drawn a line on a wall in the basement. He was almost fifteen centimeters taller than when he'd left Paris. Could Babette really not have noticed? Of course, she had grown too, even more so than he had.

Jeanot said, "The cars are much bigger. And we have a house. And I have a lot of friends," he lied. "*Beaucoup d'amis.*"

He could tell he was losing her. "Maman and Papa have big parties where a lot of people come. I have a friend who has a racing bicycle, and he stole money. Or...I had a friend."

Babette's gaze swept the surroundings, stopped to watch a young man striding by. She smiled at him. The man strode past her without a glance. She frowned.

The four had walked from the Bonjean's building to a nearby café and Jeanot and Babette were eating ice cream; their mothers occupied an adjacent table, each with a glass of wine.

Babette looked momentarily sad, and then brightened. "My parents are getting a divorce. Maman says she's tired of a husband who sleeps with all the *putains* in town. Maman says that when the divorce is final, we'll go to Nice for a month to visit her sister, and then we'll come back and get an apartment in the 17th arrondissement. That's a *good* neighborhood."

Jeanot knew this too. The apartment on the rue de la Terrasse where he'd lived was in the 17th.

"We live in a good neighborhood too, in America," he said. "There are trees and squirrels and Papa grows tomatoes."

Now she looked at him oddly. "*Pardon?*"

"Where we live, we have a yard with a big tree in the middle and there are squirrels there."

Babette nodded and stood up. She smiled, bent down to peck him on the cheek and went to whisper something in her maman's ear. Madame Bonjean smiled and also stood up, rummaged in her purse, found a bill and dropped it on the table. Then all four were standing and hugging, and as Babette and her mother walked away, Maman said, *"C'est triste.* I invited them to come and see us in America, but they probably won't." Then she turned to Jeanot with a smile. "And how was Babette? She's turned into a lovely young woman."

Jeanot shrugged. Was that what had happened? He had no idea.

Chapter 33

Jeanot traveled back to the United States alone, feeling both very proud and slightly concerned. He worried that the pilot might get lost during the flight, might land in some remote city or even worse, a foreign land. The legalities surrounding the deaths of Maman's brother and father in the same two weeks would take time to sort out, and both his Maman and Papa agreed he couldn't miss much more school.

Maman packed his suitcase and gave him a paper bag with sandwiches, two bananas, several slices of saucisson wrapped in yesterday's *Le Monde,* and a number of handwritten notes he was to hand to flight officials if he got confused, scared, lost, tearful or thirsty. They took a taxi cab to Le Bourget airport, where Maman hugged him a half-dozen times and tearfully handed him over to a smiling Air France stewardess; a short, attractive uniformed lady with brilliant red hair who called him *mon petit* and took his hand. The woman reassured Maman that she would not lose sight of him during the entire flight, and she did not. They waited for the plane to board in the lounge she said was for very important people, though to Jeanot the other men and women there looked largely average.

Jeanot slept most of the way to Reykjavik. The stewardess snuck him into the first class section and he reread the new *Tintin, Spirou* and *Mickey* magazines bought at a kiosk on Avenue Courcelle. One hour into the flight, the stewardess gave him half-a-glass of champagne, then another half. He ate a banana and a sandwich, then was given a *mousse au chocolat* from the first class menu. He fell back asleep and dreamed of Oncle Yves being lectured on music by Françoise's boyfriend, Vincent.

The jolt of the airplane landing in Iceland woke him. He disembarked with the stewardess and accompanied her to the duty-free shop where she bought liquor and American cigarettes, as well as some American candy bars that she gave him. They took off again and landed without mishap in New York and the Air France lady saw him placed on a shuttle that arrived at National Airport at 10 o'clock at night. Jeanot felt slightly nauseous when the DC-3 touched down. Another stewardess escorted him from the plane, and Papa was there at the gate to gather him. They drove back together to the house in Maryland.

Life returned to normal as much as it could without Maman around. To get home quicker in the afternoon, Papa took a cab from work rather than the bus. He arranged for the Polish widow who lived across the street to keep Jeanot at her house until he returned.

They ate out most nights, since Papa's only talent in the kitchen was omelets, and Jeanot was not fond of eggs. It was mostly Hot Shoppes or Howard Johnson. Both restaurants had large booths with vinyl-covered upholstery, orange and cream motifs, heavyish waitresses and similar menus. Hot Shoppes, however, had Teen Twists which Jeanot favored, not because he liked the sandwich so much, but because it implied he was a teenager, which he was not. Sometimes Papa invited KC and Robert, and the two boys always scrambled, competing to be the one sitting next to the girl. Papa pretended not to notice.

Papa appeared to be fascinated by the children's conversation. After ordering the meals, he would fall silent and let the talking go where it might. Jeanot and Robert went to the same school; KC, a grade higher, did not. They compared notes on the food in the cafeteria, the curriculum, recess activities, other kids, and the habits of teachers. Jeanot could see his Papa was astonished to see how quickly his son was learning English, so he made it a point to pepper his conversation with grown up words and phrases like, "I should hope so," and "I'm aware of that," and, "Really? Who would have thought?"

Jeanot was increasingly fascinated by Robert, who was always questioning and seeking answers. Travel and life overseas had broadened Robert's knowledge while somehow preserving his innocence. Robert did not hold grudges; indeed, he and Timmy Burke, whom he had fought and vanquished effortlessly, had become, if not friends, at least not enemies. Jeanot had told his Papa that Timmy seemed a lot less fearsome since his encounter with Robert. Perhaps, Jeanot thought, being half-Oriental had given Robert something indefinable, a measure of peace and acceptance. Robert never seemed sad, but he never seemed completely happy either. He didn't brood, but he seldom laughed out loud as other children did. The family had met both Robert's Vietnamese mother and his American father, a tall angular man who worked at the Department of State. It seemed, however, that Robert was almost on his own. He came and went from his house at will. He often ate with the St. Paul family in the evening and then walked home unaccompanied after giving Maman a small bow and complimenting her cooking. He had a gift for making himself belong wherever he was, and Maman mentioned she thought Robert might become either a great diplomat or a great white-collar criminal; she did not laugh when she said it. Jeanot from the start had noticed Maman was charmed by Robert's demeanor and manners. She believed the obvious French influence on the Vietnamese played a role in the boy's superb upbringing and politeness. To her, Robert was proof that colonialism worked.

KC was the wisest of the three with comments that occasionally made Papa blink. She was sure the world was going to end in a matter of months, if not days. She believed in reincarnation. She and Robert, she informed Jeanot, had a long discussion on the subject over ice cream Sundaes while Jeanot was in Paris. She was certain all her brothers, except the smallest one, were going to Hell. She readily accepted the paradox in her thinking, announcing, when challenged, that, "Some of us will come back, others won't." When Papa asked her what she thought about the future of the four of them at the table, she said, without a hint of humor, "We are going to order dessert." Pressed further, she gave Papa a long appraising look and nodded. "We're going to be all right."

For Jeanot, even after the funerals, death was still an unclear concept. On the one hand, it was awful and red and bloody like the dog who'd been hit by a police car earlier that year. The neighborhood kids had gathered around the dead animal, the braver ones poking at it with a stick even as the policeman tried to shoo them away. Some of the children had cried and one boy with a notably weak stomach had thrown up on his own shoes. That kind of death, Jeanot thought, was probably reserved for anything or anyone that played in the street.

For humans, though, it meant, at its simplest, that *you were no longer there.* Dédé was *no longer there.* Jeanot understood that his Oncle Yves was also *no longer there,* no great loss. Since the two deaths in France had happened so close in time, Jeanot wondered whether Oncle Yves and *Grand-père* had perhaps decided to go away together, a father and son journey to an unclear destination. Papa said he thought this was a good explanation. Papa himself was not an advocate of heaven, hell, or any place in between, he told Jeanot. No longer being *there* was as acceptable a notion as any.

KC's notions—somewhat similar to Jeanot's if a bit more confusing—were reassuring. All things alive came back after death, but in some other form of being. She had read it in a book and thought about it a lot and it made perfect sense. She would return as a squirrel since she liked climbing trees and looked forward to defying gravity. Jeanot thought a squirrel was too likely to be squashed by a car like the dog, and so he opted to be a buffalo. Robert shrugged and told them if he had to come back, he'd like to do so as himself, since he was perfectly satisfied with his life. Papa said the basic logic of KC's reasoning was inescapable.

That night, at least, KC had indeed read the future. They all had dessert.

Chapter 34

The year following The Deaths, Jeanot's family prospered and became champions of the American Dream.

They moved to a larger house on the same street, but two blocks away. It was red brick, three floors including the finished basement, with a detached two-car garage and a long driveway that wound from the street and through the half-acre back yard. Papa added a new kitchen—he did not do the work himself, but took a week off to supervise—and transformed the old one into an elegant wet bar where bottles were stacked on shelves ingeniously tilted to display the labels. Jeanot helped. He learned how to measure twice and cut once, how to drill, hammer, but mostly how to carry. He carried two-by-fours from Hechinger's to the roof rack Papa had installed on the Lincoln. He wrestled large sheets of plywood and boxes of tiles. He helped Papa put down a brick patio, using sticks and string to keep the rows even. Then he swept cement and sand into the cracks between the bricks and sprayed everything down with water. He helped plant trees in the new backyard, and dug out a ten-by-ten feet square of dirt so Papa could grow potatoes. Maman found the whole idea of Papa gardening hilarious, and she laughed even harder when rabbits discovered the potato patch and ruined it.

They bought a large washing machine and a dryer from Sears, and installed them in the utility room. Also from Sears came a television set larger and heavier even than the one in the Post's house. It took two strong men to wrestle the thing into the living room, install a massive antenna on the roof and run wires along the gutter downspout and into the living room.

KC and Robert came over often and had sleepovers. Jeanot's room was large enough that they could all sleep on the floor on rubber air mattresses, and they stayed up with flashlights, telling each other scary stories. KC had the best ones, almost always involving a strong and lovely girl surrounded by boorish boys. The girl would be rescued by ghosts summoned from the nether worlds, mean ghosts who took no pity on the wailings of their boy victims.

"The ghosts have claws," KC said. "They rip your throat and your stomach, and leave the guts behind."

Jeanot and Robert looked at each other.

After a moment's thought, KC added, "Actually, they rip out the stomachs first and leave the intestines all over the place, so that they can still hear their victims screaming before the throats come out. Then, the ghosts eat the boys' hearts."

Jeanot asked, "Do ghosts eat hearts?"

Robert nodded. "In Indonesia, they have ghosts in the jungle. They look like large brown monkeys."

Jeanot thought KC's gut-ripping ghosts were a lot more interesting than Robert's ghost monkeys, but he didn't say so. He did add that, "In Paris, the ghosts are called *fan-*"

"I wasn't finished," interrupted KC, glaring. Her face looked even more beautifully terrible in the dim flashlight glow.

Jeanot sighed and subsided.

KC continued. "Then the ghosts draped the boys' guts over the trees in their backyard, and wild dogs came and ate them." Smiling, she stopped and looked at Jeanot and Robert, who were now both staring, completely aghast. "And those trees," she hissed, "were the exact same trees as in YOUR BACKYARD, JEANOT!"

Robert squeaked.

"Fuck," exhaled Jeanot.

KC raised an eyebrow at him. "You kiss your *Maman* with that mouth?"

Maman and Papa bought an acre of wooded land near the Chesapeake Bay where other French families spent their summer weekends. They went camping there, which delighted Jeanot. Papa was less enthusiastic. It reminded him a bit too much of the war, he said. At night, on several occasions he woke up disoriented and frightened. Wartime horrors were still fresh in his mind, and a half-dozen times Maman woke him as he was thrashing and whimpering in their double sleeping bag.

The land was hilly, so with shovels and spades they dug out platforms in the sandy soil. They dug two of them, one large enough for Maman and Papa's army surplus tent, and a smaller area for Jeanot, who had demanded and gotten his own pup tent.

Into this sunny paradise rode Justine and Johnny Coachman, ensconced in an air-conditioned silver Mercedes Benz 300SC Cabriolet, a *German* automobile amidst the St. Pauls' Lincoln, the diplomats' and journalists' Peugeots, Renaults and Citroëns. The Boche car was driven proudly by a Francophone American and his gorgeous Parisian wife. The people stared.

It was Jeanot who first saw them drive in on the rutted track fronting the campsite. He was squatting by the road inspecting a particularly large mosquito bite when the car stopped and the driver asked him, "Does Simone Rubinstein camp here?"

Jeanot said yes, she did. In fact, he'd helped her set up a tent a hundred yards away and had dug out a small fire pit. The Coachmans were her guests.

Madame Rubinstein was a survivor of Treblinka and Professor of French literature at American University. She told Maman that she'd met the Coachmans once or twice, had found the wife pleasant and the American husband somewhat intriguing, and had proffered an invitation to the Bay without much thinking about it. That the couple came at all was a surprise; that they came in a Mercedes was astounding.

The Coachmans had three blond kids, two boys and an impossibly perfect adolescent girl, and they set their coolers, towels, umbrellas and beach chairs not fifteen feet from where Maman and Papa were basking.

The first weekend, Jeanot noted that the Coachmans kept largely to themselves. Madame Rubinstein told Papa she was mortally embarrassed by their lack of automotive savoir-faire. She left soon after her guests arrived and did not return for several weeks, even though she'd told Maman she had been contemplating renting a bungalow situated mere feet from the beach for the entire season.

No one spoke to the Coachmans, but it appeared as if the snubbing had no impact on the family of five. Jeanot tried to greet one of the boys in French and proffered a perfectly intact horseshoe crab shell, but the Coachman boy either did not speak French or pretended not to.

The Coachmans returned the next week, this time driving an Aston Martin DB2/4 Mark II, an imposing and ridiculously expensive motorcar, Papa explained, that at least was made in an Allied country. Papa told Maman this was the exact same car as was driven by King Baudouin of Belgium.

In the end, it was the ring that first caught Maman's attention and opened the portals. It was monstrously large. It glinted like a breakaway star, a diamond surrounded by orbiting planets of no lesser value. What horrified Maman was the fact that Madame Coachman was wearing it so nonchalantly, *at the beach, where it might drop from her finger and be lost forever!* Madame Coachman waved her hand, hello, in Maman's direction and the ring's brilliance was eye-searing. The impossibly perfect girl approached Jeanot who, standing at surf's edge, was poking at a dying jellyfish with the remnant of a clam shell. Monsieur Coachman poured a glass of wine into a stemmed goblet, raised it in Papa's direction and said, "*Venez boire un coup avec nous!*"

It was all so irresistibly choreographed, so perfectly natural and beckoning that both Maman and Papa rose as if hypnotized, wiped the sand from their legs and backsides, and went to meet the Coachmans.

The girl (her name was Sylvie, she was 12 and wore a two-piece bathing suit), kicked sand at the jellyfish and buried it, which was exactly what Jeanot had been planning to do himself had he not been staring at her startling blue eyes.

The next weekend over lunch on a picnic table, Monsieur Coachman revealed that he did not actually own either a Mercedes or an Aston Martin, as he had borrowed both vehicles from his brother Woody, who ran a luxury car sales establishment in Rahway, New Jersey. Monsieur Coachman hinted the dealership catered largely to New York Mafiosis. That Saturday morning, the Coachmans arrived in a splendidly sleek black Citroën DS just like, said Papa, the one the French Ambassador in Washington owned. Monsieur Coachman spent the better part of that Sunday giving rides to people who wanted to test the car's revolutionary suspension system, and all agreed that this was indeed, finally, representative of the best that French engineering had to offer. Jeanot watched all this with casual interest.

He had almost befriended Sylvie. She was a shy girl who shrugged a lot and seemed uninterested in anything her brothers did, and to Jeanot's delight, she spoke French. She adored her mother, had mixed feelings about her father and did not like cars. Jeanot could not help but try to compare her to two of the most important women in his life, Babette and KC, and came to the conclusion no comparison could be made.

Since the family had moved, KC came over less. Robert seldom visited anymore, and Jeanot was certain his two best friends had become best friends with each other. Sylvie did not have the bright presence of KC, but she was interesting in a quieter, subtler way. She told Jeanot that though she liked *him,* she generally had nothing to do with boys. They were gross, boring, loud, stupid and grabby, traits she found generally repugnant. Her brothers seldom even talked with her, which was fine.

Jeanot thought the Coachman parents seemed too perfect, and noted the children seemed too well brought up in spite of Sylvie's opinions of her brothers. Maman told Papa that neither Coachman boy spoke French, though they appeared to understand it. Sylvie was fluent, and ignored the older French boys there who were studying for next year's Baccalauréat at the Lycé Francais in downtown Washington. She dragged Jeanot up and down the beach, ordering him to pick up the carcasses of blue crabs and other rotting maritime fauna she wanted very gingerly to inspect.

So the Coachmans, Johnny, Justine and Sylvie (the boys were Randall and Richard and no one cared which was which; both answered to either name) became accepted if not embraced by the weekend community. Monsieur Coachman had an easy touch at the barbecue; even his *boudin* was brazed to perfection. Madame Coachman was a make-up expert who claimed to have learned her skills at the Comédie Française. No one really believed her, but she did accomplish wonders with mascara and the slightest hint of rouge. Sylvie broke young hearts, including Jeanot's.

Papa and some other men fished, catching skates that locals refused to eat but which Maman and the other women cooked with black butter, garlic and scallions. They ate crabs by the bushel and braved the mosquitoes to dance in the night under the stars. There were automobile rallies, trips to nearby Annapolis, contests of every sort, bridge during rainy afternoons, and horseback riding. Jeanot was placed on a large horse called Crackerjack that refused to follow the simplest commands and trotted along the trail as Jeanot bounced uncomfortably in the western saddle. Sylvie rode gracefully, and her brothers yelled as they raced along, leaving Jeanot literally in the dust.

The session on horses reminded him of the cowboys and Indians diorama on the card table in Paris, and it surprised him how quickly he'd let go of that passion. Here he was, on a horse, like his former heroes, and he was bored, uncomfortable, sweaty, mosquito-bitten and sore. The cowboy hat he'd worn so proudly as a child was now in the back of a closet, and somewhere he'd misplaced the holster and cap gun bought in Paris and shipped to America.

Families slept six to a room or tent on inflatable mattresses. They burned and tanned and peeled and thought it was the best of all worlds. They were French, happy, well-fed and well-off, and in America.

The French camping colony seldom mixed with others. A horde of Italians had taken over a section of the beach mere yards away. They played volleyball and soccer and were loud. Maman thought the men's bathing suits were far too brief and commented on the women's makeup. She herself was now wearing a one-piece suit, having decided a bikini no longer fit her style or social standing.

There were the minor scandals found in any summer community. Madame Coachman, who claimed to be writing a book, kept notes that she willingly shared with anyone interested, be they adult or child. Jeanot learned through her that a lower level consular employee was discovered in a double sleeping bag with a woman not his wife, and that the agricultural attaché of a lesser Francophone nation stood accused of exposing himself in the women's shower. The attaché denied it but was never seen again. Two young men whose deep friendship was suspect proved the suspicions true, though in truth no one really cared. A woman almost drowned but didn't, and another suffered from sunstroke. A tent caught on fire, a car was driven into the surf, and a Sears & Roebuck fiberglass outboard boat was run aground. Simone Rubinstein was hospitalized for 48 hours with poison ivy covering sixty percent of her body. During a spirited game of hide and seek, one of the Coachman boys hid in the trunk of Maman's Lincoln and fell asleep. He was not missed until later that night and found after a half-hearted search.

There was a party on the last Saturday of the season and some sixty people drank one hundred and ten bottles of wine. The girl-friend of an Agence France Press journalist drove her tiny Renault into a tree, and a fat man, an uninvited Swiss, climbed on to the roof of a cabin, jumped off, and did it again, the second time breaking both ankles. Jeanot spirited a bottle of not bad Médoc from under a picnic table and he and Sylvie drank it together. Jeanot did not throw up that night, a sure sign, he decided, that adulthood was fast approaching.

Chapter 35

Throughout the summer and into the fall of that year, Maman had been trying to find a man for Madame Rubinstein, Treblinka survivor, poison ivy victim, professor of French literature and author of several well-selling college textbooks on the French language.

Madame Rubinstein was a small and busy woman, a childless war widow with close-cropped hair, largish ears and breasts, and a taste for heavy jewelry. Amazingly, her father, Raymond Rubinstein, had been the oboe player in the production of one of Grand-Père Leopold's opera, *Mona Vana*, which had met with little success in Paris between the wars. This unlikely happenstance had forged a strong bond; Madame Rubinstein had become one of Maman's very best friends. Papa told Jeanot he liked Madame Rubinstein as well, though he found her sharp-tongued and a bit unprincipled in her amatory habits.

The two women met once a week, lunched, gossiped, shopped or went to the movies. Madame Rubinstein refused to play bridge, having, she said, watched her death camp guards enjoy the game. She always thought it somewhat *louche* that Maman was so attached to the pastime, but their friendship, once established, was unshakable.

Madame Rubinstein was not particularly interested in meeting a man. She professed to know many, most of them married, and had, she said, been with some and not with others. She owned a lovely home near American University and had furnished it with an admirable collection of Louis XVI and Napoleon III furniture. She had pointed out to the St. Pauls a small Modigliani and an even smaller Picasso sketch of a bull done on a dinner napkin. The piece, she said, was dashed off in 1919 by the artist to pay for a luncheon in Nice. It was discreetly framed and unobtrusive on a sideboard, though it was the first thing to which she drew her new friends' attention.

The house, she would occasionally tell guests, had once been the main feature in a serious European architecture magazine, which made Maman somewhat envious. The cover of the magazine had also been framed and placed in the downstairs powder room directly facing the toilet, a masterly move that somewhat annoyed Maman, since, she said, it displayed tact and discretion while guaranteeing a captive audience.

Maman had introduced Madame Rubinstein to single male diplomats, businessmen, restaurateurs, junior level consular officers, lawyers, real estate agents, two dentists and one French urologist who had come to America to study advanced surgical techniques, and had stayed. There had been soldiers and sailors and a pilot for Air France, as well as a highly decorated officer who had served in the *Légion Etrangère*. Romance had not blossomed. Madame Rubinstein, Maman told her family, had found in each man something lacking, a certain missing *je ne sais quoi*.

Maman thought she'd spotted a winner when she met Lucien Sagan, a journalist whose stories had appeared both in Europe and abroad, and whose time as a war correspondent had etched deep and elegant lines across his brow. He seemed thrilled to meet Madame Rubinstein, who told Maman she had evinced a *frisson* when shaking his hand. The two spent a weekend in Annapolis, and then mysteriously broke up. Neither Madame Rubinstein nor Lucien would comment, and Lucien soon left the United States for Sahelian Africa where he would live with Touaregs for a year and write a bestseller.

When Maman mentioned Lucien to Madame Rubinstein, the professor's forehead would knit, her lips purse, and her eyes narrow, then she would shrug, and sigh.

Just before Thanksgiving of that year, both Maman and Jeanot noticed that Madame Rubinstein seemed less dour, that her step had, if not a bounce, at least a certain looseness, and that she mentioned an unfamiliar name, Corentin Frakes, with some regularity. After a bit, Madame Rubinstein admitted Corentin was a suitor, an American born in Brittony to a couple of displaced New Hampshireans. Maman realized she did indeed know the man, had met him two three times and never once had paid him the least attention. Frakes was an accountant for a local law firm, and his existence within the French community was at best peripheral. People occasionally went to him for legal advice though he had none to give. Maman told Papa she vaguely recalled a stultifying ten minutes listening to the man describe a bird-watching expedition and wondering who had invited him, and why. He spoke French fluently with the barest hint of an American accent, and, Jeanot recalled, made slurping sounds as he drank his wine.

Smiling, Madame Rubinstein said, "Justine Coachman introduced us..."

Maman took the news with a smile but that night she slammed saucepans and burned the potatoes, shouted at Jeanot for an imagined wrongdoing and refused to watch the Ed Sullivan show with Papa. She said she found it outrageous that after all her efforts, Madame Rubinstein should choose a mousy American—even a francophone one—over her own candidates! That the latest aspirant was Justine Coachman's friend, a woman people barely knew and one married to an American with possible mobster relatives; that was contemptible.

Months later, Jeanot would learn, Corentin would abandon Madame Rubinstein. She tearfully told Maman the man claimed he was not good enough for her, and that a couple could not build a future on uneven ground. Madame Rubinstein was a little broken-hearted but mostly relieved, she admitted. Corentin had taken to spending the weekends at her home and this drove her to distraction. She felt everything had to be in order prior to his arrival so most Fridays were spent cleaning and polishing furniture and floor, washing windows and scouring the tiles in the kitchen. Having been raised a lady by her

Jewish parents, Madame Rubinstein felt her own appearance had to be perfect as well, and so she spent too much time dieting and tending to her hair and nails.

Maman was vindicated and the friendship with Madame Rubinstein blossomed once more.

Chapter 36

Two congregations, one Catholic and one Protestant, catered to the French in Washington. Sylvie, a Protestant, said that she had as *Pasteur* Jérome Casterman, a Jew, according to rumor. People gossiped that Pasteur Casterman, praying for succor to the Christian God while in a German extermination camp, had promised conversion if he escaped death, which he did. Sylvie didn't care. The *Pasteur*, she said, tended to his flock with dignity but was not altogether popular. People had strong feelings about his potentially Jewish antecedents. Jeanot, recalling the talk he'd had with Babette about his own probable Jewish origins, was sympathetic to the *Pasteur's* predicament.

Jeanot and the Catholics had *Père* Alexandre Jean Marie de Gourbillet, a short Jesuit with unfortunate teeth, a permanent scowl, round metal-rimmed glasses, and a military haircut. He was thought to come from noble stock impoverished by the upheavals of World War I, and in fact, said Papa, was 87th in line to assume the throne of the Bourbons should a second revolution return that cheerless monarchy to France.

Le Père Alexandre ran his parish laxly, giving the impression that his profession had been forced upon him rather than chosen.

He was what Jeanot had once heard a member of the congregation call "a fair to middling priest." He knew his sacraments, listened to the paltry confessions of his parishioners while knowing full well that the real sins never reached the confessional and this was fine by him. Jeanot himself once had, with heart beating a tattoo in his chest, confessed to *Le Père* about drinking and lying to his Papa and Maman. He'd been surprised and slightly appalled to find that the priest barely seemed to care. Had a real crime been committed and confessed, Jeanot decided, *Père* Alexandre would have been at a loss as to what to do. That, of course, was disappointing, seeing as so many people so regularly came to *Père* Alexandre for advice and support. Jeanot was disillusioned.

Maman was a supporter of the church. She had discovered that the Sunday post-service was a gathering spot for francophones and francophiles of all stripes. She often dragged Jeanot to church with her, claiming that it would help him keep in touch with his French origins. The French Ambassador and his wife, if they were in town, came for communion, as did the French butcher and his eight children from three marriages. Africans from Senegal, Madagascar, Mali, and other former and active colonies attended, though these families often stood in clumps off to the side. Jeanot had wanted to speak to these people from foreign places he'd read about only in books and in the pages of his favorite magazines. He never quite worked up the courage and they seemed completely uninterested in him.

The French restaurateurs, doctors, attorneys and real estate agents traded gossip. Children romped, teenagers gathered across the street, while the chauffeurs of the mighty idled their cars and smoked.

Once a month there was a *kermès* held in the basement of the church. Jeanot never liked it there; it was cramped, smelled musty, and reminded him of the cellar in France and the coal delivery men; terrifying apparitions bathed in dust and wearing burlap sacks on their heads. He did like what the parishioners brought to the sale, though— pastries, cookies, smoked sausages, *cassoulets, hachis Parmentiers* (named after the French agronomist who had invented the potato), *boudin,* and several other savory dishes. This edifying mix of northern and southern French fares was offered for sale to benefit the church and homeless people in the colonies. Maman's specialty was quiche, which, after several months of experimentation with ingredients and cooking times, was by far the most popular item on the sales tables. Each month she baked a dozen of the pies, and these vanished within minutes. It was said that the French ambassador's wife had bought several for a late afternoon cocktail party, and though Maman had not been able to verify the sale, neither did she deny it. *Père* Alexandre had complimented her several times, saying that with enough of Maman's quiche, Africa could be saved. Jeanot loved them, always insisting that Maman bake a special quiche just for him.

Jeanot knew that assembling the quiches, baking, taking them to the church and displaying them for others made Maman feel good about herself. Papa said it made her more conscious of her own piety. Someone once called her Sainte Thérèse de la Quiche and though Maman laughed at the title, there was obviously a small part of her that reveled in it. She was doing her part, she explained to Jeanot, for the less fortunate and doing so in a worthwhile community, with people who mattered and made decisions that could affect the entire planet. She thought of her family in France, she said, all of them gone now; her father Léopold and her brother Yves, even her stepmother Emma. They had valued being with the right group, with the important and the influential, the ones who, Yves used to say, farted higher than their asses. The family would have been proud of her at this moment. She had, she said, arrived, was on a first name basis with diplomats, important journalists and generals, had a home of her own and cars. She had a husband who loved her and, if he was not a household name, he did have an important position with the government of her adopted nation. His voice was heard all over the Francophone world. In Africa and Europe and Asia they listened to Roland St. Paul preaching America, offering news of the free world to those not quite as free or perhaps not free at all. People listened to her husband secretly, in basements, garages, the backrooms of taverns and inns and other darkened places, his soft voice a welcomed guest. He too, in his own way, was an important person, and this gladdened her.

Jeanot was proud when he heard his Maman speak of his Papa like this, and was proud of his Maman as well for her skills. She seemed happier and more comfortable. She had told him, "*Je suis dans mon assiettes.*" The saying had always amused him. He'd once used the phrase with KC, and she'd laughed, saying she understood perfectly.

"Everyone," she said, "should have a plate of her own."

Chapter 37

Had Maman's quiches not been targeted by Justine Coachman's *tartes aux fraises des bois,* the events that led to the near demise of the French Catholic congregation might not have occurred.

One Sunday in late October, Papa, Maman and Jeanot pulled up in front of the church so Maman could unload her dozen-and-a-half quiches for that month's *kermès.* There were six mushroom, six ham, and six asparagus; a new recipe she was not sure about, yet one she thought might impress buyers. Jeanot helped carry them in, careful not to trip. He'd stumbled once before, and the destroyed quiche had been an insignificant consequence compared with Maman's fury.

Maman found her usual table, spread the tablecloth she kept for that particular duty, and displayed the pies by group. When she was pleased with the arrangement, she instructed Jeanot to sit at the table while she went across the room to speak with other volunteers. She was trying to drum up business for the Franco-American Club of Washington, set up years earlier by a breakaway member of the Alliance Française. The member had had been unhappy with the Alliance's willingness to accept Senegalese and other Francophone African members. He had set up the new club to be all white. However, recent presidents of the Franco-American Club of Washington were more accepting. It was wrong, Maman told Jeanot, to exclude anyone. All people who lived in the present and former colonies were French citizens, according to law and to General de Gaulle, and turning them away because of color was a great sin. She explained to Jeanot that the club no longer excluded anyone; that all natives of French-speaking countries were now welcome, regardless of color.

The club boasted a membership in the low 30s, as opposed to the Alliance's hundreds, and Maman was its newly elected president, replacing an elderly American lady who, though she spoke French fluently, had never crossed the ocean. The Franco-American club was one of what Papa called "Maman's social stepping stones."

Jeanot had heard Papa complain that Maman might be over-extended, an unfamiliar term. He knew she was also president of the French Book Club, the French Bridge Club, and the recently created *Association des Français à Washington.* She was involved in the French theater, *Les Amis du Cinéma Français,* and had her eye on the *Club des Gourmands du Samedi Soir.* This last was a group of young French diplomats who met once a month for a high-end seven course dinner prepared by hired chefs from local embassies.

Maman's membership in these groups was part of a campaign to become well known in the area, and this was already bearing fruit. In a very short time, Maman had become a necessary part of the French community, and nearly every one of Jeanot's friends knew her, or had heard her name in conversation around the dinner table.

She was talking to someone, maybe a prospective member, when Jeanot called her to the quiche table which, he noticed, had been pushed a few feet closer to the wall to make room for another display. This new display was manned by Madame Coachman, who was arranging her own pies in some sort of pleasing geometrical pattern as Maman drew near. They greeted each other effusively, rolled their eyes and threw up their hands over each other's baking skills. Maman insisted on pushing her table even farther out of the way to make room for Madame Coachman's masterpieces. Jeanot looked on with interest, sensing that something mysterious and grown-up was occurring. Maman said, "*Va jouer avec la petite Coachman,*" and shooed the boy towards Sylvie who was waving at him from across the room.

Jeanot witnessed the sale of Madame Coachman's *Tartes aux Fraises des Bois* and saw *Père* Alexandre buying two for his own consumption. Maman took three quiches back home that day. This had never happened before, and during the drive back to Maryland she voiced some suspicions that Madame Coachman's presence at the *kermès* had something to do with the decline in sales. Why was the woman there in the first place? Maman thought Monsieur Coachman was Lutheran, and there had certainly been no manifestation of Catholic beliefs the few times the two women had met. Maman didn't trust the Coachman woman, she told Papa. She still wondered how and why this new arrival had found a mate for Simone Rubinstein when all of her own efforts had been for naught. This immediate bonding of Justine Coachman and Simone, Maman's best friend, had stung, she had to admit. Now this *parvenue* and probably wife of a Lutheran was selling tarts at the *kermès* and nothing good would come from this. The woman had no boundaries, showing up unannounced at the vacation site in her American husband's fancy gangster cars, and now peddling her wares at the church sale. That, declared Maman, was the problem with *parvenues*: They showed up in the most inappropriate of places and wanted to change things.

On the drive back to the house Papa said, "I don't think they're Lutheran. Where did you hear that?"

Maman couldn't remember but it somehow had stuck in her mind.

"I think Simone told me," she said. "Yes, that's it. And Simone would know."

"Hmm," said Papa, which Jeanot knew meant this was not an argument worth having.

From the back seat where he was holding the quiches, Jeanot said, "*Sylvie n'a pas été baptisée... Elle me l'a dit.*" Sylvie had told him that she'd never been baptized.

This was all Maman needed to hear, that the Coachman daughter had never been baptized. She looked at her husband. "*Tu vois?* I told you. Lutheran, for sure." Then, turning to Jeanot she added, "Not that there is anything wrong with being Lutheran, of course, or any other religion. Simone is Jewish and we love her like family!"

Again, Jeanot wondered about his own origins, and if Babette had been correct about him being Jewish, but again, he decided not to mention it.

Papa said, "I'm fairly certain Lutherans get baptized."

"Then maybe the Coachmans are Jewish," Maman said.

Jeanot, reasonably certain that Sylvie was Protestant, chose to remain silent.

At the *kermès* a month later, Maman told Jeanot to look around for Madame Coachman's *tartes aux fraises des bois*. She had, she informed him, made discreet inquiries regarding the Coachman's faith and had discovered the family was neither Lutheran nor Jewish, but no one could swear for their Catholicism either. The inconclusivity of it nagged at her. It shouldn't be that difficult, she said, to know such basic things about a person.

"Maman," began Jeanot, but Maman was already gone, searching for any signs of tartes or Coachmans in the throng.

A month later, Maman brought twenty quiches covered in Saran wrap and she and Jeanot set them up on the usual table. Madame Coachman was not there. Maman's pies sold out, though she had to let the last five go at half-price.

Jeanot found the once-a-month *kermès* was something to look forward to, far more interesting than the incomprehensible sit/stand/kneel masses recited listlessly in a dead tongue by a bored *Père* Alexandre. Jeanot had noticed that more than once his Papa had sat with eyes firmly closed, in what could only be deep Catholic concentration. Often, Papa's display of faith was marred by the slightest of snores. Maman would elbow him in the ribs and Papa would wake up with a start and a guilty glance about him to see if anyone had noticed. Few did. Looking around, Jeanot could see Sunday morning somnolence was rampant throughout the church.

Eight weeks later, Madame Coachman brought twenty-four assorted pies that Maman was pretty sure had been purchased the day before at the German bakery in Arlington, Virginia. The pies had that commercially baked look, she said, and they sold quickly. *Père* Alexandre bought two himself, then came back an hour later for two more. A restaurant owner who in the past had bought six of Maman's quiches instead opted for six of the other woman's pastries. This time, Maman left her unsold wares on the table when she departed, unwilling to be seen trundling surplus goods back out of the *kermès*.

Jeanot, meanwhile, had roamed the church after the service and found a half-bottle of sacramental wine. He beckoned to Sylvie and they drank it in their secret place, an alcove set down a short flight of stairs that they'd found two weeks before hidden at the back of church. There was a door there which looked as if it hadn't been opened in a long time, the handle and lock stiff with rust, and it was protected from view by a flowing crepe myrtle tree. Sylvie sat on a step, drank in large violent gulps and swallowed chunks of a Mars candy bar. She was angry at her mother and mostly silent though once in a while she said, "*Quelle bande de cons,*" and Jeanot knew she was referring to her mother and father who, it appeared, had not been getting along for some time. She told Jeanot her own *maman* and *papa* slept in separate rooms and rarely spoke to each other, though when they were in public, everyone smiled and grinned as if all was well, which it was not. Her *papa* often went out at night and didn't come home until very early in the morning. When he drove Sylvie to school he smelled like wine and often some of the buttons of his shirt were undone. Sylvie hated the smell. She repeated that as she swigged at the wine, keeping it mostly for herself. There was another smell she hated, she said, and that was of *Père* Alexandre who often came to the house late at night to visit. Jeanot had noticed the priest's odor as well, not unpleasant but strange enough to be disturbing. Something with licorice and another sweet aroma Jeanot couldn't identify trailed the cleric heavily, announcing both arrival and departure. It mixed with the tang of the Seita cigarettes *Père* Alexandre smoked at every opportunity.

When they had finished the half bottle, Sylvie handed Jeanot two sticks of Wrigley's Juicy Fruit gum to mask the wine odor. She hugged him fiercely, then laughed and ran away.

Jeanot rejoined the *kèrmes* just as the Coachman family was leaving. He followed Maman and Papa to the family car and could tell from Maman's stiff back and purposeful walk that things were not going well. He concentrated on chewing the Juicy Fruit, not the best flavor. He wished Sylvie had given him Doublemint, which had a brighter, longer lasting taste, and told himself he would bring a pack or two to share the following Sunday.

He chewed silently but not silently enough. From the front passenger seat and without looking back, Maman snapped, "*Arrêtes ça! Mon Dieu! C'est comme si il y avait une vache dans cette voiture!*" Jeanot didn't think his mild popping sounds were like a cow at all, but he parked the gum on the roof of his mouth until they got home.

He and Papa went to the basement to finish assembling a bookshelf. When that was done, Jeanot ran off to spend time with Robert and KC.

He noticed on his way out that Maman had gone up to her bedroom and closed the door.

Chapter 38

For Jeanot, getting Maman to the hospital would always remain a vague, shrouded event. One minute he was sitting in the living room reading the latest issue of *Tintin,* three weeks old but received in that morning's mail. The next minute, he heard Papa shouting, *"Chérie! Réveilles-toi s'il-te-plait! Réveilles-toi tout de suite!"* Then Papa was on the phone talking in a very tight and controlled voice, giving their address to the person on the other end of the line. Papa said, "Please hurry," twice, then to Maman again, *"Je t'en pris, chérie! Réveilles-toi!"*

Bare moments after that, an ambulance pulled up to the house and two men wearing white shirts and dark pants with yellow piping rushed past him as Papa waved them up the stairs and into the bedroom. Jeanot ran up the stairs himself just in time to see one of the men put a mask on Maman's face. Papa was ashen and standing next to the bed. The other man pushed him gently out of the way.

The same white-shirted man looked on the night-table, picked up a tube of pills and emptied it into his hand. "Miltowns. Did she take a bunch of these?"

Papa nodded absently. "Maybe. Anxiety. She's a very anxious woman."

Jeanot said, "She takes them in the morning and at noon and at night. Two each time."

The man looked at Jeanot and said, "Thank you, son. That's important information." Then he faced Papa and asked, "What other drugs does she take?"

Papa shrugged. "Downstairs. Dining room table."

Jeanot saw his Maman's eyelids flutter. She looked wildly around the room, took a deep breath and tried to sit up. The ambulance man put a gentle hand on her shoulder and forced her to be still. Her eyes focused on Jeanot. "Jeanot? *Ça va mon petit?*"

She closed her eyes before he could respond. Her breathing grew rhythmic and steady. Her mouth was open and Jeanot could just see redness of tongue and slightly yellowed teeth from the Pall Mall cigarettes.

"She's gonna be all right, son. Don't worry. Everything's gonna be alright."

Jeanot nodded. "She takes a lot of pills. Every day."

"Izzat so?"

"Yes," said Jeanot. "My Papa is worried. He told me to look after her." He paused and the man gave him a questioning look. "Sometimes she takes some in the afternoon or morning too."

"Always the same pills?"

Jeanot shook his head. "No. Sometimes it's little white ones, or yellow ones. Or blue. Some are blue."

The man sighed and closed his eyes. Then he squatted so his face was even with Jeanot's. He put out his hand. Jeanot looked, then tentatively shook it.

"So here's the deal, kid. We just shook mitts," he raised his right hand, "and that's my guarantee that your mom's gonna be back home in a couple of days. We're gonna take her to the hospital, and the doctors will take a look and maybe give her some medicine—"

"More pills?"

"No no. Well yeah, maybe pills, but not the same kind. This will be medicine to make her feel better, stronger." The man rose to his full height which Jeanot noticed was very high.

Jeanot said, "So, good pills?"

"Good pills," agreed the man.

The second man returned and Jeanot heard a snatch of conversation. "…goddam pharmacy, right in the middle of the dining room table…"

A third man appeared with a folded stretcher and opened it. They lifted Maman onto it, and carried her down the stairs carefully, keeping her as level as possible. Two men loaded her into the ambulance while the third man spoke with Papa.

"We're taking her to Sibley. It's the closest hospital. She's not in any danger, but she may be dehydrated. That's what happens with drug add—" He saw Jeanot, corrected himself. "People who accidentally take too many of those drugs. They may want to keep her overnight, do some tests."

Papa nodded. His color had returned. "May we go with you? My son and I?"

The man shook his head. "No. we can't have passengers, I'm sorry. Regulations. You can take your own car and park it near the emergency room. You know where the hospital is, right?"

Papa did. He gathered a few items from the bathroom—brush, comb, toothbrush and the Colgate tooth powder Maman always used— and some fresh underwear and stockings from Maman's dresser. In their bedroom closet, he found a skirt and blouse she often wore and a pair of slippers. He dropped everything into a bright red and white beach bag.

The ambulance had arrived with sirens but left silently. Papa and Jeanot took the Lincoln, Papa driving a bit too fast.

After a few minutes, he said, "She'll be fine, Jeanot. It was an accident."

Jeanot didn't answer. Papa said, "She'll be home tomorrow."

"Or maybe the next day," Jeanot said. "One of the men said the doctors will want to take a look at her."

"Tests," Papa said. "Maybe she got food poisoning. Maybe it wasn't the pills."

There was a momentary silence. The car hit a pothole and rocked a bit.

"It was the pills." Jeanot knew.

Papa slowed to a crawl and made an overly careful right turn into the hospital parking lot. He slid the Lincoln between a Ford and a Chevrolet, backed in and out until he was perfectly centered. Then he looked at Jeanot and said, "*Oui. Je sais. Tu as raison.* It was the pills."

The admission saddened Jeanot. Part of him had wanted Papa to prove him wrong.

When Papa asked where Maman was, a nurse told them to wait, then returned to her paperwork. Papa stood there until she looked up again.

She said, "Sir, you should sit down. A doctor will be with you as soon as possible."

Papa found a pay phone. He fished change out of his pocket and called Doctor Marianne Rouget whose name he had on a card in his wallet. She arrived twenty minutes later looking ever-so-slightly disheveled. Jeanot noticed her lipstick was on crooked. She spoke briefly with the nurse at the registration desk, then told Papa, "We're lucky. I know the attending physician. Let me go speak with him. Go to the cafeteria. Get some coffee. I'll meet you there in fifteen minutes."

Jeanot got a Coke, a donut, a Danish that had turned stale and cold French fries on a paper plate. Papa got a cup of coffee into which he forgot to put sugar, but he didn't seem to notice.

There were patients and doctors and nurses and visitors, and not one person paid attention to Jeanot, who ate his donut and then his Danish. It struck him that a lot of people were here for the same reason he was. Somebody they loved was sick, or had eaten something bad, or been in a car accident. Somebody was in pain and the ones who cared for that person were powerless to do anything except maybe sit in the cafeteria and eat donuts.

Papa had his hands around the paper cup of coffee as if warming them. Jeanot edged closer so that their legs touched, and Papa smiled.

"*Ça sent drôle ici, unh?*"

Jeanot sniffed at the air and it did indeed smell funny, a strange mélange of antiseptic and old people, cold coffee, cigarette smoke, day-old hamburgers and crushed potato chips. A woman at an adjoining table emanated waves of lilac scent and a man seated next to the closed window puffed irritably at a cigar.

Dr. Rouget appeared in one of the cafeteria entrances and Jeanot waved her over. She sat at the table, nodded once and lit a cigarette.

"*Bon.* She's fine. She's not awake yet, but should be within an hour or two. The ambulance people said there were a lot of pharmaceutical drugs involved. I only prescribed Miltown. What else is she taking? Does she have a second doctor she sees?" She paused for a moment and squinted at Papa. "Doc*teur* Bianchi, perhaps?" She pronounced the second syllable of his title with obvious distaste.

"I don't know," said Papa.

"Yes," nodded Jeanot. "We went to his office a lot. Twice a month, maybe more."

Papa looked at Jeanot quizzically. "Really, Jeanot? Twice a month?"

"More. Sometimes every week. And then we went to the pharmacy and the Canadian lady who speaks French gave Maman her pills in a little white paper bag. And sometimes she would give me a pack of gum, too."

Dr. Rouget turned to Papa who now looked as if he would cry. She said, "I can't speak about Doc*teur* Bianchi," and she accentuated the *teur* again, "that would be unethical. But I will say he is known among his colleagues for dispensing prescriptions… freely. All with the best intentions, I'm sure, but your wife is not the first of his patients to end up here."

Now Papa looked furious. "I'll kill him, that—"

Dr. Rouget interrupted. "You'll do no such thing, Roland. You and Jeanot will go home, or go and find something to eat, and they'll release Marité tomorrow. I will come to your house after she returns, and we will all talk about this. But this evening, you'll rest. If you want, go through the house, see if she's hidden drugs anywhere."

"Hidden?" Papa looked shocked.

Jeanot looked at the expression on his Papa's face and felt the guilt welling up, overpowering. Papa had told him to watch over his Maman, to tell him *everything*, and he hadn't. Now, something terrible had happened, something that might not have happened if Jeanot had been honest in the first place. It was his own fault that his Papa looked stricken. Jeanot was terrified of his father being scared.

Jeanot said, "In the old desk. The secret drawer that's in the middle. She keeps some there. Also, in the kitchen, under the knife drawer." He paused, added, "And behind that book on Paris at night. And maybe another place too. Maybe in her red shoes in the closet. I'm not sure."

Jeanot looked at his Papa's face and realized he had just said something terribly wrong. Papa's eyes were streaming tears that he tried and failed to wipe, and a sob shook his body. Dr. Rouget took one of his large hands in two of hers. "Roland, écoutez moi. This is not the end of the world. In fact, it's a very good opportunity to address the problem. Because," she added, "there *is* a problem here. Your wife is an *habitué*."

She left, a small busy woman whom Jeanot liked even though he could not fully understand what had just happened.

They went to Maman's room. She was awake but groggy. Jeanot found the clear tubes and bottles hanging on hooks and going into her arm both repulsive and fascinating. She looked very small in the bed, not like someone he knew, and a bolt of panic shot through him as he thought of Dédé and his uncle and his grandfather, all gone now. Dédé had looked sort of like this when he'd died; small, shriveled and unrecognizable. Jeanot took a step back, stood a little distance from Maman's bed, but Papa pulled up a chair and sat as close to her as he could. He stroked her forehead and whispered something to her that made her smile.

She motioned with a tired arm for Jeanot to come closer and he did, still scared, still wondering if death was hovering in this room. He was certain that it could be, flying invisibly over the three of them and ready to destroy everything in one quiet sigh.

Maman said, "I'll be home tomorrow and we'll make crêpes, *d'ac-cord?* And maybe KC and Robert can come over too, *et on aura une fête, d'accord Jeanot?*"

He nodded because he had to and because Papa was at last smiling. She fell asleep then, her head turning to the right on the pillow. Before they left the room, Jeanot made sure to check that his Maman's chest was moving beneath the sheets.

They ate at the Howard Johnson near their home and Papa mostly pushed his food around. He called Maman's room twice to make sure she was all right, and the third time, he told Jeanot, a nurse with a gruff voice picked up the phone and told him not to call anymore. They would go back to the hospital in the morning and bring her home.

The physician kept her three days and twice talked earnestly with Papa, something about *addiction,* a word Jeanot didn't know. They had removed the tubes from her arm on the second day and Jeanot, relieved, finally decided that she wouldn't die. He felt as if he could breathe again.

When they brought her home, she insisted they first stop at the Giant food store so she could buy everything to make crêpes. Papa pushed the metal cart around as Maman took items from the shelves and when no one was looking, Jeanot snuck in a box of Whitman Samplers chocolates he would wrap and give her later.

When they finally did get her home, she went straight to bed and fell asleep. Papa asked if they should make crêpes anyway, but Jeanot thought they should wait until Maman was better, and so they did.

Over the next few days, the house was full of visitors and the story that Papa always told them was that Maman had indeed accidentally taken too many pills one night. It could have happened to anyone, he said. Doctor Rouget came to see Jeanot's parents, and the they did not include Jeanot in their discussion. He went through the house very thoroughly and found twelve hiding places where Maman had hidden drugs. Worried that there might be consequences if he flushed them down the toilet or threw them away, Jeanot hid the pills he found in the box in his bedroom, where he had once kept his cowboys and Indians.

Chapter 39

Madame Coachman came to visit, bearing flowers and accompanied by Sylvie. Maman pretended to be asleep so she wouldn't have to see her, so Madame Coachman talked quietly with Papa in the living room. Sylvie and Jeanot went into the backyard and he took her to the creek behind the house. They both sat on the rocky little beach and Jeanot pointed out where the black snake lived and where the giant turtle used to be.

Sylvie was uninterested. She said, "My mother said your Maman is *une habituée*."

That was the second time the word was spoken. Jeanot said, "*C'est quoi, habitué?*"

"A drug addict. Do you know what that is?"

Jeanot had a vague notion. Sylvie said, "Haven't you seen *I Want to Live?* Susan Hayward was astounding!"

He hadn't.

"Maman took me to it though she wasn't supposed to. She lied about my age so I could get into the theater, because she thought I should see it and learn about 'the dangers of drugs.'" She idly tossed a pebble into the water. "Maybe your mother should see it too."

"Why does your mother say that about my Maman?"

Sylvie pursed her lips. "I think they don't like each other. I think it has to do with the pies."

He looked at her blankly.

"The church pies. My mother's are better than your mother's."

"They're not!"

"*Père Alexandre* thinks so. He bought four of them but only two of your mother's." Sylvie said this without a trace of malice. "And everybody knows *Père Alexandre* really knows pies."

"My Maman said your mother didn't even make the pies. They came came from Giant food!"

Sylvie sniffed. "She made them. I know. I helped."

Jeanot took off his shoes and waded into the creek. Sylvie followed suit. She said, "Actually, my mother did buy them, but not at Giant. There's a bakery near our house and she went there. And my dad got really angry because she sold them at the church for less than she paid for them, and he's very careful with money." She splashed water on her arms and neck. "But if you tell anyone, I'll just say you're lying."

Jeanot understood. This was a piece of knowledge he would nurture and not pass on, not even to Maman and Papa, though he might tell KC or Robert. He asked, "Why did you tell me?"

Sylvie shrugged. "I'm mad at my mother." She segued briefly into French, "*Vraiment furieuse!* She said we were going to buy me shoes at Woodward & Lothrop, and instead we went to Sears. So I didn't get the shoes I wanted, and the kids at school will know, they'll see the Sears shoes and laugh at me."

Jeanot's entire wardrobe, including underwear and socks, came from Sears & Roebuck. "What's wrong with Sears?"

Sylvie gave him an odd look, then twisted her face into a grimace. "*Nobody* shops at Sears. Only stupid ugly poor people shop at Sears. All my friends know that. *Everyone* knows that."

Jeanot decided he would tell the secret to both his Maman and his Papa as soon as the Coachman mother and daughter left. His Maman would feel much better and perhaps not have to take pills ever again. His Papa would feel better too. Jeanot thought he would go visit KC today; she dressed at Sears. He would never talk to Sylvie again. Nobody would die.

Fin

About the Author

Thierry Sagnier is a writer whose works have been published both in the United States and abroad. He is the author of *The IFO Report,* (Avon Books), *Bike! Motorcycles and the People who Ride Them* (Harper & Row), *Washington by Night* (Washingtonian Books), *Thirst* (Pigasus Press), and *The Fortunate Few* (NCNM Press).

His short story, *Lunch with the General,* published in Chrysalis Reader, was nominated for a 2013 Pushcart Prize, an American literary prize honoring the best "poetry, short fiction, essays or literary what-not published in the small presses." He is also the author of *Writing about People, Places and Things*, an online collection of essays chronicling his thoughts on writing, family and friendships, and his bout with cancer. His novel, *Montparnasse*, set in Paris in 1919, will be published in 2019 by Apprentice House.

Sagnier was born in France and came to the United States in his early teens. He has worked and written for *The Washington Post* and several other newspapers and magazines, produced videos and short films for the Canadian Broadcasting Corporation, and was a columnist for Canada's *Le Devoir.*

His short plays were selected for production by the East End Fringe Festival in Long Island, and have been produced in Virginia and at New York City's Ta Da Theater.

He currently lives in Virginia.

Apprentice House is the country's only campus-based, student-staffed book publishing company. Directed by professors and industry professionals, it is a nonprofit activity of the Communication Department at Loyola University Maryland.

Using state-of-the-art technology and an experiential learning model of education, Apprentice House publishes books in untraditional ways. This dual responsibility as publishers and educators creates an unprecedented collaborative environment among faculty and students, while teaching tomorrow's editors, designers, and marketers.

Outside of class, progress on book projects is carried forth by the AH Book Publishing Club, a co-curricular campus organization supported by Loyola University Maryland's Office of Student Activities.

Eclectic and provocative, Apprentice House titles intend to entertain as well as spark dialogue on a variety of topics. Financial contributions to sustain the press's work are welcomed. Contributions are tax deductible to the fullest extent allowed by the IRS.

To learn more about Apprentice House books or to obtain submission guidelines, please visit www.apprenticehouse.com.

Apprentice House
Communication Department
Loyola University Maryland
4501 N. Charles Street
Baltimore, MD 21210
Ph: 410-617-5265 • Fax: 410-617-2198
info@apprenticehouse.com • www.apprenticehouse.com

CPSIA information can be obtained
at www.ICGtesting.com
Printed in the USA
LVHW03s0423111018
593108LV00001B/233/P